Praise for Waterwight Flux ~ ~ ~

"A great wrong must be righted in this hunt for the truth. McHargue again effectively offers images from dreamscape and myth in this intriguing follow-up novel . . . the author goes beyond the expected with her original, striking characters . . . The plot is fast-moving, with action, danger, emotion, and moral choices; beneath all of this is a subtle environmental message embodied in the two scientists' meddling with nature . . . Imaginative characters that powerfully tap into myth."

~ Kirkus Reviews

Waterwight Flux

Book II of the Waterwight Series

Remember who you are!

Laurel

Waterwight Flux

Book II of the Waterwight Series

Laurel McHargue

STRACK PRESS

STRACK PRESS LLC   Leadville, CO

Waterwight Flux
Book II of the Waterwight Series

Published by Strack Press LLC
Leadville, CO

FIRST EDITION 2017

Library of Congress Control Number: 2017963566
McHargue, Laurel, Author
Waterwight
Laurel McHargue

ISBN: 978-0-9969711-2-6

Edited by Carol Bellhouse and Stephanie Spong
Cover Design by Trif Andrei and Trif Paul, TwinArtDesign

For

Patricia M. Bernier
2 January 1929 – 19 October 2017

Table of Contents

~ 1 ~

[Celeste]

YIKES! WHAT HAVE I DONE? Celeste wondered after poking a hole in the sea-life-filled cloud. The rising waterspout frightened her, but she knew it would deliver the trapped creatures safely back to their world below the rippling turquoise surface. How she knew that remained a mystery to her.

She marveled at the lightness of her body and speed of her flight until—

Wait a minute. What's happened to me?

Her wings fluttered and she dropped precipitously as she struggled to look at her body, a body that just moments ago was that of a teenage girl. She saw milky white feathers and reptilian legs when she focused beyond a small, flesh-colored beak.

She had a beak. And feathers. She was a bird, a dove, and if she didn't flap her beautiful wings soon, she'd be a dead dove.

Catching herself before smashing into a rocky outcropping below, she spread her wings and felt them arrest her descent. She lifted and dropped in a graceful rhythm as if buoyed upon gently rolling waves. Testing her wings, she turned left and right, climbed and plunged, raced and rested, until soaring over the mountain range felt like something she'd done her entire life.

Images of throwing a spear—*but how could I throw a spear with these wings?*—and flying away with two other doves after an enormous tower of water crashed to shore flashed through her memory and disappeared.

I remember flying, but this feels different. Celeste was troubled. She scanned the land below until she found a bulbous boulder on which to perch. The sun was setting on the horizon, glimmering on the water and casting a magical glow all around.

The moment she lit upon the boulder, it shook lightly and made a curious sound, a sound that made no sense to her. She cocked her head and cooed softly, a response that felt both foreign and natural, and then flew away from the trembling pile of stones, which continued to echo bizarre vibrations. When she turned to look back at the mountain range, a stony profile highlighted by the shadow it cast caught her attention. Her heart skipped a beat, but she figured it was just the way a little bird's body might react to being surprised.

Returning her attention to the sky, she flew up and up until the land below blurred along with memories of frightened faces and scary underwater places. The higher she flew, the more blurred her visions became until there was little left to trouble her, though she had no idea where she was going.

The rattling, throaty "caw" of two enormous black ravens startled her from her reverie. When the birds approached from either side, she fluttered, uncertain of their intentions. They flew together in sync, and when the tips of their wings touched hers, a jolt of pure energy surged through her.

Images of an old, one-eyed man delivering a package beyond a slippery doorway also surged through her mind, and a puppy, and the smell of bacon—*bacon?*—and for a moment, swirling dizziness threatened to knock her from the sky.

But her companions buoyed her upward, ever upward, beyond layers of stratus into thinning air. Higher still—into the colorless, frigid atmosphere of a dimension she'd never imagined—she couldn't understand why her wings were not completely fatigued. She felt strong enough to fly around the entire world.

Despite her exuberance, a nagging voice far back in her consciousness whispered, "Run away!" and she was reminded of a girl with skinny legs and unruly dark hair and green eyes, green eyes, green eyes with flecks of gold, vibrant viridian eyes, so many eyes belonging to so many people with legs and arms and wings and voices and voices in her head comforting her, warning her—

"Kra-ka-ka-CAW!"

The sharp voices of her winged companions shook her back into her white-feathered body and turned her focus to what she acknowledged must be their destination. The vision stunned her.

Undulating in brilliant overlapping strands of iridescent pinks and oranges and blues and purples and yellows like countless silk scarves hung out to dry on a windy day, nacreous clouds spread across the heavens as far as she could see. Celeste anticipated how it would feel to fly into the pearlescent layers.

But why are we here? And will they bring me back to the planet soon?

Reflexively, she closed her eyes for a moment upon entering the first dazzling layer and noted increased pressure surrounding her. Her companions remained at her wingtips, providing a sense of reassurance, but when she opened her eyes again, she screeched her first "Rooo-oo!" when she saw an approaching threat.

The two wolves were gigantic, even from a distance. They looked hungry. Celeste wondered how the advancing beasts could run across the silky clouds without falling through. She was trying to make sense of everything in a time and place where nothing made sense, yet she also recalled a faraway place where similar anomalies were the norm. Her tiny head hurt.

Her winged companions remained unfazed by the apparent peril and kept her between them as they closed the gap with the wolves. Looking into the animals' intense eyes triggered another overpowering memory of lean, hungry dogs, and she lost her fear.

Where are they now, the dogs who trained me to leap and fly, the dogs who kept me safe from the shapeshifter? Celeste feared for those who had remained on the hilltop and in the village after the towering water crashed down. She couldn't remember what happened the moment it fell, only that she was then drawn toward a rising cloud filled with frantic sea creatures.

Perplexed by memories of being a girl, Celeste fluffed her feathers, cocked her head, and focused her attention on the wolves' lush coats.

The animals slowed to a trot and then stopped. When they sat to look up at the ravens and their guest, feathery wisps of color swirled around them, and a vision of Thunder flashed in Celeste's mind. Thunder, with his ever-changing patchwork of Easter egg colors and buttery-soft fur—he was on that hilltop too.

The ravens released Celeste and settled onto the backs of the wolves, who turned to face the direction from which they first appeared. Celeste remained fluttering above, unsure of what else to do. An eerie silence and a strange heaviness filled the atmosphere, and she slowed the flapping of her wings until she realized she didn't need to flap them at all to stay aloft in the space above the silky strands.

A massive cloud wave billowed in the distance and rolled over the waiting group, buffeting them gently, and then a piercing white light cut through the colors.

Celeste squinted and turned away from the blinding beam.

~ 2 ~

[Harmony]

"**COME QUICKLY, HARMONY!** We need to hide." Harmony was torn between Sharon, who gestured for her to follow, and the others, who stood staring at the sight they'd just witnessed in the sky.

After the gigantic, creature-filled water bubble was nearly out of sight in the darkening sky, Harmony felt it spill its contents back into the newly transformed ocean. She wondered if the others felt the ground shake when the tunnel beneath the bubble collapsed. None of them had seemed to notice when she had lifted her stubby arms to push away the ominous bubble.

None but Sharon, who appeared startled by what she had done.

"Hide? Why?" Harmony frowned. She didn't want to leave all the pretty people.

"They're mean. They'll want to hurt us. Especially you. They don't like people who are different."

"Friends." Harmony pointed to the entranced group, giggling when she said the word. After living under water with sea creatures her entire short life, she wasn't used to talking. Her hooked yellow teeth made it difficult to enunciate clearly.

But she could giggle, and when she did, the music of it mystified those around her. It had entranced the flying girl to follow the sound right into the sandcastle world Harmony had built for friends. Everything was happy there until the laser-eyed wizard delivered a flying frog toy to the girl with pretty black curls.

"Not friends," Sharon corrected, "bad people. Hurtful people. Come on, before they see us leave."

Sharon reached for her sister's hand and pulled her away. But Harmony had never run before. She'd barely walked, contorted as her legs were, and she tripped right away. Blue tears sprouted from her huge yellow eyes and she wailed an unearthly sound that pierced the atmosphere and brought everyone to their knees.

Harmony wondered why her sister looked frightened and why all of the villagers covered their ears and squeezed their eyes shut, huddling on the ground as if defending against an unfathomable threat.

She was even more confused when Sharon lifted her from the ground and held her against her chest. It felt like her sister was trying to muffle the sound of her cry. She didn't like the feeling of confinement and the rough jostling as Sharon ran far into the forest until she could no longer see the village.

Harmony stopped crying and lifted her twisted little face to her sister. When Sharon smiled at her, Harmony had the strange impression that the corners of her long-lost sibling's mouth had never turned that way before.

"I'm so sorry, Harmony. Are you okay?" Sharon sat the girl down against a tree and looked her over. "Just a little scratch, see? You'll be all right." She used a dry corner of her maroon cape to dab at the bluish blood on her sister's knee. "Huh. I guess this new skin isn't as strong as I thought it would be."

Just as Sharon uttered the words, Harmony's wound healed completely, leaving behind only a small drop of blood.

"Go home now?" Harmony asked. She wiped the drop of blood from her knee and looked at it, perplexed, before licking if from her finger. "Hungry."

"Yes, we're going home now. Blanche said our house is gone, but it couldn't have just disappeared, could it?" Sharon looked into her sister's eyes and Harmony saw her shiver. "And I'm hungry too. Here, have one of these." She pulled a fungus from behind the tree and brushed it off before handing it to her sister, and then found one for herself. "They don't taste great, but they'll have to do for now."

Harmony ate the brown object without complaint, but it left her far from satisfied and exceedingly thirsty.

When they resumed their trek, Sharon had to stop repeatedly for Harmony to catch up. But Harmony was in no hurry. She marveled at her new surroundings, stumbling as she turned in circles to peer up into the sparse leaves in the treetops. This world was nothing like the one she had just left. The air was thin and dry and nothing floated in it. It felt empty.

Sharon appeared agitated. "Come on, Harmony, we've got to get home before it gets too dark. I'd carry you again, but you're going to have to learn how to do things on your own now, just like I had to when my—when our parents disappeared. Believe me, it'll make you stronger, and you're going to have to be strong to live in this stupid world." Sharon looked back toward the village. "And we don't want anyone following us."

"No friends there? Not one?" Harmony couldn't imagine her sister wouldn't have a single friend among the pretty villagers.

"I told you, they're all mean. There's only one girl who might understand us—that older girl, Blanche—but I don't trust her either. Now, hurry up."

Harmony didn't understand the word trust, but recognized it wasn't the right moment to ask about it. She'd already learned many new words in the short time she'd been on land, and her ability to absorb new information was as keen as her ability to absorb water. It wouldn't take long before she'd adapt to her surroundings and blend in with the others.

It seemed to take forever to get through the forest and Sharon increased her pace frequently, seemingly forgetful of the struggling child behind her. Finally the trees cleared. Though it grew dark, Harmony sensed they'd soon reach their destination.

It had been so easy in the past to swim wherever she wanted to go in her tranquil, watery world. This walking, this trudging, was no fun at all. And the atmosphere . . . it was so very dry. Her body felt heavy and a dizzy spell threatened to knock her over. She focused on remembering the pretty people and the way they spoke, and a surge of excitement over the possibility of seeing them again revived her.

When Harmony finally reached the last tree, she saw her sister running back and forth across the clearing beyond, apparently searching for something.

"Are we home now?" Harmony's voice was different. It was no longer the voice of a four-year-old.

"Harmony?" Sharon squinted back toward the trees and gasped.

~ 3 ~

[The Village]

SHORTLY AFTER THE GREAT bubble emptied its
creatures and collapsed back into the sea, a cold fog rolled
down from the hill and enshrouded the villagers. They
remained looking skyward, though the fog was thick, until
they were brought to their knees by a piercing cry that
seemed to surround them from all sides, like the fog itself.

All were on their knees except for Maddie and Chimney,
who were off gathering food for what they hoped would be a
celebration.

Maddie was happy to disappear with Chimney and leave
behind the flood of voices and feelings cast upon her during
the time leading up to the threatening deluge. Her ability to
experience what others were feeling had started when Celeste
first touched her.

Her power frightened her at first, but she soon grew
accustomed to her new role as the one who could sense what
everyone was feeling. An empath, they called her. People
would come to her for comfort, and being the one to bridge
the communication gap between Mac and Teresa had gifted
her with the warmth of their love.

But when Celeste had returned with Ranger and the
glorious jaguar and the other cats, and the villagers had
followed her to the Overleader's house, Maddie's empathic
powers had become overwhelming. It took a quirky young
boy's suggestion for her to distance herself from the crowd

and disappear with him to regain her composure, and for that, she would be forever grateful to Chimney.

The two new friends were on their way back to the village when they heard movement in the forest.

"Shh! Maddie, don't move." Chimney froze in place with Maddie by his side. They held their breath and watched as an unknown teenage girl in a dark cape passed by within feet of them. Behind her, a bizarre little child limped along. When the girl was almost past them, she turned toward Maddie and Chimney—who believed they were invisible—and smiled, her crooked yellow teeth glowing like her orbed eyes.

As soon as the strangers were out of sight, Maddie and Chimney stared wide-eyed at one another.

"Did you see that little limping . . . person? I think she saw us, if it even is a girl. And who's that older girl? They both have weird pink hair! Who are they? Where do you think they're going?" Chimney squeaked and twitched.

"I don't know, Chim, but I got a really weird feeling about both of them. It's like I know the older one, but the child? The little one trying to keep up? My heart ached when she smiled at us."

"Mine about froze. Let's get back, and fast."

~ ~ ~ ~ ~

Back in the village, when the ear-piercing noise stopped, the people opened their eyes and stood. The fog was gone, and so were Sharon and Harmony.

It took a while before anyone noticed.

"I told her her house was gone." Blanche stared into the darkening forest, her brows creased tightly.

"She'll be back, especially now that she has a sister to care for," said Mac. He still had his arm around Teresa. Blanche turned away from the couple and frowned.

As if reading Blanche's thoughts, Teresa reached out her hand in a gesture of comfort, but her touch made Blanche flinch and move away.

"I really don't think we should be worried about them," said Nick. "I'm going back to the beach. Celeste must still be there. I'm gonna find her, and when I do, then maybe we'll know if it's all over."

He glanced at the man in the swimsuit and the woman by his side with a quizzical expression—never having seen either of them in their human forms before—but didn't seem to want to waste another moment trying to figure out who they were. His eyes lingered for a moment on an emerald scarf hanging from the man's swimsuit.

"I'll go with you, bro. We'll find the little flying dude." Thunder turned to Eenie with their brood gathered around her. "You be good now, darlin'. We won't be long."

"I will go as well." Ranger paced, his agitation palpable. "She was mine to protect. I cannot fail her again."

"Do be careful, Love." Eenie licked Thunder's cheek and then watched as the three ran back toward the water.

Still restless from the spectacular events, the villagers looked around at one another as if taking inventory. Finally they noticed the strangers in the group. With all eyes on him, Orville placed his arm around Riku protectively and made a hasty decision.

"We've come from the water and are here to help." He did his best to camouflage his French accent. "This is my friend Riku and I am . . . Finn." He figured it would be far easier to fit into the community as a survivor of a global catastrophe than as someone they'd all remember as Celeste's frog with the delicate wings and battle shield feet; no one would ever recognize Riku as the lizard that had terrified them.

When Maddie and Chimney emerged from the forest, Orville was happy to have the group's attention diverted.

He'd need time to figure out what his new role would be now that he was transformed into his original body as a man. His mind drifted to Celeste and he wondered if he'd ever hear her voice or share her dreams again. He sensed she was very far away, beyond his ability to help, and it troubled him.

Maddie spoke first when she and Chimney joined the group.

"We saw a teenage girl and . . . an unusual child heading toward the Overleader's house. Does anyone know who they are?"

Blanche continued to stare into the forest as she spoke. "The girl *is*, or at least *was*, the Overleader before the water changed back. Her name's Sharon and the other one is her sister. At least that's what she told us, but I wouldn't trust anything she says now that I know the truth."

"But that little one." Chimney scrunched up his face. "She's . . . not right."

"Seems like many of us, of you, haven't been quite right for a while now." Mac released Teresa and examined his arms. "I might not have any special powers like the rest of you, but we all *look* different now, and that hasn't changed since the water receded."

With Celeste missing, Orville believed the danger was not over, but didn't want to alarm the villagers. He looked around at their expectant faces. "Something very good has happened today, yes? May I be so bold to request that Riku and I dine with the good people of this village while we consider our new situation? We are, as you all must be, weary and hungry."

The villagers looked at the bags Maddie and Chimney had brought from the forest.

"Sure, mister, we have lots," said Chimney. Orville noticed the boy studying him intently.

Without another word, the throng followed the food gatherers to the community tables.

~ ~ ~ ~ ~

Down at the beach, Nick, Thunder and Ranger watched as people and unusual creatures emerged from the receding water and looked at one another in a state of confusion.

Nick scanned the beach and then the empty sky. "Where are they all coming from? And where will they go?"

"Those are some seriously wet dudes," said Thunder. "Guess they were in the water, but how'd they survive?"

"And where is our Celeste?" Ranger paced in circles around the two and they all looked to the sky, but there was nothing to see.

"She's not here," said Nick. "We need to warn the others we may have visitors soon. Look. Some of them are coming this way and they'll eventually find our village. If Celeste doesn't come back tonight, I'll search the land at first light tomorrow. There's a lot more land to explore now that the water's moving away, and if she's injured—"

"I will be there to help," said Ranger.

"Count me in too, bro-dudes," said Thunder.

~ ~ ~ ~ ~

Overhead, a colossal dragonfly soared unnoticed, breathing fire into the darkening sky.

~ **4** ~

[Celeste]

WITH MEMORIES OF TWO doves suspended in midair above a still, silent girl in a garden, Celeste felt confused by the ominous presence approaching from beyond the swirling clouds. Sensing the blinding beam was growing stronger with each beat of her heart, she squeezed her lids closed more tightly.

"Oh! But I do forget sometimes," a familiar voice bellowed, and Celeste felt the light go out. "Open your eyes now and look at me, little dove."

Little dove. Little Paloma. Those had been her names once, hadn't they? But when? Where? She turned to watch as the iridescent colors parted and an old man appeared wearing a cape and a patch over one eye beneath a floppy hat.

"You recognize me, do you?" His voice inspired both familiarity and fear. "Yes, you remember George, the ham man."

But Celeste was a dove, a bird, and George—the ham man—had delivered a winged, wind-up frog to a girl in a sandcastle. Who was that girl? And why was she remembering that girl and that place and . . . *Where am I?*

"You are in Asgard as my guest, bold one. I and my companions there below you are the only ones remaining in this realm now. The others have been forgotten and have disappeared into oblivion. AH-HA! Perhaps we should rename our home Oblivia! What say you, minions?" The man guffawed, and as he did, great swirls of color washed over his audience.

The two ravens flew to the old man's shoulders and the wolves trotted to him, flanking each side. They all faced Celeste.

"But I jest, and there is no time left for foolishness. I have brought you here because you are my connection with those who still would believe in me. You have heard their chanting and felt their doubts. Would that I could make them continue to believe, but I cannot. Belief in a god such as I must come from the believers; it cannot be forced."

The word 'ritual' resounded in Celeste's mind accompanied by an uncomfortable feeling of having all eyes on her as the name Odin was repeated over and over around a shrinking pond. It made her heart squeeze tightly. *So you are Odin.*

"Yes! The many reports of my death are clearly unfounded. I believe one of your great men once said something to that effect."

And what can a little bird do for a god with powers to part the heavens and save a child from captivity?

Celeste couldn't speak her thoughts, but she didn't need to. Odin, apparently, could hear them.

"I see, child. You forget. But you must never forget who you are! Did not another ancient one remind you of that?"

". . . fly away once more, and never forget who you are." I remember. *But what am I? Who am I? A bird? A girl?* Still suspended in spectacularly shifting colors and wary of those who seemed to expect something of her, Celeste felt more lost and confused than ever. She shivered and her feathers puffed out around her.

"You are both bird and girl in this new world that continues to shift in ways beyond my control. I will need you to be both, if we are all to survive. Come to me and I will show you what we face." Odin held out one upturned hand to her.

Celeste was uncertain, but Odin spoke softly and there was a pleading expression on his wizened face. Besides, what else could she do? Where could she go? She didn't even remember how she had ended up in the magical atmosphere surrounding her. She flew to his hand, and when she perched upon it, was grateful for its warmth.

She watched as he circled his other hand slowly in front of him. Wispy clouds dispersed downward into a dizzying vortex. When a dark hole opened beneath them, she gasped with fear. Vertigo seized her like a thief on a precipice and she dug her claws into Odin's hand to keep from falling into the void.

"Do not fear, small one. You cannot be harmed in my realm and I will not let you fall. Look below and see with new eyes. There is still work to be done."

When Celeste dared to peer through the opening, she understood what Odin was talking about. She remembered the silver-pink ooze that had threated the survivors of The Event, and she remembered throwing the Spear of Sorrow. The following moments were coming back to her.

When the spear-like tower of water crashed down, only the Overleader had been affected by it, but in Celeste's moment of joy at seeing the water turn clear again, she became a dove. Two other doves—Teresa's doves!—whisked her away to Old Man Massive's mountain, where they left her to release the sea creatures looming far and wide in a menacing bubble over the sea and land.

And then the ravens, Odin's companions, brought her to this breathtaking realm above it all.

"You see, yes? It is not over." Odin pointed to a place on the planet far below them, and although the tip of his crooked finger all but blotted out the tiny sphere, Celeste could see.

Crystal turquoise water by the shore near the village extended for miles out to sea, but then it became murky until farther out, near the center of the sea, a small area of sickly silver-pink appeared. Celeste cocked her head and peered into Odin's sad eye.

"You must return with my messengers and gather information. Travel the new world and its new peoples. I fear another power is at work below, hidden and more dangerous than I had suspected when I saved you from the siren song of the child. You are the one who understands the needs and desires of your people. My birds have served me well over the centuries, but like me, they are old and tired now. They cannot translate as they once did. If you cannot do this, Celeste—if you will not do this—I will surely die. *We* will surely die."

Without a moment for questions, Odin's ravens swept up on either side of Celeste and launched her from Odin's hand. Through the hole in the clouds they shot toward the planet below. Even if Celeste had wanted to, she could not break free from the wingtips flanking her, for they held her within a powerful magnetic field.

An odor of rotten eggs rose to greet them from a small patch of churning, steaming water below.

~ 5 ~

[Harmony]

HARMONY WATCHED SHARON jump backward and wondered if she had frightened her sister. Excited by her decision to try to look more like the girls she had seen in the village, Harmony expressed her happiness as she always had back in her water world—with light and sound. Her light throbbed in shifting colors of ethereal pink, then blue, then green, and this pattern of three repeated several times before dying out. Her celestial melody accompanied each surge of color.

When she completed her initial transformation, she stood taller and straighter. She noticed a look of astonishment and tears pooling in Sharon's eyes.

"Ha . . . Harmony?" Sharon rubbed her eyes in the sudden darkness after the light vanished. She walked over to where Harmony stood motionless. "Is that you? Those lights! That sound! Were you singing? How'd you do that? That was the most beautiful—"

"Harmony. Yes. It's . . . me." Harmony was as surprised as Sharon appeared to be. She extended her arms and looked at each hand, and then grabbed Sharon's hands in hers and compared them. She released her sister and took several steps, watching her feet as she moved. There was no limp. "I'm just like you now!"

But when she giggled, she exposed her hooked teeth which sparkled below enormous yellow eyes. Harmony noted the aversion in Sharon's expression.

"Not like you then," she said. "But now you won't leave me behind again!" She ran a quick circle around the clearing before returning to Sharon and stopped, close to the older girl.

When Sharon took a subtle step away from her sister, Harmony knew she'd have to be careful with how she interacted with others. She didn't want to be like the sharks that frightened away all the other fish.

"I'm sorry, Harmony. I was so excited about getting you back home, but it looks like we're too late. There's nothing here. Blanche was right."

"Not gone. Just . . . hiding. Come out, come out, wherever you are!" As Harmony spoke the childish incantation in a voice that seemed to be maturing, her eyes shone like moonlight on water and reflected a warm glow over the open space.

"Wait! Over there!" Sharon ran toward something reflecting in the distance and Harmony stayed right with her, matching her footsteps exactly, though not making any sound at all as she ran.

When they reached the glimmering spot, Sharon frowned.

"Oh. It's just the crystal doorknob." She plopped down ungracefully next to the front door of what was once the entrance to her house. It lay flat on the ground.

"Open it," said Harmony.

"What do you mean, 'open it'? It's not even attached to anything anymore."

"Open it," she repeated.

Sharon stood, shrugged off the oppressive cloak and gave Harmony a questioning look. Then she turned back to the door and stood motionless for a moment. "This is silly, you know." Nevertheless, she bent down and grabbed the shiny crystal doorknob and turned it slowly.

Click.

Eyebrows raised, she looked back over her shoulder to see Harmony standing there wearing the cloak and looking taller.

"Open it now. Hurry," Harmony ordered, and without further question, Sharon lifted up on the doorknob. Hinges creaked as she raised the door and a dank draft wafted up from a hole below it.

Harmony glanced over Sharon's shoulder and her eyes illuminated a stairway. "Let's go." She nudged Sharon onto the first step and after closing the door behind them, followed her down a length of crooked wooden stairs until they turned into a badly damaged room.

"It's the kitchen!" Sharon stumbled over detritus strewn across the floor and opened one of the cupboards. "Yes!" She pulled out several cans of spiced ham and searched for an opener. When she found it, she sat on the floor against a cabinet and opened two cans. She handed one to Harmony, who sat close by.

The two ate hungrily in the closed space eerily illuminated by Harmony's eyes.

"How did you know?" asked Sharon.

"It was a door, and doors open."

"But—"

"No buts." Harmony cut her off.

"Hey, you're not my mother." Sharon frowned again and Harmony felt her sister staring at her while she ate. When they finished, Sharon placed her hand on Harmony's. "I didn't mean to snap at you. Our parents. What did they do to you? Why did they hide you from me? How did you survive, and where did you live these past, what—ten years?"

Harmony dimmed the glow from her eyes and gazed into her sister's eyes as if trying to find something hidden deep inside. "I saw the frightened look on your face when you first saw me," she whispered. "Imagine my birth. Imagine a parent's horror."

"You were just a baby! It wasn't your fault! That was *you* crying in the night, wasn't it? They told me it was only the wind. Tell me what they did to you."

"I only remember cold, and needles, darkness, and—" Harmony's eyes lit on a long filet knife leaning against a corner and stopped talking.

"I'm sorry. No more questions tonight, okay? You must be as exhausted as I am. I think we might be able to get to the bedroom if we can get past that beam."

The girls worked their way through a crushed doorway and crawled under a fallen support beam. Sharon kicked at a door and it crashed to the floor, raising a dust cloud that choked them. When the dust settled, they found a mattress under more debris. Together they lifted one side to clear it off, and without a word, settled down on it back to back.

Sharon fell asleep within moments. Harmony closed only her nictitating membranes. She was too stimulated by the day's events to sleep, and didn't really need to anyway. Her opaque lids dimmed the glow from her eyes but allowed her to remain alert to her surroundings. She removed the cloak, finally dry, and spread it over Sharon. Then she sat back up and tried to make sense of things.

Though it had happened years ago, Harmony still remembered the sensation of splashing around her tiny body and then floating on a vast sea. She remembered the steely eyes of the people who had thrown her into the water. Too young to know fear, she remembered giggling, and then the sensation of sliding through a phosphorescent tube.

Harmony shook her head to relieve the throbbing pain between her temples. She wondered how long she'd have to wait before Sharon would wake up. She'd need to keep the older girl close by if she wanted to survive on dry land.

While she waited, Harmony slowed her heartbeat and scrutinized the ruined room.

So, this could have been my home.

~ 6 ~

[The Village / Orville]

THE ANDROGYNOUS ARCHERS wore no clothing for indeed, there was nothing to hide. With bow in hand and an arrow at the ready, the archers had witnessed Sharon and Harmony disappear into the ground. They headed back through the forest to keep eyes on the village from a safe vantage point.

With gelatinous skin that adjusted constantly to the surroundings, the archers could hide anywhere, especially in the growing darkness.

~ ~ ~ ~ ~

Orville was eager to hear what Nick would say when he, Ranger and Thunder returned to the village.

"We need a plan," said Nick.

"Did you find her?" asked Chimney. Orville noted the boy's distress after seeing Nick's expression. Chimney dug his toe into the dirt and frowned before mumbling, "She saved us, you know. It doesn't make any sense she'd leave us now, does it?"

"It was not her decision, child," said Ranger. "We will find her. Or she will find us. Do not despair."

"Of whom do you speak?" Orville knew that if he hoped to maintain his cover as Finn, just one of many people released from the bizarre water, he'd need to watch what he said. He couldn't let on that he was just as anxious about Celeste as they were. He noticed Ranger sniffing the air around him suspiciously.

"A girl who could fly." Ryder scanned the heavens. Orville believed if anyone could spot her, it would be the boy with eyes that could see across miles and through skin, even copper skin. His power had helped him set Chimney's broken leg after his fall into the fissure.

Orville wondered if Ryder would recognize him in his new skin. The boy had repaired his broken frog wing too, and had cried when he realized the frog had lost too much blood.

"Celeste can't help us if she's not here," said Nick. "And like I said, we need a plan for all these people and . . . things heading this way. We need to handle this by ourselves. We barely have enough places for our own people to stay," he cast a sideways glance at Orville and Riku, "and then there's the food issue."

Maddie placed her hand on Chimney's shoulder. "Chimney can find lots of food, and Teresa? Now that you can see again, do you think it'll be easier to grow more in the garden?"

Teresa smiled and looked at the young ones gathered around the group. "Yes, I think so. And now I'll be able to teach the others."

"Celeste was supposed to be their teacher."

Orville knew Nick's words weren't meant to be offensive, but noted how Teresa looked to Mac for reassurance, smiling at the handsome young man who had protected her when she was blind and unable to communicate.

Mac drew Teresa closer. "She'll be back, Nick. Chimney's right. She wouldn't leave us after saving us without a good reason."

"I feel so useless," said Nick. "I wish I could reverse time and go back to—"

"Hush!" Ranger barked, his ears standing straight and his gaze locking onto a tree in the woods. "Something lurks." Without another word, he ran toward the trees, and Thunder was by his side in an instant.

Orville watched the noble creatures and marveled at their willingness to confront a potential threat. They, and he, all shared an unusual connection with Celeste. They all wanted to believe she was safe, and would return.

~ ~ ~ ~ ~

"Be careful, dude. Let's not run right into trouble." Thunder's colors swirled faster with excitement.

"Smart. This way," said Ranger, and the two veered off at an angle, positioning themselves behind a large tree trunk not far from the perceived threat.

"What now, boss?" Even when Thunder whispered, his voice echoed through the woods.

"Show yourself!" Ranger commanded the indistinct form not far from their position. An eerie and confusing response followed.

"We will not harm you / It is not our intention / Opposite is true."

Ranger looked at Thunder, who stared straight ahead. Several voices spoke as one in harmony. The effect was mesmerizing. Even more mesmerizing was what approached them.

With three unique heads atop one shared, twisting, two-armed body, the archers moved silently toward them. Long, slender necks allowed their heads to turn in every direction, and with limbs that appeared to move as easily forward as backward and sideways, the archers could move stealthily.

Shiny black hair from each head braided together and met in a massive coiled pile like a whip undulating between the three heads.

One head was distinctly masculine. Deep brown eyes like swirling pools of dark chocolate peered from under thick black brows that matched closely cropped facial hair. Another had glacier blue eyes and softer features with full, pearly lips. The third inclined neither to the masculine nor the feminine, but instead, was violet-eyed and childlike.

They stopped within feet of the stunned observers.

"What . . . who are you? State your intentions." Ranger regained his composure while Thunder stared, speechless.

"Many call us Merts / Doorways to hidden places / We will watch for you," they spoke.

"I do not understand. Speak clearly, Merts," said Ranger.

"Leave us to our task / We work alone together / You need not fear us."

All but Merts' eyes and hair and the bow and arrows they carried shifted and blurred as they moved. The effect was disconcerting.

"Dude!" Thunder stared, his furry brows raised high.

"Mother watches too / But great challenges await / Those who still believe."

"Whose mother? Still believe what? Tell what you know, Merts." Ranger sounded vexed.

"Back to your people / They grow in number and fear / That is dangerous."

Thunder finally shook himself from his trance and looked back toward the village. New people approached from the hill beyond. "Hey, boss, check it out."

Ranger looked back and the hairs on his hackles rose. He turned to tell Merts he was not finished with them yet.

But the archers were gone.

~ ~ ~ ~ ~

Merts hadn't gone far. Leaving their bow and a quiver of arrows in front of Ranger, they launched their hair up into the nearest tree. The black whip intertwined with bare tree branches and lifted Merts from the ground. They blended in with the tree trunk high above the animals. It was the perfect camouflage.

"Why would they leave their weapon, boss?" Thunder paced around the longbow.

"Perhaps as a sign of peace." Ranger sniffed the air. A fresh scent of seawater lingered, and he easily could have located the archers. But the scent of fear in the village was more powerful.

"Come. We are needed. I sense no threat from Merts."

The two got to the village just as several strangers ambled toward the group.

~ 7 ~

[Celeste]

CELESTE BRACED FOR IMPACT. Just when she thought she'd plummet into the steaming pink water with the enormous ravens by her side, her guardians swooped into a breathtaking arc and hovered. They seemed to focus on a single point below the surface, though she couldn't see beyond an occasional reflection of sky through the steam.

She tried to communicate with the shimmering black birds but got nothing from them.

Resuming their flight, they soared over an endless expanse of rolling liquid until the steam and odor disappeared and the water became blue again, the color Celeste remembered seeing after the Spear of Sorrow disappeared into its depths. Daybreak cast a serene glow over the panorama and for a moment, she felt like a girl again, gliding over ripples that giggled.

The thought frightened her, and she sensed a shift in her body. A heaviness flickered through her being and she believed the ravens felt it too. They moved in closer to her until the sensation passed.

Land appeared, though it resembled no land she knew. Mountains of mud rose from a shoreline that pulled at them as it receded. For miles and miles there was nothing but mud in various configurations and an occasional struggling, doomed sea creature.

We need to get them back to the water, Celeste thought. They were close enough to touch, and she struggled to break away, but the ravens held her steadfast between them. *Stop! Where are you taking me?*

They looked at her then with their brilliant black eyes and her head filled with images of foreign lands and thriving villages and cities with towering buildings and children laughing and families gathered together and—

"STOP!" she screamed, and the abrupt shift in her weight and intensity of her command severed her connection with the birds. Although she didn't fall far, her awkward impact with the ground knocked the wind out of her and left her sinking slowly in the slime, her long black hair a muddy mess across her face.

Startled, the ravens flew circles around the teenager, squawking and pecking at her lightly.

Celeste gasped and struggled to sit up. She coughed and spat mud, and when she opened her emerald green eyes and saw the ravens circling, she grabbed handfuls of slime and readied herself to throw it at them. But she sensed another flux. Flinging the mud from her fingers, she watched as they transformed to wingtips and kept watching as her legs shrank out of the mud into bird's legs. When she shook the growing dizziness from her head, she saw her beak and knew her transformation was complete.

The ravens locked wings with the muddy dove and lifted her from the ground. They resumed their tour of the planet, and this time, stayed low against the landscape.

Celeste thought she might be dreaming, and for a long while, she accepted the thought. The visions in her brain faded and she closed her eyes, allowing the ravens to carry her where they wished and enjoying the breeze tickling her through her filthy feathers.

Her bliss ended abruptly when she opened her eyes under cold water. The ravens had dunked and were dragging her through a mountain lake. When they raised her back into the air, their throaty "caws" sounded like laughter. She was not amused, but now she was clean and had to admit, it felt better.

The lake water was clean like the mountains surrounding it. No more mud. Here and there, signs of green growth appeared along with flashes of movement. Mountains became plains and Celeste recognized groupings of people and assorted wildlife wandering around, denser in some places than others. Occasionally a person or an animal spotted the three linked birds flying overhead, but no one expressed surprise.

She grew weary. It seemed they had traveled around the entire planet, and perhaps they had. The sun was setting—or was it still rising?—when they came across a village that shook the fatigue from her tiny bones.

It was their village. Her village. She recognized their faces and tried to remember their names, but there were new faces too, and she noticed others approaching the village from the hilltop where she—was it she?—had hurled an evil spear into the water.

She sensed unease in a small group facing the newcomers and wondered why the dog and the multicolored jaguar kept looking into the woods behind them. *Ranger, his name is Ranger, and the jaguar's name is—*

A bolt of lightning blinded her for a moment before it struck the hillside, and then another and another closer to the people below. The people screamed and scattered.

Celeste struggled to free herself. She could help them, if only she could break away from the ravens, but struggle as she might, their magnetic grasp only grew stronger. And then, everything below was blotted out by an icy white cloud.

Breathless once more, she recognized where the ravens were taking her this time. She stopped struggling. The moment she saw the first wisps of rainbow-colored clouds, a surge of joy unlike any she had experienced overwhelmed her and she cooed a delighted song. Nothing on the planet below could compare with the beauty of her new celestial home.

Odin greeted the returning messengers with open arms. The ravens perched on either shoulder, and Celeste landed lightly in his right hand.

"Tell me, travelers, how fares the planet?"

The ravens peered into Odin's one eye and delivered their images, which Celeste watched in his eye's reflection. When she saw the teenage girl splat into a muddy landscape, her breath caught in her throat and she sensed a looming flux. With the first lightning bolt that seemed to come straight from Odin's eye, Celeste slid from his hand and landed on her human feet in front of the great god.

"Come, child, do not fear." His words were kind and his arms reached out to hold her, but she jumped back.

"What's happening to me? I can't control this!" She stared at her hands, spreading her fingers wide in anticipation of seeing feathers appear, and with her first teardrop, she sank into the swirling clouds. Fear gripped her as she imagined herself plummeting from the heavens to a swift death below.

"Oh, child, you must believe in yourself for others to believe in you. If only the same were true for me." Odin reached down and grasped Celeste's hand from the clouds. "Have I not told you the importance of your task? Do you believe I would let you fail, or fall from this great height? Now come with me and rest your troubled spirit. We will watch over you."

Odin led Celeste to a glowing room with an enormous bed made of soft, buoyant clouds. She was nearly asleep before he draped a light cloud cover over her, but she heard him summon his wolves.

"Watch over her. I know not the cause of her transformations, but we must not let her fly away."

As he lumbered off, rumbling booms filled the atmosphere.

~ 8 ~

[Harmony]

HARMONY LIKED not needing to sleep. It was such a waste of time. The things she was able to accomplish in her underwater world were as limitless as her imagination, and with each new artifact she found on the ocean floor, she expanded her magical sandcastle. Sure, much of what she fabricated was made from sand, but Kumugwe had saved her life and granted her much power.

"My home is now yours, creature," the sea god had told her long ago when he pulled her from the surface of his waters.

She was too young to understand him then, but it didn't matter. Kumugwe fed her and cared for her and taught her how to live and breathe in his world. A lover of music—his not-so-secret pleasure was harmonizing with the whales—he expressed delight in the sound of her laughter and called her "my funny little Harmony."

He made sure she was never at a loss for playmates. From baby seals to giant orcas, all manner of sea life tended to her whims. Nevertheless, she knew she was a unique creature in the sea world and wondered if she'd ever meet another like herself.

Several years after The Event, Kumugwe opened a water tunnel and showed her a distant girl standing on a precipice.

"If you can lure her to you, you can keep her," he told her. "Look! She's going to jump!"

Harmony didn't know who the girl was or why she would do such a foolish thing, but she was determined to succeed in capturing a playmate like herself. She began to sing a song Kumugwe had taught her, and in her excited anticipation of studying the girl, she giggled and giggled, sending mysterious bubbly tunes throughout the silvery-pink water.

It hadn't taken long before she had the girl trapped in her sandcastle. Kumugwe had taught Harmony how to see into the minds of others, so she learned everything she needed to know about the girl's family. She knew what her parents looked like and how they spoke and what her favorite foods were, and she even learned enough about the dog to make him nearly alive.

But she'd never heard the girl's name.

By the time her new playmate was sliding down the first seaweed hallway, Kumugwe had animated the family Harmony had created for the new girl. Harmony could tell he was delighted by her resourcefulness. He was a good father.

If only Odin hadn't interfered. Harmony was almost ready to introduce herself to her new playmate after secretly studying her for a long time, but then the pesky sky god delivered a strange package. Curious to see what was inside, she allowed the girl to open it. It took her too long to figure out the girl was trying to escape, and as hard as she tried, without Kumugwe nearby, Harmony was not strong enough to keep the winged metal creature from stealing the girl away.

But now she had a real sister who was still asleep in the dusty depths of their crumbled home. She soon grew bored of waiting for Sharon to wake up and had no idea how long people were supposed to sleep anyway. Quietly, she left the bed and crawled through the debris to the stairway. A sudden intense thirst made her feel panicky. She needed water.

She pushed the flattened door up at the top of the stairs and gasped when a gust of wind pulled it from her hand. In total awe of the atmosphere above her, she walked into it cautiously. The ground was covered in an icy white substance. Instinctively she rolled in it, melting it with the heat of her parched body and renewing her dehydrated cells. When the sensation of shivering frightened her, she returned to the safety of the dreary space below.

Harmony had grown herself to be as tall as her sister, and explored other rooms in the damaged structure to find clothes to fit. In a closet of another room were garments that must have belonged to the woman who'd given birth to her. Who was that person? She searched for clues in scattered items around the room.

Boring garments, trinkets, scientific magazines and books, and various bottles holding fragrant, slippery substances were all she pulled from the mess. There were no photographs, no paintings, no artwork. No books other than technical ones. There was nothing to illuminate her biological parents' personalities beyond their obvious devotion to science.

And then she saw a shiny object like the front doorknob behind a damaged full-length mirror.

The door was ajar, and much like the one on the ground above, this one led to a stairway. She opened her eyes wide for maximum illumination and saw the stairway curve out of sight far below. Down she went, taking care not to fall through the occasional missing or damaged step, until she came to another door where the stairs ended. But unlike the other doors in the house, she couldn't open this one easily.

She wondered if Sharon knew about the door and the space behind it.

With great effort and much surprise at the strength in her newly matured arms and legs, Harmony slid the door open just enough to squeeze through. Her eyes lit on a room undamaged by the disaster that had struck the rest of the house, and as she gazed around, she trembled. The metal table, the surgical instruments, the beakers and chemicals and charts covering the surfaces of every wall—this was where her parents had tried to fix her. She turned to run from the room when an unusual schematic caught her attention.

She knew where they were.

Far away, she heard Sharon calling her name, but she wasn't ready to share her revelation.

Quickly and quietly she returned to the bedroom and replaced the mirror, ensuring the door remained hidden. She busied herself with clothing on the closet floor just as Sharon walked in to find her.

"I was worried. Did you even sleep?" Sharon's voice sounded crackly. Odd. Old.

"Yes, of course, I didn't want to wake you, but the thing I was wearing when you found me didn't fit anymore." She giggled at the obvious truth. "You're okay with me wearing these, right?"

"Yeah, yeah, of course. But what . . . how—"

"And I went outside just a moment ago and there's a cold white substance all over the ground and falling from the sky. Are we in danger?" Harmony wasn't ready to discuss her transformation yet either.

"Cold? White? Are you talking about snow?"

"I don't know. I've never seen, well, anything on the outside of the sea. Is snow dangerous?" Harmony's language was improving, as was her ability to influence her sister's behavior.

"No! No, it's just that it hasn't snowed or rained since before The Event. I'd like to see it, but wow. I feel achy all over. Please tell me I'm not changing back into that old body again!" A look of fear flashed across her face.

"No, you'll be fine," said Harmony. She was glad for the distraction. And as much as she wanted to get to know her sister and learn about life on this side of the water, she couldn't wait until Sharon fell asleep again so she could spend more time in the laboratory below.

She was going to find the people who tossed her into the sea.

~ **9** ~

[The Village / Orville]

THE BLIZZARD HIT with a fury. But just as suddenly as it had started, it stopped, leaving Orville and everyone around him stunned. If the lightning bolts weren't enough to frighten them, the cloud that swirled around them certainly got their attention. Wind-whipped ice crystals stung Orville's cheeks and blinded him until the cloud vanished.

Orville remembered snow and wondered if the villagers' memories were as bittersweet as his. Snow meant holidays and sledding and families gathered for feasts. But the families were gone now.

"Look, Katie! That big white cloud turned everything cold, just like you can do!" Lena threw a handful of snow at her twin sister and when Katie returned the gesture, the girls laughed and tumbled in a substance neither of them had likely seen before.

For a brief moment everything seemed suspended in time and a slow smile spread across Orville's face. The magic of the moment was soon shattered, however, by a boisterous newcomer.

"Don't trust a single one. They're watching us, you know, they're watching us, and don't you say no. Not a single one. Clouds—they'll getcha, they will. And you'll never come back. Come back. Come back."

In the confusion of the storm, the villagers had lost track of the newcomers. Several of various ages, all with copper skin, eyed one another suspiciously and moved a distance away from the loud one. Even the children stopped their spontaneous play when they heard him ranting.

Orville approached him slowly. Clearly distraught, the disheveled gentleman appeared wild-eyed and jumpy. "Hello, friend," Orville spoke softly, as if to counteract the man's agitation, "I'm Finn. What's your name?" He extended his hand as an offering of good will to the man. The others watched.

"A name? A name? What's in a name? Ha! Finn? Like a fish? What kind of name is Finn? Not your name. Not your name. Kindly remove your fin from my face, sir!"

The children giggled, and Orville persisted. "The kind people of this village may need help rebuilding, sir, and like you, I have just come from the sea."

"Rebuild? Rebuild, you say? A mason, you'll need. I'm Mason. A mason. I'm Mason. There's work to be done and we must find them. Find them and stop them and so many colors." He stared at Thunder as he ranted and the children laughed again.

"Well, Mason," Orville glanced over his shoulder at the wide-eyed spectators, "the village could probably use more laborers." He looked at the other newcomers and saw they were bedraggled and hollow-eyed. "Chimney, son, I understand you might have something for all to eat. May we work together to find shelter before nightfall? Come tomorrow, we will think more clearly."

Blanche appeared irked that the man with the gold-flecked jade eyes seemed to be taking control. "He's my brother, and if you don't mind, I'll tell him what to do."

Orville knew he shouldn't expect the girl who had been so cruel to him when he was a winged frog to be any different now that the threat of the pink ooze had passed. "I mean no offense, *mademoiselle*, but it has been my experience that with food and rest, many things are made easier." His French accent slipped out.

While Orville spoke, he noticed Chimney studying him. He wanted to hug the boy who had fallen into the fissures with him and had saved Thunder's two cubs, but the time wasn't right.

"We got lots, sis, and I'm hungry. Hey, Bridger, can you do that thing that you do and make some little rooms or somethin' for them new guys?"

Bridger nodded, and Blanche huffed back to her house.

"Mud. Lots of mud. And feathers, feathers, find the feathers." Mason shook himself while he spoke.

"Come, Mason, we'll find whatever you need tomorrow. For now, calm yourself." Orville coaxed the man into town and the others followed while Bridger and Ryder discussed where to build the new shelters.

No one saw Orville's eyes bulge and his tongue whip out to catch a passing insect when he turned away from Mason. And no one but Orville noticed when Riku bent over because a patch of lizard skin flashed down her back and threatened to transform her completely. But when the two looked at one another, Orville knew they had each sensed the other's flux.

And when the ground rumbled briefly, Nick's eyes opened wide. "Stop!" he yelled, and everyone turned to look at him. "No, I mean . . . never mind. I just, ah, I just tried to stop that shaking, but—" Nick didn't finish, and Orville could see he was perplexed.

He could also see Ranger and Thunder studying the forest, and trusted they would remain on high alert for any other surprise visitors.

~ ~ ~ ~ ~

Merts returned to where the girls had disappeared into the ground. They sensed uneasiness in the surroundings and anticipated the girls would reappear at some point. They also knew the villagers would need more than what Chimney and Maddie had found that day to eat.

Moving in a way even the most attentive creatures wouldn't sense, Merts hunted small game, and with each new kill, their braided hair whipped out to retrieve the arrows and bounty. When they were satisfied they had gathered enough, they deposited the animals at the edge of the forest and created a ruckus to attract attention.

Bridger and Ryder were closest, and by the time they found the food, Merts were well hidden high in the trees.

Ryder alternately squinted and opened his eyes wide, searching for what had made the commotion and left the food.

"I can't do it anymore," he whispered.

"Do what?" Bridger looked frightened.

"I can't see like I used to. Quick! Make a shelter."

Bridger pointed to some materials and willed them into the shape of a small hut, the way he had made survival boats not long ago, but nothing moved.

"Uh-oh. Whaddawe do now?" he asked.

"I don't know, buddy, I don't know." Ryder removed his glasses and rubbed his eyes. "I guess we bring these animals to Blanche and see what she says."

"Stuff's still messed up, isn't it?" Bridger worked hard not to cry.

"Don't worry, Bridger. We'll figure things out."

~ ~ ~ ~ ~

The dragonfly flew a high, wide circle over village and forest and beachfront before returning to its home. Merts saw its flames and wondered what it was.

~ 10 ~

[Celeste]

CELESTE STRUGGLED TO WAKE from a dream that threatened to hold her captive.

"Once upon a time there was a lost little bear who was afraid of being alone, but she didn't need to be afraid. She would never be alone."

"Tell me more!" the child begged. *"And why is she alone now? See?"* She pointed to a lone girl standing on a rocky island in a picture book.

"Never alone. Never alone. She's never alone." The man stood and closed the book, which crumbled into a pile of sand at his feet. Something about him seemed familiar.

"But wait! Don't leave! Please don't leave me alone! I'll die!" The child pleaded with the man when he stared at the sand pile, but then he turned, walked away, and disappeared in a cloud.

Suddenly suspended above a serene mountain lake, the child wept. One teardrop fell onto the mirror-like surface below, and from it, concentric ripples expanded and swelled until the child could see tsunami waves crashing on every shore around the planet.

She stopped crying then, fearful of what another drop might do, and when she had calmed herself she heard a heartbeat coming from deep below the water. But it was not a normal heartbeat.

Thud-thud-clink, thud-thud-clink, thud-thud-clink.
A plaintive cry for help arose over the heartbeat . . .

"Who's there? Who's making that noise?" Celeste shook herself awake, scaring the wolves who sat guard on either side of her nebulous bed.

The wolves howled and Odin appeared.

"Now, now, beasts, the child is already frightened! Be gone!" The animals trotted noiselessly away just as Odin's ravens landed on his shoulders.

Celeste tried to get out of bed, but could get no leverage on the swirling surface on which she had somehow slept. She floundered under the wispy cloud cover. Tossed from side to side by the billowing bed, she recalled a similar time, a time when an undulating bubble of a bed had rocked her into a deep sleep.

"Cease your struggle, spirited one, and you will accomplish what you intend."

Celeste couldn't see Odin through the cover, but knew he could see her. She sensed the grin on his face.

"There's nothing here to push against! How am I supposed to move when there's no resistance?" She lay back in frustration.

"Ah, but how easy it is to move without resistance! Why is it that mortals expect everything to be difficult, and when expectations become reality, they protest? Rise, child, and tell me what you learned on your first circumnavigation of the planet."

The cloud cover vanished and Celeste hesitantly extended one foot over the side of the bed. Feeling nothing beneath her foot, she looked to Odin for reassurance.

"Rid yourself of expectations and stand."

Odin had already assured her he wouldn't let her fall, but her self-preservation instinct was strong. Sure, gods and their supernatural creatures could go wherever they wanted without fearing death, but she was no god. She moved her other foot to where the floor should be, and even though she still felt nothing but space beneath her feet, she stood.

"And now you believe in me?" Odin's question sounded like one a child would ask.

"Of course I believe in you. Unless I'm still dreaming, I just slept inside a cloud and haven't fallen through these beautiful, colorful strands yet because of you. Am I still dreaming?"

"These dreams, child, tell me, what is it you fear? Are not dreams mere fanciful games in your head?"

Celeste couldn't imagine the god was being serious. "Are you telling me you've never had a dream? I wish they were just games. Then I wouldn't have to worry about things like that strange heartbeat."

"Tell me more," Odin persisted, and his words brought Celeste back to the frightened girl in her most recent dream.

"I'm not sure how to explain it," she began, wondering how much she should share with the eager-eared god. "It was just different, that's all. Not like my heartbeat. But you wanted to know about what I learned below."

"Yes! Yes, indeed. You saw a planet recovering from a great deluge, you saw the sea receding and living things returning to the land, you saw things both foreign and familiar, and you saw the troubled waters still churning."

Celeste noticed he hadn't mentioned the blinding lightning bolts she suspected he had hurled to prevent her from getting too close to people she might recognize in the village.

"I guess I learned that I failed. I thought I'd found the key to stopping the ooze—and maybe even finding my parents—but if there's still some pink liquid down there, it could grow again, right? Can't you make it go away? You're a god. Can't you just swirl your hand like you did with the clouds and make it go away, or fix it?"

"Is that what you believe is my obligation? To make all the bad things go away? To fix all the mistakes made by creatures who cannot foresee the consequences of their actions? If that were the case, child, I would have died from exhaustion long ago!"

"Then what good are you?" Celeste planted her hands on her hips and stared into the old god's eye. Fear flashed through her body when she realized that with one swirl of his hand he could send her to her death in an instant. Instead of quavering, however, she remained resolute. He had told her to stand. He had told her he needed her. She continued to stare.

Odin squinted back at her, and then released a burst of thundering laughter that blew the clouds around her and threatened to knock her onto a passing cloud.

His laughter shook the ravens from his shoulders and they fluttered around the bold girl who willed herself to stay put despite the flurry surrounding her.

Celeste thought Odin's laughter at her affront was odd, and as the wingtips of his ravens tickled her face and forced her to close her eyes, she sensed a lightness in her body and knew another flux had occurred.

When she opened her eyes again, her wingtips were trapped in the magnetic field of Odin's black-beaked guardians.

And Odin had stopped laughing.

~ 11 ~

[Harmony]

HARMONY SENSED SHARON staring at her as the two climbed the stairs to the door. She wondered if the adaptations she was making to her body were too rapid, but she wanted her sister, and others, to accept her.

"Wait a minute, Harmony. Before we go outside, I'm just wondering how you're feeling. I'm sure you've noticed that you're starting to look like me. Come here and let me take a look at you." She sounded like what Harmony imagined a caring mother would sound like.

Harmony turned back and smiled at her sister, and as she did, her hooked yellow teeth flew from her mouth in every direction. Sharon flinched, raising her hands to her face to keep from being hit.

"Ouch! That was unpleasant." Harmony rubbed her cheeks and smiled again. She ran a finger over her new teeth. "Pretty?"

"They're . . . perfect. Mine aren't even that nice." Sharon frowned.

Harmony had made herself tall and slender, as tall as her sister, and with luxurious pink hair all the way to her lower back, she presented a stunning appearance. She wondered if her sister was angry at her for changing the way she looked, but didn't know why she would be.

"We'll go back to the village now?" Harmony turned to climb the stairs.

"No!" Sharon snapped.

"But you said they were mean to people who were different and I'm not different now. I fixed it, didn't I?" She sat on a stair. It didn't look like they'd be going outside soon.

"What do you mean, you fixed it? And your eyes . . . they're still not right." Sharon scrunched up her face.

"Well, I saw what the others looked like and studied you as you slept—"

"You *what*?"

"I mean, I noticed how you looked right before I fell asleep—and I thought I'd like to look like you." Harmony sensed she needed to watch what she said to her sister, a girl who seemed unhappy and angry. Humans were more complicated than she'd thought.

"So, you can make something happen just by thinking about it?" Sharon asked.

"I guess so. I've just done it a couple times since I came out of the water and met you. How wonderful it was that you were waiting right there for me! Maybe *you're* the one with the power!" Harmony thought this was a great idea and laughed, delighted by the sound of her own melodious voice.

But Sharon shook her head slowly.

"And how did you even get back here? I have so many questions about . . . everything. Were you on an island? How did you survive? And yeah, why are you back now?"

Harmony didn't know how to describe what her life had been like since the water god had rescued her, so she motioned for Sharon to sit next to her.

"Do you trust me?" Harmony asked. "I realize you don't know me well yet, but I am your sister."

Sharon nodded.

Harmony drew her sister's face close, touched foreheads with her and gazed, unblinking, into Sharon's eyes.

By projecting bits of her history this way, Harmony wouldn't have to struggle to find the right way to express what she had experienced in her short life. And she could also absorb some of Sharon's moisture.

"No way!" Sharon pulled away when the images stopped flooding her brain. "How long have we been sitting here?" She slumped against the wall, breathless. "I've never even heard of Kumugwe. He gave you everything! Why would you ever want to leave that world?" She looked into Harmony's orbed yellow eyes quizzically. They weren't quite as startlingly huge as they'd been moments earlier.

The question was like a slap in the face, and Harmony cried. Huge blue tears spilled down her copper cheeks and washed over her irises, changing them from yellow to a beautiful shade of sea green.

"I want to go home!" she wailed, but knew she couldn't. Not yet. She saw Sharon wince and remembered a similar reaction when her cry in the village made people cover their ears. She closed her eyes and calmed herself.

Harmony had stopped transmitting details of her life right before the part when Kumugwe showed her the girl on the precipice. She didn't know how Sharon would feel about how she'd lured the girl to her sandcastle as a playmate, only to lose her to a winged toy frog.

For some reason, she wanted to impress her older sister. And then, there was the job she needed to complete. She needed to find the girl and bring her back—back to her real home under the sea—but not as a playmate this time.

~ ~ ~ ~ ~

"The girl who escaped is the same one who returned my spear to me," Kumugwe had told her. He had felt its return the very moment Celeste had hurled it toward the sea, and he had seen her face. But when he sent the water tower crashing down to stop the old woman from hurting her, he'd lost sight of the girl with wavy black hair. "Bring her back to me and I will reward her greatly, as I have you."

Harmony believed there were other reasons Kumugwe wanted to find the girl. She had heard him singing songs of lamentation with the whales about rumored invaders with wicked intentions.

"If she is strong enough to return my mighty spear, perhaps she will be strong enough to rid us of our hidden foes," he had said.

"But you are mightier than everything in the sea!" Harmony had told him, and she believed it with all her heart. "Can't you find them? Can't you make them go away?"

"They have powers I do not understand, my little Harmony, and though my guardians are well dispersed throughout my salty realm, they have failed to find the source of our great disruption."

Harmony would make Kumugwe proud of her for discovering where the intruders were. And wouldn't her biological parents be surprised when they finally came face to face with her again after all those years? She remembered the look of disgust on their faces when they threw her overboard. She wondered how their faces would look when she'd walk back into their lives looking as she did now.

She couldn't let them know her true intentions, though, or who she was. At least not right away.

~ ~ ~ ~ ~

"It'll be okay, Harmony. We'll rebuild our home. Now dry your eyes."

Harmony took a deep breath of dry air and felt her sister patting her on the shoulder. When she opened her eyes again, they remained a sparkling sea green.

~ 12 ~

[The Village / Orville]

WHEN RYDER AND BRIDGER approached from the forest with the mysterious feast, Orville saw the newcomers eying the limp animals hungrily. He also sensed another flux was imminent.

"I don't feel good," he heard Chimney whisper to Nick, who stood with his eyes closed as he rubbed his temples.

"I know what you mean. Something's not right. I tried to stop things for a little while, but I couldn't. I feel . . . heavy."

"Me too. I feel like everyone's staring at me."

"They're not. They're all just hungry. But did you feel that tremor? Maybe things are just settling down now that the ooze is gone. Maybe that's why we feel like this. Something's definitely changing. Hey, maybe we don't need our powers anymore." Nick patted the boy on the back, something Orville had wanted to do.

"But I liked it when people didn't notice me." Chimney scrunched his shoulders and twitched. "And what if Celeste can't get back?"

Nick frowned. "She has to come back. She will come back. We'll find a way to get her back."

"Hey guys, check this out." Ryder entered the gathering. "No idea who left them there, but they're fresh." Displaying several rabbits he had grasped by the ears, he held out both arms.

Orville noticed that Bridger could barely lift the burden he held in his shirt, and helped him unload more small game.

"Nice," said Nick, refocusing his attention on the younger boys before scanning the forest. "Hey, Chimney and I were just talking about how things feel different now. Do you know what I mean? Does anyone else feel kinda weird?"

Orville knew his premonition about a flux had been right.

"Yeah. My vision's off," said Ryder, "and Bridger can't move anything to build the new huts. Do you know what it means?"

Nick shook his head. "Here, let me help. Hopefully we'll be able to get a fire going after that freak storm."

Several from the group still gathered on the street helped the boys while two of the newcomers gathered firewood.

"I can't remember the taste of meat," said one of the newcomers.

"Meat, meat, pleased to meet you! HA!" Mason piped up when he noticed the activity. "A hand, shall I give you a hand? But then I'd only have one. That won't do, won't do at all. I'm the handyman. I'm the mason, so I must have two hands, two arms, not eight. Eight arms lead to trouble. Haven't talked for days, so many days, but not dead! Not dead yet! The ol' gray mare, she ain't what she used to be, that's for sure. Imagine eight arms beating that drum. One-two-three, one-two-three, one-two-three."

Orville smiled at the man's erratic behavior and noticed how the others stayed out of his way. Blanche returned from the house and asked what all the commotion was about, and when she reached the group, she pointed toward the hilltop.

Though it was far away, Orville could see the approaching horse was larger than normal. And there was something odd about it. As it pranced closer, he could hear the clanking of what appeared to be its body armor.

"What's that between its ears?" someone asked. "And what's it dragging behind it?"

The group gathered closer together spontaneously, except for Mason, who busied himself with skinning the animals as he muttered about an "incessant drum." He seemed to take no notice of the approaching beast at the end of the road.

Lena walked to where Nick stood, and when she spoke, Orville listened closely to the child who could anticipate what was about to occur.

"The horse is frightened, Nick," she whispered. "She didn't always have a peacock stuck to her. Go ahead and stop her. Find out who she is."

"Does this mean we have our—"

Lena nodded yes before Nick finished his question, and before Orville could suggest caution, he saw the young man close his eyes in concentration and felt all around him freeze in space and time.

~ ~ ~ ~ ~

Nick stopped the horse and everything around the village. Even the crackling flames in the fire pit became an ethereal sculpture. He trotted to where the creature froze in mid-stride and stood before her in amazement.

What sounded like body armor was, in fact, the horse itself. Silver-gray sheets of metal with cogs and rivets at every joint emphasized its powerful anatomy. More unusual was the apparent fusion of a brilliant blue peacock's head between the ears of the horse's head.

Nick walked behind the horse to see what was dragging behind her. "I guess that makes sense," he mumbled when he recognized the iridescent colors of the long peacock tail feathers dragging behind the horse like a train on a wedding dress. One of the feathers had shed from its tail and lay just behind the others, and he picked it up. It was longer than he was tall, and the glowing eye at the end was larger than his own head.

He returned to the horse's head and saw no malice in her heavily lashed amber eyes. He wasn't as certain about the peacock head that seemed to have sprouted between the horse's ears.

In any case, he'd eventually have to start time again and the peacock-horse would require attention in the village. He replaced the feather where he'd found it and ran to the hilltop to determine how far his time-stopping extended.

"Please let Celeste be on her way here," he said to no one.

The view from the hilltop startled Nick. For as far as he could see, green grasses rose from mud and leaves sprouted from soggy, gnarled shrubs and trees. He saw no fissures, no water, and no Celeste. He thought he caught a glimpse of something large flying above and for a moment, feared Sharon might have resumed her murderous vulture form. If that were the case, he didn't want to leave the villagers defenseless.

Happy to know he still had some control over his surroundings, Nick returned to the village, touching the silvery-blue texture of the horse's metallic mane as he passed her. It was surprisingly soft.

~ ~ ~ ~ ~

Orville sensed he was back in time when he saw Nick standing where he'd been before he'd used his power, and watched the glorious horse complete her trek to the village.

She stopped before the amazed crowd and fanned her peacock tail, its crystalline structure reflecting every bit of ambient light.

Orville looked at the stunned crowd and thought that even Thunder with his fur—a palette of swirling pastels—couldn't compete with the iridescent awesomeness of the tail attached to the metal beast.

No one spoke for a long while until finally, Orville moved from Riku's side and walked slowly toward the towering horse. The silence was broken when he extended his hand toward the horse's muzzle.

"Finally, someone with guts." A grumpy voice came from the peacock. "Do you think maybe me and Layla could get a little somethin' to eat and drink? We're parched."

Orville turned back to the crowd and smiled, but still no one spoke.

"What? Am I talkin' gibberish here? Can anyone out there understand what I'm sayin'?"

"Welcome, and yes, we understand you." Orville spoke for the group. If there were any benefit to the turmoil the planet had endured, it was that regardless of the survivors' origins, when they spoke in their native language, all could comprehend what they were saying.

"Chimney, please show Layla and her, ah—"

"Lou. Just call me Lou," the bird said. "We're together, if that ain't already obvious, but she don't talk much."

"Would you take our guests to the pond? We were just preparing food as you arrived."

The other children accompanied Chimney and the horse to the pond, cautiously staying clear of her huge clanking hooves.

"Clank-clank-clank. One-two-clank. That's the lullaby. That's what they want you to hear when they're watching you while you sleep. They're always watching, you know." Mason skinned the last of the small game, wiped his hands on his trousers and walked into the woods.

~ 13 ~

[Celeste]

CELESTE WAS LOSING HERSELF. Each time she became a dove she felt light and free and unencumbered by the concerns of others. With the brain of a bird, she found Odin's breathtaking realm enchanting, and believed that if she remained there long enough, his wolves and ravens would befriend her.

She believed the sky god was powerful and benevolent. Why, then, did the tiny voice in her head tell her she must fly away? And how would that even be possible?

"So small and yet so bold. There is a reason you were marked, little Paloma, though even I have yet to discover it." Odin sat upon his massive golden throne and gestured for his ravens to leave her.

Marked? What does he mean, marked? she wondered.

"Come, perch on this great armrest and I will describe it for you."

Celeste had forgotten Odin could hear her thoughts when she was a bird. She wasn't sure if he could read her mind in her human form. She'd have to consider her thoughts carefully. She perched near the tired god.

"I do not imagine you have seen it before. Even I failed to notice until just now when you turned your beak away from me. Turn from me now and let us see what this means."

Celeste took two small hops, turning her back on him, and fought the urge to turn back around. Was he playing some sort of trick on her? She had to remain calm.

"A solitary droplet on the crown of your head and beneath it, three concentric ripples. Is it a raindrop? Perhaps a teardrop? Are raindrops and teardrops any different, save for the origin? No one could have noticed this beneath your dark curls, and even on your smooth feathers the image is blurred, but yes, that is what I see."

Celeste remembered a girl's teardrop triggering tsunamis. *I must never cry again.*

"Ah, but you will, little bird, you will. Tell me, though, why such a thought should occur to you."

You say you need me, and that makes me feel both honored and frightened. What if I'm not as special as you think I am? I don't want to cry because you might think I'm weak, and I don't want to disappoint you.

Even though Celeste's tiny brain filled with confusion, she hoped he wouldn't question her thoughts. She needed to learn more about Odin's intentions. She knew very little about the gods, but her instincts told her she must earn this one's trust.

As if sensing conflict, Odin's wolves bounded into the room and sat at their master's feet, whining softly. Celeste had to think of them too. If Odin did die, so would they.

And what does it even mean for a god to die? Where does a dead god go? It makes no sense that you would fear death, though. She remembered the chanting of Odin's name around the shrinking pond. *Couldn't you hear them calling you every night?*

"The insincere ranting of children. Pshaw. They called my name because one brash girl told them they must. They do not truly believe."

Nick had told her as much the first night she arrived in his village. *Nick!* The thought of him made her feel like a girl again. *But I am a girl.* "I'm not a bird!"

Her last words startled them all, for her transformation happened quickly. Sitting on Odin's armrest with her long legs dangling into the clouds, Celeste reached to the back of her head to see if she could feel the markings Odin had described. All she felt was a tingling in her tangle of hair.

"Yes, child, you are a girl. And who is this Nick?"

How could she describe the young man who had trusted her unconditionally when his village was about to be destroyed, his gorgeous eyes, his selfless way of helping others, his arms around her as they flew together?

"He's just one of the boys I remember from the village." She felt blood rise to her cheeks.

"I see." Odin nodded slowly. "And the thought of this particular boy shook you from your feathers?"

Celeste wondered the same thing. *I have to stay a girl, I have to stay a girl, I have to stay a girl.* She repeated the demand in her mind several times before speaking. If Odin could read her mind, he'd ask about her repetition.

"I'm not sure, but he reminded me that you're right. They don't all believe in you. And why should they? They were desperate for rain for years, and you could have provided it. Why didn't you rain on them, at least once? Maybe that would've kept them believing." Celeste was glad he didn't question her mental *stay a girl* chant.

"And we are back to your naïve belief that the gods should answer the demands of their mortals. Do you know how many voices have been raised to my kingdom over the centuries? Have you considered, perhaps, that I may have been focusing my efforts on keeping the troubled waters from consuming even the weakest believer? Ah, but even my deep-water brother cannot control his domain."

"What do you mean?" Celeste was confused.

"Kumugwe is the one sea god still living, though perhaps his fate is tied to mine. Neither he nor I understand the new power that shook the planet years ago. He told me of a child he had rescued, and most recently, about the new playmate she had lured from a cliffside. I knew it must be you. Perhaps Kumugwe would have saved you from your slow death as he had saved the crippled child, but I could not take that chance."

"I don't know anything about a child," said Celeste, though she remembered the sound of a child giggling. "So, you delivered Orville to me to save my life."

"I had to be sneaky." Odin raised his brows and grinned like a little boy. "If he knew I was there, his sea beasts would have caused trouble for us all. We gods do not tolerate interlopers."

Celeste suddenly missed Orville terribly. "And you must have saved Orville's life too, then."

"Indeed. He fought the mightiest of battles to protect you. I reached him just in time. And as I could not risk sending him to you in his weakened, fleshy body, I rebuilt him with steel and sea metals. Kumugwe would not miss the amount of copper I, ah, borrowed from his stores." He looked behind him as if expecting the sea god himself to be listening.

Celeste wondered why a powerful god would care about one girl and was troubled by a sense of obligation she felt for what he had done for her. She didn't like the idea of owing him anything, but if he could help her find her real parents— not the creepy ones who tricked her in the sandcastle—she would do what she could to assist.

"Send me back to the village now and I'll see what I can do to make them believe in you again." Celeste was certain she could make the villagers believe. "After all, you are real. Do you think I could convince them?"

She thought that if they all believed again, Odin would watch over them.

"If only it were that easy, child. There is much to be done in my realm, and we must find a way to stop the hidden threat below. If not, all will be lost. But you believe in me, and that is a start."

"What do you mean, there's much to be done? How can I possibly help up here?" Celeste felt anxious to return to her people.

"Patience, my friend. You must have patience."

~ ~ ~ ~ ~

She didn't know the sky god had no intention of releasing her from his control. Ever.

~ 14 ~

[Harmony]

HARMONY WANTED TIME to explore the lab more by herself, but realized she'd need Sharon to help put all the pieces together. The story of their parents was like a puzzle in her sandcastle, and she wasn't even sure if Sharon could see the completed picture.

"Sister, I don't want you to be angry with me, but I found the lab right before you woke up." Harmony noted a flash of confusion contort Sharon's face.

"Oh, yes, I almost forgot about that room. Is it as damaged as the rest of the house?"

Harmony continued to study her sister's face and wondered why she looked embarrassed and uncomfortable. Was she not being truthful? The thought that her sister was pretending to know things made Harmony sad, but she masked her disappointment.

"No, it's all in good order. I guess since it was so far under the house, it was safe. And what *did* happen to the house?"

"I have no idea. I was . . . away . . . when it happened. Do you remember what I looked like when you found me? That achy, ugly old woman? I was trapped somewhere else when it happened." Sharon scrunched her eyebrows together.

"Yes. And now you're as different as I was, or maybe you're just the same as you should be. What do these topside fluctuations mean? Does dryness make things change?"

"Dryness can't change people," said Sharon. "I used to think it was the ooze that changed things, but now that it's gone, there must be something else going on."

Harmony reminded herself to find moisture. A lifetime underwater had altered her physiology drastically. If she didn't rehydrate soon, she'd have to take more water from Sharon's body.

She'd never purposefully done it before—she'd never needed to—but when Harmony had held her sister's forehead to her own, her body drew away some of Sharon's life-giving water. When Sharon slumped against the wall, it had been more than just the relayed information that had left her exhausted.

"You said you wanted to see the snow. Let's go now, before it changes too." Without waiting for a response, Harmony ran up the stairs and threw open the door. The snow was melting in the warm sun and she rolled herself in what remained until her clothes were soaked.

"It's just like I remember it." Sharon's wistful smile was fleeting. "Hey! You're getting those clothes all wet! Let's go back downstairs and get you some dry ones before you get sick. And then maybe we can check out the lab again. It's been a while since I've seen it. Our parents didn't really like having me down there for some reason."

Harmony studied her sister's face, sensing her bitterness, before speaking. "I saw something, you know. Something we should talk about. It's a plan. I think it's their plan for a new lab, and I think I know where they are."

Sharon's eyes grew wide. "Show me. I'll know what to do."

Though Harmony appeared to be Sharon's age since changing herself, she needed to remember that Sharon still considered herself the older sister, the one who would make decisions. She knew their roles would change soon, but for now, she'd continue to learn from the girl who knew more about topside than she did.

Harmony refused a change of clothes back in the musty bedroom—the wetness against her skin revived her—and noted the startled reflection of her sister behind her when she removed the large mirror from the hidden doorway.

They moved hastily to the bottom of the long stairwell and Harmony could feel Sharon's quickened heart rate when she opened the laboratory door. Her own heart rate remained steady.

Once inside the lab, Harmony watched Sharon take inventory of her surroundings. "Is this how you remember it?"

Sharon pulled her hand from the cold metal table. "Yeah. This was where they did . . . things to you." She shivered. "What did you want to show me?" She stared at the sterile tools on the table.

"Look. It's a plan for an underwater vessel." Harmony pointed to the intricately detailed schematic.

"And you think they actually built this? You know where they are?"

"I can't be sure. I think I saw something like this on one of my swims a while ago, but I didn't know what it was." Harmony's sea-green eyes glowed intensely when she thought of her ocean home.

"But wouldn't Kumugwe know if they were down there somewhere? He could help us find them. And maybe he could even give me my powers back. I'd love to be a shark again."

Harmony had much to learn from humans. She felt protective of her sea-god father and couldn't imagine he'd hide knowledge of her birth parents' existence from her. Was it possible they were responsible for the destructive force against which his powers couldn't compete? And if so, there'd be no way for him to link them with the damaged child he'd rescued. No. He would never have hidden this from her.

"My—his home—is more expansive than topside. Hidden things pose no threat, so he wouldn't waste his time on them. No, I don't believe he knows where they are. And I don't know about your powers or if he can do anything about them."

"So you think our parents are hidden in this vessel underwater somewhere. How will you find them again? And how will I be able to go with you?"

Harmony walked around the room silently before responding. She held up a scalpel. "Tell me, sister, why? Why would you want to find these people?" Her eyes glowed so brightly it forced Sharon to squint.

"Because I'm grown now and I want answers. Don't you? Maybe we don't know the whole story. Maybe they were forced to do what they did. Maybe they're old now and need our help. I just feel like your return and the water turning blue again is some kind of sign. Don't you want to ask them questions? Don't you want to find out who they really are? Don't you want them to apologize?" By the time she finished talking, Sharon was shaking.

"No, sister. I don't want any of that. But I'll help you, and I'll stand by your side when we meet them." In fact, Harmony wanted exactly what her sister wanted, and more.

"We'll need a plan, then," said Sharon. "And if they're as powerful as we both think they are, then maybe we shouldn't go alone. If we can convince her, we could bring along that girl from the village."

Harmony was ready to spend more time with the other humans. Maybe her runaway playmate, the girl who'd thrown the spear, would be back to the village by now. She'd never forget that girl's face through the mesh of the metal frog's pouch as she screamed "Away!"

And she couldn't understand why anyone would want to escape from the magical sandcastle she'd built just for them. It made her sad.

Finding her birth parents wasn't what Kumugwe had sent her topside to do. She wanted mostly to please the god who'd given her everything, and she wanted to go back to the only home and the only father she knew. But when she'd found the schematics, she also wanted to find the creators. The fact that she and Sharon were their offspring had to be more than a coincidence.

"I'll help you convince as many as we need," she told Sharon, "and we'll find our parents soon. Don't worry. I'll keep you safe."

Harmony would do her best to keep her promise to a sibling she didn't yet really know . . . or trust.

~ 15 ~

[The Village / Orville]

MERTS RECOGNIZED the mumbling man was no danger. The archers waited for Mason to acknowledge them.

"Two heads are better than one, they say, and they know because they're watching you. Watching you all the time. So why not three heads? Three heads. That's the ticket. Three heads with three brains. Why didn't I think of that? But I did, just now, three heads with three brains. Better than one head, one head with a bird brain. Bird brains are flighty, flighty little bird brains, but I hear things, and I see you watching me." Mason shifted his gaze from the sky to the trees to over his shoulder to the creature in front of him, never lingering on any one object.

Merts, whose three mouths spoke only in haiku, paused before communicating with the rambling man.

"Keep your mind open / To what the bird is thinking / She must find her way."

"Music, beautiful music, that's who you are. Lovely, lovely all, you can watch. No trouble with you watching, that's for sure. Bird brains have wings, and feathers fall. Watch for the fall and prepare for flaming feathers."

Merts's three heads tilted as they tried to make sense of Mason's disjointed expressions.

"Don't think, don't think, food's what we'll need, food and shelter. You bring the meat and I'm pleased to meet you. Shake your hand? No, sir, no, ma'am. Gotta say, bloody pleased to meet you. Won't shake your hand but shook some bloody meat." He looked at his hands and wiped them on his pants again as he walked away from Merts without a goodbye.

"This man is special / We must reflect on his words / Puzzle pieces, all."

Merts sensed activity from where the two girls had disappeared into the ground. They launched their braid into a far tree and swung themselves through the forest, ever alert to potential dangers. If the girls were going back to the village, the archers wouldn't be far behind. Although they were not aware of the girls' intentions, they believed something wasn't quite right about the one who looked like the others in the village. As for the disfigured child, Merts felt a certain kinship with her.

~ ~ ~ ~ ~

Orville noted the wide berth the children still gave Layla on their return from the pond. Smoke from fresh meat sizzling over low flames engulfed them. Layla appeared hesitant to approach the fire, but Orville saw Lou smack his tail feathers against her back legs, nudging her forward.

"Now we're talkin'. So, what's a bird gotta do to get a little taste of what's cookin'?" Lou cocked his head forward when Layla bowed her head low. "Just one tasty morsel will do. She don't need nothin', being metal and all, but I could eat a horse! No offense, Layla."

Layla shook her head, her mane making jingling sounds against her neck, and Lou fanned and shook his tail. The villagers gasped at its beauty.

"I hate it when she does that," said Lou. "Makes me dizzy. Didn't mean to startle youz, but it helps me feel balanced. Kinda like holdin' your arms out when you're walkin' a thin line, I s'pose. But what do I know. I'm just a bird. Didn't used to be, I don't think, but what do I know."

"It's . . . it's beautiful. If I could do that, I'd never want to hide again." Chimney dug his toe into the ground and looked embarrassed by his confession.

Orville smiled. He'd grown quite fond of the quirky boy before his most recent transformation. It was difficult for him not to reveal himself, but everything was new again, and he'd have to be cautious. And then there was Riku.

"Kinda hard to hide when you're fused to a hunka metal this big. Again, no offense, Layla, and please don't do that shaky thing again."

Layla hooved the ground and looked at Chimney, who appeared to be doing the same thing. Someone announced "Food!" and for a while, all conversation ceased.

~ ~ ~ ~ ~

"Ain't nobody gonna ask how this happened?" Lou pecked gently at a spot between Layla's eyes and a pleasant echo reverberated in the metal creature.

"Please, yes, tell." Riku spoke timidly. The others stared at her for a moment as if seeing her for the first time. "We all have witnessed unusual things. You are not the first."

The copper-colored group nodded, and many looked to see Thunder playing with his colorful cubs near the pond before returning their gaze to Lou.

"So there I was, mindin' my own beeswax, when 'lights out.' Next thing I know, I wake up in this cold room with metal everywhere and a guy and this dame starin' at me. I can't move, and they come at me with this huge needle and I'm out again. I wake up again and this is what I look like, only the guy and dame ain't too pleased. Somethin' about ain't no way we're gonna fly. Before I can say a 'howdy-ya-do,' ZAP! Poor Layla here gets an electric shock in the butt and we're gallopin' into a little chamber. Door opens and WHOOSH! We're floatin', no, sinkin' real fast in this weird water. I think to myself, I'm a goner, for sure."

Every eye in the group was on the storyteller.

"I'm holdin' my breath and sayin' my prayers and wonderin' why I'm sinkin' to the bottom of an ocean attached to a metal contraption—no offense, Layla—when outa nowhere comes these bubbly-headed things with eight long leggy things with suckers on 'em. They latch onto Layla and pull us to this cave place where there's lotsa other weird conglomerations and some humans too, I think, but they're all, like, asleep or something. Next thing I know, 'lights out' again."

The newcomers from the beach furrowed their brows, and one finally spoke.

"I remember a cave, and octopuses."

"Me too. Like a dream. A long, long dream."

The others nodded.

"How did you all escape?" Orville asked. "How did you survive down there for all this time?"

"And did you see a girl who could fly?" Nick asked. "Maybe she did something to save you?"

"Honest truth? Couldn't tell youz. Next thing I know, Layla's walkin' outa the water and here we are, but never seen no flyin' girl."

The newcomers nodded their agreement, and silence filled the air.

Orville looked at his skimpy swimsuit and felt embarrassed. "May I suggest, *s'il vous plait*, that we all find shelter for the night? Might we impose on those of you with homes for a place to rest our heads this night, even if it be on your bare floors?"

"Layla and me'll stay put. She don't never lie down, and seems I've been asleep for so long it'll be a miracle if I ever sleep again."

The group split up and each of the homes hesitantly invited newcomers. Thunder led Layla to a place where his family slept, though it was decided that he and Ranger would take turns walking the perimeter of the village throughout the night.

~ ~ ~ ~ ~

When everyone in Blanche's home was asleep, she tiptoed into Chimney's room and shook him awake.

"Come on, Chim. We're going to find Sharon and her sister. I think they know things. Important things."

"What? Why? I don't want to leave. Leave me alone." Chimney was barely awake.

"We've got to get away from these crazy people, they're dangerous. Now, come on." She tugged on his arm, but he pulled away fiercely.

"No! You go. I'm staying here. You might not, but I have friends here." He rubbed his eyes and pulled his covers back up. "Sorry, I didn't mean that, but really, don't go. We need you here, and those girls just aren't right. Please, Blanche. Please stay." Tears brimmed in his eyes.

Blanche pushed his long bangs from his forehead with uncharacteristic tenderness.

"Okay, Chim. Okay. You go back to sleep. We'll figure things out in the morning."

She closed his door quietly, grabbed a small bag she had placed by the front door, and when she saw Ranger was at the far end of the village, crept quietly into the woods.

~ **16** ~

[Celeste]

CELESTE NOTED there was neither day nor night in Oblivia, as Odin had started to call his beclouded home, but her erratic fluxes were taking a toll on her energy.

"Sleep now, child, for when you wake, your training begins." Odin conjured up another silky bed.

Celeste didn't question her buoyancy in Odin's ethereal realm any longer and fell into a dreamless sleep. When she awoke, hours or days or months later, she shook her feathers from the cloudy cover and preened herself.

Where am I? What am I? Her thoughts were vague and as she looked about, she was plagued by a disorienting dizziness.

"You are here, with me, little dove."

Something about the way he addressed her didn't feel right. She didn't like it, but couldn't put a finger on why. Perhaps it was because she had no fingers.

Oh, yes. I'm a little dove in the glorious realm of Oblivia.

"You shall fly with me today—your presence renews my vigor—and together we shall bring rain to the dried lakes and shrunken ponds."

But I don't know how to make it rain. Celeste had a sudden urge to coo a happy tune. Everything around her was so very beautiful and for a fleeting moment she felt light and carefree.

"Ah, my tweet friend, do not ruffle your feathers over matters so trite. It is I who shall teach you everything. Come, now, to my table, and we shall feast!"

Celeste was hungry, though she didn't know for what. She flew at a distance behind Odin as he lumbered across several layers of undulating clouds and wondered how his footsteps could still produce booming reverberations in the atmosphere.

"Thunder!" he told her, winking at her over his shoulder. "Preparation for the rain we shall soon deliver. Stay close, now, for we must enter the hall together."

Odin's ravens and wolves appeared from flowing clouds just as an enormous door, elaborately engraved in silver and gold, lifted from beneath them. Before the great door opened away from the waiting troop, Celeste glimpsed scenes of tragedy and triumph, floods and fires, humans and creatures never before encountered. Most made no sense to her. She wished to study it, but as soon as they were together on the other side, it swung closed behind them and sank back into the clouds.

"Spectacular, is it not? It tells all, and though I have studied it over the centuries, I remain yet unenlightened to the final chapter of our history. But let us not worry about such inevitabilities! Feast your eyes, and then your mouths, minions!" Odin strode to a grand table laden with meats and treats of every imaginable type.

Celeste's hunger overwhelmed her, but when she gazed at a roast covered in crispy fat, she couldn't imagine eating it. A brimming bowl of dates and berries beckoned her, yet she kept returning to the juicy roast with its aroma visibly wafting its way to her.

She longed to sink her teeth into the heavenly meat, but she had no teeth in her tiny beak. Her contradictory thoughts confused her. After plucking a few sweet berries from the bowl, she flew over the table to where the roast taunted and repelled her. Away and back she flew several times before an urge to fill her stomach with something hearty overcame her.

THUMP!

Celeste landed in an enormous bread bowl on the table near a roast big enough to feed an entire village.

"Well, well, look who has returned! Tell me, girl, have you willed this flux, or will this continue to occur randomly?" Odin's words had a harsh edge.

"Well, maybe?" Celeste brushed the crumbs from her clothes and crawled off the table, startled and embarrassed. "I really wanted to taste this roast. I wonder—"

"Eat, then, and quickly! There is no time for idle wondering. Bird or girl, you will come with me today and learn the ways of rain." Odin stuffed his cheeks with bread and treats while he talked, and Celeste had to look away as crumbs flew from his mouth.

The roast tasted as sumptuous as it smelled. *Heavenly,* she thought, and chuckled. She saw Odin watching her intently as she ate, and when she reclined back against the chair, her hands patting her full stomach, he rose. When he stood, the great door lifted back up from the clouds and opened.

Celeste scratched her head and let her fingers linger where she knew the markings were hidden beneath her hair. "Isn't it silly to have a door up here? I mean, the heavens are yours. Can't you eat wherever and whenever you want without going through this door?"

Anger flashed across Odin's face and his wolves whined, crouching near him. The ravens flew to either side of him, but didn't land on his shoulders. And then, he laughed.

"Silly? You call the door to our dining hall silly? You have much to learn, girl. And learn, you shall. Come." Without answering Celeste's question, Odin strode back through the door.

Celeste wondered if he knew the truth about the door. She was last to cross to the other side, and when it slammed shut, it buffeted the clouds beneath her and knocked her over.

Odin didn't turn to see her, but she heard him chuckle. It took her several moments to stand—she was still figuring out how to leverage her solid body in the ephemeral clouds—and before the door disappeared again, she glimpsed an engraving at the very top of an enormous gossamer-winged creature with a long, thin body. Flames shot from its mouth and there was something or someone who appeared to be riding atop it.

"Hold my hand, my celestial Celeste. It is time to fly." Odin stretched back his hand to her.

Celeste took his hand hesitantly, and an intense wave of power surged through her. Without a moment to think about what was happening, she was plummeting through a cloudy vortex from the heavenly realm. Odin pulled her along with him until the planet below came into focus.

"Here, we pause a moment to consider where we shall direct the rain. Shall we cause a frightful storm, or deliver gentle sprinkles to the planet? And where shall we deliver our gift?"

Celeste looked at Odin and thought he appeared much younger, but no longer trusted appearances. She looked at the expanse of water on the planet, an area of silvery-pink ooze slowly expanding far from the nearest shore, and remembered throwing the orichalcum-encrusted spear from the hilltop near the village. She remembered the water turning normal after the spear sank out of sight and wondered if the change had been coincidental.

It couldn't have been.

Why, then, was the water turning again?

"Well, my funny friend?" Odin looked at her expectantly, his hand entrapping hers like a snare.

Celeste didn't want him to know she was thinking of the survivors in the village, especially Nick. Odin clearly enjoyed her company, and for a moment, she felt compassion for him. She knew what it felt like to have no real friends. She knew what if felt like to be lonely.

But with his power and reinvigorated youthfulness, he could help—or destroy—whatever he pleased.

"Show me how to rain on a mountaintop. So many are still covered in ash, and I wouldn't do any damage there." Old Man Massive's ash-covered profile flashed in her mind and she wondered what he would tell her to do. He would tell her to remember who she was.

"Splendid idea." In a moment, they were closer to the planet. "Now, focus your attention on one spot of water." Odin watched as Celeste gazed at a point below. "Do you feel the heat within its particles?" He placed one finger on the back of Celeste's head where she was marked, and when she smiled, he continued. "Good! Now bring it to you, slowly, bit by bit."

"Holy moly!" Celeste's eyes grew wide as a thin stream of water rose from the vast ocean. It appeared she was controlling a small bit of water by believing she could do it.

"A fast learner! I knew 'twould be the case. Now, disperse the bits and create a cloud like those you remember seeing before a storm. You will need more bits than that tiny stream, so bring them to you." Odin smiled when a gush of water rose from the ocean and scattered into clumpy particles below them. "Yes! And now push your little cloud over a mountain—that one will do—and when you are ready, keep your gaze upon it and squeeze your hands together." Odin released her hand and held her by her shirt collar.

Celeste was swept into Odin's enthusiasm over her achievement, and though she wished for him to release her, she couldn't deny her own delight at what she was about to do. Staring at her tiny dark cloud, she squeezed her hands together and the cloud burst apart, dropping rain on the mountain in a single splash.

"Well done! Well done, little friend! You shall soon learn how to control the squeeze more prudently." Odin laughed and patted her on the back, sending her reeling across the sky.

Celeste let out a cry, but quickly discovered she could fly again as a girl. Without thinking, she flew back to Odin and reached for his protective hand.

"I can still fly!" she shouted. "And that—making rain—that was incredible! What's next?" She had never felt so powerful, but the feeling frightened her.

"One lesson at a time! We must return to Oblivia where you will rest before our next lesson." He clung to her until he had her tucked neatly into bed with his wolves standing guard.

She sensed his desperation to keep her in his realm. She pretended to sleep.

~ 17 ~

[Harmony]

IT WAS DARK when Harmony and Sharon rose from their underground home.

"We'll have to be quiet when we get near the village," Sharon told Harmony. "Those animals aren't friendly, and who knows what else might have shown up there from the water."

"But I feel like I could probably talk with anyone right now, especially if they've spent time under water. I just don't know where they've been, though. I guess I never really did much exploring away from my—Kumugwe's home."

"We're not going there to socialize, Harmony. We're going to find that girl named Blanche, the one who pulled me up at the beach. She knows the villagers are weak-minded. I'm certain she'll be on our side."

"What do you mean?" Harmony walked side by side with her sister, subtly brushing arms with her as they ventured into the forest. Each little brush drew moisture from her sister's skin. She needed to stay focused in this foreign, dry world. She needed to stay hydrated. "What's a side, and why would she want to be on ours?"

Sharon put her hand over her mouth and Harmony heard her chuckle. Her sister looked perplexed and stopped for a moment.

"Wait a sec, I just felt a little dizzy. Must be the darkness. Being on our side just means she thinks like we do and will want to help us. The others are useless. And they're afraid. We need to be the ones in control and making the rules. Blanche gets that."

Harmony decided not to question her sister's line of thinking. Instead, she would observe the interaction with Blanche and learn more about her sister and the others. She hid her disappointment that they wouldn't be mingling with the villagers. Several seemed like they could be good people, if given the opportunity. Maybe they wouldn't look at her with fear in their eyes now that she had changed herself to look even more like them.

She was happy that Kumugwe had given her copper skin and an ability to share it with others so she might look like them. Like the octopuses that populated the vast sea and occasionally visited, her blood was also copper-based, a gift from a father who knew she'd need the ability to process oxygen in her new world.

She remembered Kumugwe telling her, "Should any human now be touched by our waters, they too will be gifted with a coating like yours, my little music box." Harmony knew how much Kumugwe loved hearing her giggle.

All of the humans she saw when she had walked from the water were copper. All except Sharon. Harmony had been perplexed by this, quickly sharing her gift with the old lady who was really just a teenage girl, but now she wondered if it had something to do with what side the people were on.

Sharon stopped suddenly and grabbed Harmony by the arm. "Shh! I hear something. Quick! Behind this tree."

Harmony allowed herself to be pulled behind a tree and heard a commotion on the ground. It sounded like someone falling. She remembered her own fall and her scraped knee.

"Youch! Dammit!" A muffled voice rose from the ground.

"Blanche?" Sharon whispered. "Over here!" She stepped out from behind the tree and pulled Harmony with her. Blanche jumped back, startled.

"Sharon?" Blanche squinted in the darkness and approached the girls cautiously. "Who's that? Who're you with?"

"It's Harmony," said Sharon. "Let's not talk here, okay? We were just on our way to find you. Thanks for saving us the trip. Come on. Follow us back to the house."

"What house?" Blanche asked.

Harmony felt the girl staring at her.

"Just . . . just follow us. You're not going to believe what we've found."

It didn't take long for the three to reach the door in the field. The glow from Harmony's eyes glinted off the doorknob, and when Sharon pulled open the door, Blanche hesitated.

"Come on down. Harmony will close the door. Don't worry, we're not monsters."

Harmony smiled at Blanche as the reluctant older girl stepped through the door onto the stairs. She sensed her softly glowing eyes were mesmerizing Blanche, who nearly lost her footing again. Harmony grabbed her arm to keep her from falling down the stairs, and in the process, absorbed some of her fluids.

"Wait a minute, I feel weird. Let me sit a minute. Don't close the door yet, okay?" Blanche rested on a step and the sisters waited. "Is this what's left of your home?" She peered down the stairs, and Harmony noted goosebumps on the girl's arms.

"The last time I was here, this place felt like quicksand right before it started to spin around. Then it sank out of sight."

Harmony looked at her sister and saw surprise in her face.

"Okay. I think I'm okay now," said Blanche. "Listen. I came over here to see if I could find you, but I never really expected you to be here. I want to know what you know." Blanche looked at Harmony again. "And are you telling me this is your sister? The same sister that just came from the water? How can that be?"

"How can any of this be?" Sharon shrugged her shoulders. "Flying frogs and girls and talking animals and who knows what else? But come on. We think we've found clues in the lab. If you'll join us, we may even be able to find some answers."

"But why do you need me? You were coming to get me. Why?"

"Because you're the boldest person in the village," said Sharon, "and what we're about to do will take guts and action. Just please come down and we'll show you."

Harmony closed the door and illuminated the stairs, observing both girls keenly as they worked their way through the wreckage and down into the laboratory below.

"Wow! What is all this? It looks like something from the future, or maybe the past." Blanche held her hands close to her sides.

"I think my parents might have had something to do with The Event. And Harmony thinks they might still be alive. Look at this." Sharon showed Blanche the schematic for the submarine. "She thinks she might know where it is. We're going to find it. And we're going to find them, if they're still alive."

"But, what then? How long ago did they leave you? And what did they do to your sister?" Blanche's gaze darted between the schematic and the sterile tools lining the countertops. "What's your plan for when, or if, you find them?"

Sharon's expression changed, her features becoming animated. "What then? Don't you see? Can you even imagine how powerful they'd have to be if they're the ones who shook the planet?"

Blanche looked confused, and Sharon continued.

"I bet they'll need help soon. Apprentices! With Harmony's knowledge of the sea and your knowledge of people and what they want, we can work with them and, you know, help! And when they get tired of their projects, well, we'll be right there to take over for them. I think I know enough about you to know you like being in charge, am I right?"

Blanche looked to Harmony as if for some kind of response, but Harmony kept her face a blank page.

"And if they don't want our help? What then?"

"You and your 'what thens'. Then, well, we'll just have to convince them. They can't keep going forever. It's just that simple. So, are you with us?"

"I don't even know where we'll begin, but yeah, I'm in. I'm assuming you have a way to get to a submarine somewhere beneath all that water?"

Blanche and Sharon looked to Harmony, who stood silently processing the girls' discussion. When she realized she was expected to say something, she spoke.

"Yes. I know a way. You won't like it, but it will get us there. When will you be ready to leave?" Harmony was amused by the expression on both girls' faces.

It looked like fear.

~ 18 ~

[The Village / Orville]

CHIMNEY'S FACE WAS WET with tears. "She wanted me to go with her, but I said no. She said we'd figure it out in the morning, and now it's morning and she's gone."

Maddie took his hand and led him to the attic stairs. "Come on, let's go see Finn. There's something about him that makes me trust him. He'll know what to do. But I sure wish Celeste would come back."

"Yeah, me too. She was awesome." Chimney strained his neck and dried his eyes.

~ ~ ~ ~ ~

Orville and Riku had slept in the attic space, the tiny room where Celeste had stayed for the short time she was there. He heard someone knocking softly on the door.

"*Oui?* Yes? Come in." Orville's voice was groggy.

"Sorry to disturb you, but we have an issue." Maddie glanced at Riku, who was still asleep on the small cot. Orville sat up from his makeshift bed on the floor and rubbed his eyes, which seemed larger than before.

"It's my sister, Blanche, the bossy girl, remember her? She's gone and I think she's in trouble." Chimney blurted out the words, waking Riku, who quickly sat and opened her arms to the distraught boy. He went to her and sank into her arms. "How could she leave me?"

"And where is it you believe your sister went, lad?" Orville pulled on a pair of baggy sweatpants he'd found in a box under the cot.

"Hey, you sound like someone," said Chimney.

"I am, indeed, someone." Orville tried again not to sound so French. "Now, why are you fearful? Perhaps your sister is gathering food for breakfast?"

"No!" Chimney pulled away from Riku's embrace. "That's my job. All she knows how to do is cook what I bring and tell us what to do. She said she was going to find that mean girl and her scary little sister cuz she thinks they know things. But their house is gone—we saw pieces of it flyin' in the air!—so where is she? And did you hear that big thunder boom before we went to bed?" He looked at Maddie, who nodded. "What if . . . what if it got her and she's dead?"

"No, lad, thunder would do no harm." Orville patted Chimney's knee and tried to think of something to distract him. "So tell me, how is your leg?" He knew he'd made a mistake the minute he spoke the words.

"It's fine. Hey! How'd you know about my leg?" Chimney looked at the man from head to toe. "Lemme see your eyes."

Orville knelt down in front of the boy and smiled.

"It's *you*! I knew it was you! Well, I didn't till just now. How'd you do that? How'd you turn into a man?" Chimney threw his arms around Orville and held him for a long time. "Please don't ever leave us again."

Orville saw Maddie looking from him to Riku and back again, and she placed her hand on his shoulder. "It *is* you," she said. "I didn't know if I could still do it, but I can feel who you are now. Welcome back, Orville. Why did you lie? None of us has been quite normal lately."

Orville looked at Riku, who nodded for him to explain.

"Do you recall, Maddie, my reception by your people? The planet is still changing, yes? And although I have much wisdom, do you believe anyone would listen to a frog? A frog who almost got Chimney killed?"

Maddie nodded and looked at Riku again. She extended her hand toward the woman. "May I?" she asked, and when Riku nodded, she touched Riku's arm. "Oh! You poor thing! Trapped in that horrible lizard for so long!"

"It was not horrible, until that witch-girl found me." Riku looked down at her hands.

"So, can we tell everyone?" asked Chimney. "Can we tell 'em it's you, Orville? I bet with Ranger and Thunder we can find my sister and save her from those witch-girls, and you'll be able to find Celeste, won't you? You can contact her, right? Like you used to?"

"I'm afraid I haven't been able to contact her since my transformation, Chim, but I think you are right about telling the others. I am no more a frog than Riku is—how you say?—a lizard. We must not keep secrets. Perhaps I am here again, with Riku, to help the people of this village, at least until your sister returns."

"But nobody wants her to be in charge anymore. Will you do it? Come on! Let's tell 'em you're in charge and then we'll go find Blanche."

By the time they got downstairs, however, Orville heard a commotion in the street and hurried outside. People were murmuring and pointing toward the end of the road.

Thunder, walking alongside Mason, appeared to be carrying a boy on his back as they approached the village. The jaguar balanced an enormous load of something bluish-gray and walked slowly in an apparent effort to keep the load from tipping. As they drew closer, Orville could hear Mason chanting.

"Pat-a-brick, pat-a-brick, Mason man. Build me a home as fast as you can. Pat it and mold it and mark it with an 'M.' Make-a-many houses for all of them."

He repeated the nursery rhyme over and over until the crowd parted to let them pass through, and Orville saw Thunder wink at Chimney and tilt his head for the boy to follow.

Once Chimney started to follow, the others fell in behind him. Mason carried a sleeping Bridger piggy-back style until he got to the other side of the pond, where he knelt and let Orville lift the boy from him. Orville held the boy gently in one arm.

Thunder crouched slowly until his belly was on the ground. "Mornin', dudes. A little help here, if you don't mind?" Stacked on a pallet strapped around him were piles and piles of dried mud blocks.

"We will make lines, yes? And pass these out to—let me see—*un, deux, trois*, three separate stacking places!" With his free arm, Orville directed the people into three lines, and by the time all of the coarse bricks were offloaded, they seemed to understand what to do with them.

It was time to think of the future. It was time to build. Mason focused on the piles, mumbling incoherently and drawing figures in the air with his hands. He appeared to be conducting an orchestra.

Bridger woke and stared, bleary-eyed, into Orville's face. "I tried to do it myself, but it kept zingin' in and out." His head flopped back on Orville's shoulder and he was asleep again.

"What the little dude means is, he tried to swirl up some shelters, but his swirly power kept short-circuiting. You can see the little piles of brush over yonder." Thunder nodded his head toward the trees.

"Anyway, I saw him and the conductor there holdin' hands and walkin' outta town last night, so I followed. 'Houses, houses, homes need houses,' big dude kept sayin'. So we walked to where the beach used to be and he starts cuttin' out big ol' mud slabs. Kid helped best he could—had enough in him to put this contraption together—and here we are. Worked all through the night. Where's my little darlin'? There she is." Thunder shook the pallet from his back and walked to where Eenie was stretching from her slumber. The two disappeared back around one of the houses.

Orville then watched as the crowd gathered around him slowly. Although he was still a stranger to most everyone, he sensed they expected something from him. Riku and Chimney stood by his side.

"It would appear that we have work to do." Orville had never been a leader before The Event, and didn't want to alienate anyone. "Chimney's sister has left, and our world remains in flux. Will you help? Can we work together to move forward somehow?"

Several of the villagers nodded their heads.

"Blanche left? Where'd she go?" asked Mac.

"Said she was going to find Sharon and her sister," said Chimney. "And I think they're bad." He disappeared, but Orville could see little chunks of dirt dislodged from the ground where the boy stood.

"Then she's no longer welcome here!" someone shouted.

"She's turned her back on us," said another. "Good riddance to her."

"Ban her from the village! She's always been a bully!"

Orville sensed an uprising and felt Chimney move in closer by his side.

"Friends! Let us not jump to hasty conclusions," he said, but in his heart, he agreed with them. "We will keep watch, yes? And in the meantime, let us regather in the street shortly to identify our strengths. We will need laborers, gatherers, cooks, hunters, and—" he looked at the sleeping child in his arms and then at Riku, "care givers."

Except for Mason, who continued to conduct his piles of bricks, the people slowly dispersed to the village. Orville could see the uncertainty—and fear—in their faces.

As he walked back to the house with Riku by his side and Bridger in his arms, he knew he was carrying far more than one small child.

~ ~ ~ ~ ~

Far above the village the dragonfly flew unnoticed. It saw all that was happening below.

~ 19 ~

[Celeste]

ALTHOUGH CELESTE did her best to feign sleep, she sensed Odin's wolves were restless. One or the other would sniff her face throughout her mandated slumber, and each time, she struggled not to giggle. Their whiskers tickled her. A couple of times she sensed Odin looking in on her. She closed her eyes tightly then and didn't move a muscle.

She pondered Odin's question about whether or not she could control her fluxes. The possibility excited her. Each time she'd shed her feathers in the past, it happened when her desire for something was strongest: to break from the ravens, to hear Odin describe the marking on her head with a clear mind, to taste the succulent roast, to remember the boy who wanted to stop time for her.

Could it be as simple as staying focused on her desires to remain a girl?

If that were the case, she couldn't let Odin know. She would have to lose focus and become a dove again to test her theory. There were problems with that, however. For one thing, Odin could hear her thoughts when she was a bird, and that was dangerous.

Even more dangerous was the feeling of freedom she felt when she flew with wings. Ideas and images flashed in her tiny brain then, but they never seemed to stick. The heavenly realm was far away from troubles on the planet. She didn't even have to flap her wings to stay aloft in Oblivia.

Celeste let her mind drift for a moment on simple, unimportant things: the feel of wind in her hair, the rustling of leaves on trees before The Event, brushing her teeth—when was the last time she'd done that?—reading a boring book. She tried not to remember how much she loved reading stories about beautiful horses because that would keep her in her girl skin. Boring, boring, the endlessly boring routine of life at the children's home.

Her wings fluttered.

The wolves leapt from where they rested, and whined.

It worked. Her little bird heart beat rapidly, joyfully, but she needed to remember the danger. She needed to remember what she loved more than the carefree euphoria of her feathered life. She needed to remember Nick.

She bounced back into her bed.

The wolves whined louder when her girl's body buffeted the clouds around them, and she saw Odin sneak a peek into her space to see what had caused the commotion. Celeste forced a yawn to hide her smile and rolled over to see him watching her.

"What a wonderful sleep," she lied. "Is it time for my next lesson already?" Though she felt bad about lying, she needed more than anything else to convince Odin of her loyalty and happiness at being his new companion. She had to, if she hoped to find a way home.

"Ah! Refreshed and eager! The day begins well. I've brought you both berries and flesh, not knowing which you might desire this morn." Odin disappeared for a moment and returned with a platter of food.

"I'll enjoy both now, friend. Thank you." Celeste accepted the tray, studying his face when she called him friend. It was sometimes difficult to read his expression with his one squinty eye and hairy face, but she thought he looked pleased.

"We shall depart shortly. The beasts will bring you to me when you have finished." He turned to leave, but Celeste could tell he wanted to stay.

"You're a wonderful teacher, Odin. I'll see you soon."

He glanced back at her with a silly grin, looking like a little boy again. Celeste's smile concealed the pang of sorrow she felt for the lonely old man.

She tossed several large chunks of meat to the wolves and devoured everything else on the platter, anxious to get on with her day and advance her plan to return to her own people. The wolves licked their chops and rubbed their heads against Celeste.

"No more whining anymore, you two. Understand?" She scratched them both behind their ears and they licked her hands. These were not the emaciated dogs who had trained her to fly, but they behaved as if starved for affection. "Now, take me to your leader!" She laughed at the ridiculous command and followed the wolves over several layers of shimmering clouds.

When she saw Odin waiting on a distant cloud, she left the wolves and flew to him.

"Ah! You fly more gracefully than a dove!" Odin appeared markedly younger than he had before, though in terms of centuries, he was still quite old. "This shall make our work easier! A massive storm is on your horizon this day, and wind to ripple the waters!"

"Sounds like fun!" Celeste giggled, and Odin's goofy little-boy grin returned.

"I'm ready whenever you are," she said, and when Odin extended his hand to grasp hers, she protested. "Let me prove I can do this on my own! Let me fly by your side. If I should fall, you'll save me, right?"

"I will never let you fall." Odin made a move to pat her on the back, but patted her gently on the head instead, much like did with his wolves. Celeste recalled the last time he'd patted her on the back and sent her flying across the heavens.

The possibility of falling was very real. After all, she had just discovered she could will her fluxes between dove and girl, or at least she believed she was the one willing the fluxes. She'd just flown as a girl for the first time since ascending to Odin's realm.

Celeste convinced herself she was in control. She'd practice her fluxes again later when it was time to sleep, though the thought of sleep eluded her.

Storm cloud training was a breeze, and as Celeste circled the planet with Odin delivering rain to dried lake beds, the thought crossed her mind that she was in a position to do great good for the people below. Was she being selfish in her desire to return to one small village when the entire population was at the mercy of the elements? Could she learn to be satisfied with the friendship of one powerful god who already appreciated her and needed a friend?

Exhausted, finally, when it was time to leave the rain-drenched planet behind, Celeste ate with gusto before excusing herself from the grand dining hall.

"And tomorrow? What will we do tomorrow?" She forced a smile, though she fought to keep her eyes open. Physical and emotional exhaustion finally sapped her remaining energy.

"Perhaps we shall give Kumugwe a wake-up call in the morn. It surprises me still you never met the old curmudgeon while his little sea witch held you trapped. Yes! We shall have great fun tomorrow!"

Celeste flew to where he sat at the far end of the table and delivered a tiny kiss to his nose, the only place on his face not covered in hair. He beamed. "Good night, Odin. I'll whip up my own bed tonight and be ready for tomorrow's work."

Tomorrow was an important day. She had big decisions to make. Would she stay? Would she go? Which version of herself would benefit the most people?

People. Old Man Massive would tell her to remember who she was, and she was a person, not a god like Odin and Kumugwe. Even the idea of becoming a god sounded wrong to her. Sure, she'd be able to control things that affected many people's lives, but what right did anyone have to wield such control? Certainly not a teenage girl.

And after witnessing such childish behavior from Odin, certainly not an old sky god, either. No, she would shake her lofty ideas from her head and remember who she really was: a lonely girl in need of mortal friends who were struggling as she was to make sense of their bizarre lives.

Despite her efforts at staying awake to work out her plan, the silky, undulating clouds lulled her to sleep and into a troubling dream.

Thud-thud-clink, thud-thud-clink, thud-thud-clink.

The unusual heartbeat grew stronger as she flailed out of control above the water. Its incessant pace drowned out the sound of her own panicking heart. Along the shoreline, hermit crabs black as tar snapped their claws in the air as people approached. She tried to scream, "NO! Turn back! There's danger ahead!" but no sound escaped her constricted throat. Why were they heading into danger?

No longer falling, she held her hands to her ears to stifle the thud-thud-clink, thud-thud-clink, but to no avail. Sadness washed over her and an octopus—perhaps the one from the sandcastle—looked at her from far away with pleading eyes. It seemed to be hiding something powerful and awful.

Far behind the octopus, water tunnels glimmered silvery-pink like the one that had lured her to the sandcastle, and they were filled with more people. She could see their frightened faces. Nick was there! And another. Why were they in the tunnels? They were in great danger, but when Celeste screamed at them to turn back, a great bubble spread from her mouth and encased her.

Her scream deafened her, and then the bubble floated her away from the people into a dark, silent ocean.

~ 20 ~

[Harmony]

"WHAT DO YOU MEAN, we won't like it?" Blanche asked Harmony. "I'm all for leaving those pitiful villagers on their own. I wish Chimney had come with me, but he has lots of friends. He'll be fine. So how do we get there?"

"We'll need water tunnels," said Harmony. "But before we go, I need to ask you both something about another girl." In her enthusiasm to find the people who had discarded her as an infant, she'd almost forgotten about finding the flying girl. "Have you ever seen a girl with long dark hair and emerald green eyes? A girl about our age? One who could fly without wings?"

Blanche and Sharon both appeared startled, and Blanche spoke first. "Yeah, her name's Celeste, or Paloma, I'm not really sure. Came here with a creepy flying frog and convinced me to help her steal a spear from your house."

"Yeah," said Sharon, "I remember they called it the Spear of Sorrow, as if it had some kind of evil power in it."

Blanche continued. "She threw it into the water and it cleared up and moved away after that. That's when you came out of the water," she pointed to Harmony, "and Sharon turned back into a regular girl. Weird. Anyway, she disappeared after that. Haven't seen her since."

"And what do you know about her, sister?" Harmony hoped Sharon would be truthful.

"She was a troublemaker," said Sharon. "How do you know about her?" The question was an obvious deflection. Harmony believed her sister knew more and hoped she wouldn't have to steal the information from her sister's memory.

"I think I saw her passing by underwater once, but she disappeared from there too. I was just curious, that's all. Seems like she might have some unusual abilities and I thought maybe someone like her could be useful." Harmony didn't need to tell the real reason for finding the girl with two names, or that she'd nearly killed her out of sheer ignorance. She was learning more about what human bodies needed to survive each moment she was topside.

"I wouldn't count on ever seeing her again," said Sharon. "So, water tunnels don't sound so bad, if they're anything like the one that pulled me through the sea before my last, ah, transformation, when you met me. It was a little scary and fast, but I survived. Is that how our parents moved a submarine lab underwater?"

"I wondered that myself," said Harmony. "See here on the schematic? It actually looks like they might have built it right under this lab. These markings look like water. I think this house was built right on top of a huge water tunnel."

"Then, shouldn't we be able to access it somewhere? You lived here for years, Sharon, wouldn't you have known about a water tunnel under your house?" Blanche spoke with sarcasm. She stood with hands on hips and waited for an answer.

"I stayed away from the lab," Sharon said flatly, "but it shouldn't take us long to find another door. Harmony, light the way around the room and let's check out the floor and all the walls."

The three girls searched every inch of the lab with the glow from Harmony's eyes, but found no obvious door. Then, Harmony stared at the surgical table.

"The table. It's there." She strode to the cold metal surface and tried to push it out of the way, but it didn't budge. "It's got to be here," she muttered. Even with all three girls pushing, the table remained stuck. Harmony stepped back and stared at it again.

"Open it," she told Sharon, much like she had told her to open the prone door in the barren field.

Sharon didn't question her sister this time, but lifted the top from the table easily. It was like a magician's box, appearing see-through beneath the surface, but in actuality, hiding a passageway within.

"No way," Blanche whispered. "I'm not going down there."

"I'll go. I can see." Harmony climbed into the passage and felt rungs beneath her feet. After several minutes had passed, she called to the girls, her voice a faraway echo. "Come down! There's a tunnel! I'll wait for you at the bottom."

When the three girls were regrouped at the bottom of a long ladder, Harmony turned up the light in her eyes. Warm, sea-green ripples of light danced along the muddy walls of a surprisingly wide path, the end of which remained out of sight.

"Listen! I think I hear water," said Blanche. "Let's go."

The three walked cautiously along the dank, slippery path until they saw a dim glow beyond, which cast ripples of light on the walls like those from Harmony's eyes.

"Wait a minute." Blanche stopped the group. "Are we walking into some kind of trap? And if you're doing that ripply thing with your eyes, Harmony, knock it off. It's making me dizzy."

"You know as much as we do, Blanche, and leave my sister alone. You're either in with us or not, so make up your mind now. You know the way out."

Blanche put her hands on her hips and huffed. "Fine. Let's go then. But don't tell me you're not a little freaked out by this whole thing." She continued toward the glow and the others followed.

Something shiny glinted ahead. At the end of the path, an enormous cavern opened over a large pool of clear water. Scattered about the cavern were remnants of unidentifiable machinery. Large piles of sheet metal, pipes, bolts, rivets, gears and blowtorches lay about on the ground, and poking out from random places in the cavernous dome were larger relics from a time before The Event. Light reflected off of many more submersed metal objects.

"No way! How cool is this? Your parents built a submarine right here! Or maybe they just found one! Maybe there were people still in it and they're working together now!"

Several moments passed, and Harmony sensed the girls were as baffled as she was in her attempt to understand what they were seeing.

"So, now what? How do we find these water tunnels?" asked Blanche.

"Give me a minute. I'll be right back." Without waiting to explain, Harmony dove into the clear water. It took every bit of control she could muster not to keep swimming until she was back with Kumugwe again, back in a world where she could breathe without feeling as if she'd shrivel up and die.

But she couldn't go back to him yet, not until she'd found the flying girl, so instead, she sent out a giggle that summoned her nearest hermit crab friends. She explained to them what she was searching for, and was rewarded with an answer. They followed her until she left the water, remaining barely submerged near its edge while she walked back to the waiting girls.

"You were underwater forever! Can you *breathe* under there?" Sharon sounded concerned.

"Yes. It took a while for my blood to adapt, but I'm actually more comfortable underwater than I am topside. And I have good news. We know where the submarine is."

"We? Who's we?" asked Blanche, and Harmony looked back over her shoulder at the shiny black crabs.

"No! No way! Are those things real?" Blanche took several steps back as the crabs crept onto land toward them.

"There's no need for alarm. They're friends. They'll get you to the submarine."

"Ah . . . hold on, what do you mean they'll get us there?" It appeared that Blanche was reconsidering her decision to join the sisters.

"They make the water tunnels," said Harmony.

~ 21 ~

[The Village / Orville]

"I SAW HER in my dreams last night," Orville told Riku as they walked back to the house. "She's out there somewhere, very far away, and she's in trouble."

"Shh . . . do not let Bridger hear you. Talk when we are alone."

Orville looked at the weary child in his arms and knew she was right. There was no need to startle the child or anyone else in the village, but he also felt responsible for telling them what he saw in his dream. He believed Celeste wasn't the only one in danger.

"I'll take him," said Maddie, and when Orville passed Bridger to her, she frowned. "It's gone again. I can't feel anything. He's powerless too."

"We are in another time of changes, Maddie, but do not fret. We will recover." Orville fought a sudden desire to leap, and his shoulder blades ached as if wings strained to burst from them. He looked at Riku and caught a flash of fear on her face.

He grasped her hand and experienced her fear as she struggled to suppress an instinct to crawl along the ground. Startled, they both realized they were feeling what the other was feeling, a power only Maddie previously possessed.

"I'll put him to bed and check on the other little ones," said Maddie, leaving Orville and Riku.

"I didn't just see her in my dreams, I felt I was with her, much like I just felt I was in your head, Riku, and you were in mine, *oui?*" When Riku nodded, Orville pulled her into his arms and held her tightly for several moments before letting her go. "I had a connection with the girl and I tried to speak to her, to tell her not to fear, but she is fighting something strong."

"What does she fight? Where is the girl who feared me when the old woman made her weep in the horrible house? I tried to communicate with her that day, tried to tell her to run away, to shun the Spear of Sorrow offered under the guise of a gift, but in the body of a gigantic lizard, I only frightened her."

"This is what I cannot grasp," said Orville. "I sensed a powerful, deadly undersea threat, yet what I saw surrounding her was beauty unlike any I have witnessed on the planet. Why does she dream of sea creatures when I believe she is far above? This is why I fear danger. Her dreams of past have been prophetic and have brought me to her. I do not know what is coming, but I feel an irrational fear. I have rescued her from near death both above and below the waters before, driven each time by an insistent voice in my head and certain knowledge that I was meant to find and help her."

"Is there any connection? Any sameness? Any, ah, thread?" Orville could feel Riku's struggle to find the right words.

"I did not see him in this dream, but I sensed the presence of the old wizard who saved me from the Overleader's clutches, the same old man who sent me, transformed, to rescue Celeste from the child under the water, the giggling child who tried to stop our escape from the frightening sandcastle."

"Then he is watching over her as well? This is good, his presence?"

"How I wish I could be certain. This, to me, is unclear, for if that were so, why do I—why does she feel threatened by a power even greater than his?"

Their discussion was cut short.

"Why the long faces, beautiful people? No offense, Layla. Don't tell me somebody burnt breakfast, cuz I could eat a—I could eat whatever's cookin'!" Lou sounded perky. "You'd think I'd never be hungry with Layla here doin' all the work for both of us, but that ain't the case at all."

Orville and Riku smiled at the incongruous horse-peacock fusion and walked with them to where the villagers were gathering.

"We are planning for the future, and hope you can help," said Orville. "Tell me, Lou, do you remember anything else from your time with the man and woman before you lost consciousness? Can you recall any details about your surroundings? Anything at all?"

"Don't much want to remember cuz of the awfulness of it all, but lemme chew on it a bit and get back to youz after I've tasted a little something. I'm feeling peckish—Ha! Ain't that the truth!—after our recent journey. Never used to be so hungry before this most irregular nuptial."

As if wired to the peacock's brain, the monstrous mechanical horse clanked to where the closest group gathered to eat. Orville took Riku's hand.

"I will keep my mind open. Perhaps Celeste will feel my presence and tell me what to do. I fear the fluxes will continue until she can return to us. If she can return to us. Until then, Riku, we must do what we can to keep those in our new village safe, especially the little ones. If *we* are startled by the changes within us, can you imagine their fear?"

"So small, and so alone. Yes, I can imagine their fear. No mothers, no fathers, and for how long? The poor darlings." Riku looked like she would cry.

"We, too, are torn from our homes and families. There is no shame in grieving, but for now, *ma chérie*, my love, let us be strong for one another. Whether we want them to or not, they look to us for guidance."

Riku bowed her head and nodded, and Orville lifted her chin gently with one finger until she looked into his kind eyes. She smiled then, and they spoke no more, but walked hand in hand to join the others.

"Welcome back, man-frog. I knew it must be you." Ranger greeted Orville. "The others have been told. There are no surprises. Do you know where she is?"

"Celeste . . . no. But she lives, and we will find her. Today, however, will you take Chimney in search of his sister? I fear she does not want to be found, and the others are right. She could be a threat. Perhaps at the end of the day you will redirect the boy's attention to those who need him here. And tell me, have you experienced anything unusual today?"

Ranger looked at Orville and cocked his head. "There is no usual," he said, and walked away toward Chimney.

The villagers had gathered into work groups and appeared ready to receive instructions. Staying busy would ease the sense of uncertainty that hung over them like a damp sheet. They dispersed as soon as Orville suggested tasks for each group, leaving Layla and Lou behind.

"Layla and me'll catch up with the dog and the funny boy, if that's all right with you, boss. And I just wanted to tell youz somethin' I remembered while we was down under."

Orville raised his eyebrows and felt his nictitating membranes blink. It felt odd, but didn't startle him. Lou continued.

"I ain't never been a big dreamer, see, cuz only sissies talk about their dreams and I ain't no sissie, but before Layla here woke me up and dragged me outta the water, I had like a big screen vision of this girl—gonna be a real looker when she grows up—flyin' around in some psychedelic clouds.

Seemed like some kinda message, but don't be spreadin' around I told you about some stupid dream. Youz asked if I remembered anything, and there it is. Let's go, Layla."

Orville watched the clanking contraption head toward the trees and then studied the ground at his feet, his brow furrowed. Riku tickled him under the chin and then held his face in her hands until he smiled.

"Where'd everyone go?" Returning from another search around the faraway shoreline, Nick looked around the empty street as he walked toward the couple.

Orville filled him in on what he'd missed, including his and Riku's true identities. Nick didn't seem surprised.

"Her scarf—you had her scarf! But wait, does that mean—"

"We do not know what it means, Nick, though it was given to me by someone who wants to keep Celeste alive." Orville remembered his dizzying transformation from metal frog to copper-toned man as he sped through the water tunnel, and the wizard with Celeste's emerald green scarf. "Here. This is yours now." He took the scarf from his pocket and handed it to Nick.

Nick accepted the gift as one would accept a precious offering, and raised his eyes to the sky.

~ 22 ~

[Celeste]

CELESTE WOKE from her dream with a startling "Rooo-oo!" and felt utterly disoriented. She hadn't intended to start the day as a dove, but after careful consideration of her desire to escape from Oblivia and Odin's realm, she chose to stay that way. She'd fallen asleep before finalizing her plan, and now bits and pieces of frightening and familiar images plagued her tiny brain.

Odin's wolves ran from her bedside. She knew they preferred the warm touch of the girl over the fluttering unpredictability of the white dove. They would bring Odin to her. There was little time to plan her escape before the god would be near her and could read her mind.

I'm a bird now . . . stay a bird to keep distance from Odin . . . convince him I need to practice on my own today before, before, something about Kumugwe—Celeste was finding it difficult to focus. She needed her girl brain, and with a final shake of her feathers, she was herself again.

"Ah! There stands my buddy!" said Odin. "Is that the right word? Buddy? Sounds undignified." She saw him smile when she whisked away her cloud bed. "Your lovely locks float around you as if submersed in water."

He frowned then.

"You were remembering my foolish idea of introducing you to Kumugwe this day, but we have no need for foolish ideas! Today, let us take time to discuss your transition to your new home! I want you to feel like Oblivia is yours as I feel it is mine."

"Great idea, buddy! And yes, that's the right word for good friends. I think I was just dreaming of my new home here as I awoke." Celeste decided she would play along with Odin's schedule for the day while she planned her escape. "Tell me more about how you make decisions about the planet below and how I'll be able to help you with your weighty responsibilities."

Celeste offered her hand to the god and they floated to the dining hall. While Odin droned on about seasons and storms and floods and droughts—spewing food from his mouth when he got particularly excited about a future event—Celeste smiled and nodded and made her plan.

She'd have to break away when no one was looking, and that would be tough. Between Odin, his wolves, and his ravens, she hadn't been alone yet. How would she convince Odin she needed some time to herself?

Ah, of course.

Halfway through her meal and Odin's childish rant about how the planet's people were unworthy of their protection, she surreptitiously stuck a finger down her throat and vomited onto the table, wrapping her arms around her belly and furrowing her brow.

"Oh, no! Gross!" she said, lifting the tablecloth to wipe her mouth, and then made herself vomit again.

"My good buddy, is the food not to your liking? Have we dined too long?" He scrunched up his nose and squinted his eye in disgust.

She didn't like having to lie, but her life—her future—was at a tipping point, and if she didn't act quickly, she feared she'd never be able to experience a normal girl's life.

Normal. What's normal anymore? The thought haunted her.

"No, no, the food is wonderful. It's just that, well, I think I might have the flu or something."

"The flu? I do not know such a thing. It must be the food. It was the pheasant, yes? It was *off.* I tasted it myself. Food, be gone!" he boomed, and the entire feast flew from the table and sank into the clouds below.

He wasn't making it easy for Celeste.

"No, truly, it wasn't the food. People, ah, humans just get sick every now and then. Oh, no! Here it comes again!"

Odin nearly fell over after jumping back from the table when Celeste threw up again, a mixture of panic and fear flashing across his face. "Oh! My! Oh, I . . . I . . . What do I do?"

"It'll be okay, really, I'll just need some time to rest." Celeste couldn't have hoped for a better response from the stammering, bumbling god.

"Yes! Of course! How foolish of me. Take whatever time you need! Time is abundant, the future is forever, you must, ah, mend yourself? Beasts! See to it our buddy gets rest!"

The wolves looked at one another and the ravens fluttered around Celeste's shoulders.

"That won't be necessary, please. If I could just have some time alone, maybe rest until dinner, perhaps that's all I'll need to feel better." She clutched her belly again and covered her mouth. "Or maybe I'll need till morning. I'm afraid I don't feel up to going anywhere today, Odin. I know how much you wanted to continue my lessons."

"Nonsense! Back to bed, poor little buddy. You have but to call my name when you are well again. I shall check on you when I raise the moon."

Perfect, she thought. She'd have plenty of time to disappear before nightfall on the planet below. Although she could have flown away from Odin then, she chose instead to walk away as slowly and pitifully as she could manage. Odin and his companions would be happy to give her the space and time she needed.

She crossed over several more layers of clouds before making a bed, and then waited and watched to ensure she wasn't followed. When she saw no signs of observation after what felt like a painfully long time, butterflies in her stomach told her it was time to go. The only sure way she knew she could make it to the planet in one piece was to return to it as she had left it—as a dove. She was not yet completely certain of her ability to fly on command as a girl again.

She'd have to be fast once she transformed, for if Odin sensed her shift and read her mind, he'd never leave her alone again.

She cleared her mind. As soon as she saw her little beak and without looking back, she shot straight down through the clouds below and into the breathless atmosphere between the heavens and the planet. With her wings pulled in tightly by her sides, she fell like a speeding arrow. At some point she'd need to open them to slow her descent and land safely, but for now, the thrill of her fall filled her with giddiness.

I'm free! She witnessed the planet growing larger and more beautiful with each passing moment. Soon she would be home.

~ ~ ~ ~ ~

Looming above her and closing the distance between them even faster than Celeste was falling, Odin's huge black ravens were in pursuit.

~ 23 ~

[Harmony]

"HURRY!" HARMONY SHOUTED, though not at Sharon and Blanche. She stared somewhere beyond the muddy dome overhead and shuddered.

"Hurry where? We're right here! What are you looking at?" Blanche was already acting freaked out around the shiny black crabs, and Harmony realized her sudden bizarre behavior—shouting at something unseen—wasn't helping to gain the teen's trust.

"Sorry, I didn't mean to yell. I just got this feeling that she . . . I mean we . . . should hurry." Harmony was startled by the feeling. An image of the flying girl she'd lured to her sandcastle, the girl Kumugwe had asked her to find, had flashed in her mind. The girl was in danger.

"Just tell us what we need to do, Harmony." When Sharon spoke, her voice sounded odd. She sounded like a girl much younger than a teen. She frowned.

"It won't hurt, but you'll probably feel quite dizzy when it happens. You might want to close your eyes. It'll make it easier." Harmony beckoned the girls toward the crabs in the water. She stared at Sharon as she did, noticing the subtle change in her sister.

"Wait a minute." Blanche stopped several feet from the water's edge. "Just exactly what's about to happen here?"

"The crabs can make water tunnels for you, but you'll just have to trust me and come over here. You need to be near them. They won't hurt you, I promise, and I'll meet you both when we're down under."

"I'm ready, scaredy pants," Sharon said as she marched to the water's edge and stood by her sister's side, mere inches from the crab's eyes and wriggling antennae. She turned her back to the water and closed her eyes.

Harmony gestured for Blanche to do the same, and after several tense moments, Blanche took her place next to Sharon, but glanced over her shoulder at the lurking hermit crabs.

"You should close your eyes too. Honestly, it won't hurt." When Harmony spoke, her sea-green eyes glowed softly. The effect calmed the older girl, who took one more look over her shoulder before closing her eyes. Harmony turned her gaze to the waiting crabs and giggled a complex, ethereal melody.

Two shiny crabs responded instantly. Harmony watched as the claws they shot from their shells expanded rapidly until they were larger than the two unsuspecting girls. A moment later, the claws opened and the cavern echoed with the sound of swirling, churning water.

"Wait a min—" Blanche opened her eyes and screamed at the monstrous claw looming over her, but her protest was cut short.

The claws engulfed the girls, clamped shut, shrank as swiftly as they had grown, and retracted back into each small, hard shell.

Harmony dove into the water and watched as each girl reemerged as a miniscule version of herself inside her own little water tunnel behind the crabs. As the tunnels lengthened and expanded, the girls grew until they were returned to their normal size. Harmony swam between the two tunnels and smiled at the stunned girls, whose expressions changed from startled fear to astonished amusement as they slid through the glowing, slippery tubes that shot deeper and deeper into the water.

"Can you hear me?" Sharon shouted to her sister. She seemed mesmerized by the beauty of Harmony's movement through the water. Harmony nodded yes, and her long pink hair undulated like a rippling fin behind her. "How much longer?"

"There is no time here." Harmony's words floated through the water and jostled the tunnels gently. "We are there when we are there. Sleep now." Harmony yawned deeply, inhaling massive amounts of water, and when she exhaled, the stream of water she released rocked the tunnels back and forth.

Though she could see both girls fighting an urge to close their eyes, they finally yawned and were soon sound asleep, slipping and endlessly sliding toward the darkening ocean floor.

Minutes or hours or days later, Harmony woke them with a gentle thud against something that absorbed their impact. They opened their eyes to discover they'd been deposited upon a sandy ledge inside a much smaller cavern with Harmony standing over them, reaching for their hands to help them to their feet.

"Oh, wow! Where are we? And how long were we asleep? I had some seriously crazy dreams!" Blanche shook her head and pulled her hand from Harmony's.

Sharon turned her back to the others.

"Hey, are you all right?" Harmony put her hand on Sharon's shoulder and when Sharon turned around, she looked frightened. And younger.

When she spoke, her voice quavered. "What's happening to me, Harmony? What are you doing to me? And where are we?"

"Please don't fear, sister. We're close to where our birth parents have been working since they left you. Tunnel travel can make you feel . . . unusual."

Harmony saw Blanche studying a noticeably younger Sharon.

"You've had a restful sleep and now you should eat before we decide how we'll announce ourselves to them."

Harmony motioned the girls to a ledge within the cave where she'd prepared an unrecognizable feast. She was surprised when they ate the unusual food without hesitation.

"Where are they?" Sharon's question was abrupt.

"Let's see. How can I describe this?" Harmony closed her eyes and hummed a pleasant tune while she thought, and smiled when Sharon and Blanche, looking confused, swayed with the rhythm.

"While you were traveling here, the hermits told me where to go. They wouldn't answer any of my other questions, though. I think they're afraid. Not far away there's an old octopus, and her name is Zoya. I never knew of her while I lived with Kumugwe, but his realm is vaster than yours on dry land, and I never ventured far from home. I know this sounds unbelievable, but our birth parents have established their submarine laboratory *inside* this poor creature."

Sharon and Blanche stopped eating, their attention fixed on Harmony.

"I didn't have the hermits deliver you right to their door because we need to consider our arrival. I know nothing about these people, Sharon. How will they react when we find them?"

"Well, I can tell you they won't be happy to see us. Why would they? They abandoned both of us, and never even gave me the time of day when I was little." She looked at her smooth copper arms. It sounded like she was about to cry.

"Could they hurt us? And if they did, who'd know? Who'd ever find us?" Blanche shook her head and mumbled something that sounded like "idiot."

"I have many powerful friends here," said Harmony. "Should you ever feel threatened, they will take you back topside. I don't believe there's anything more they could do to hurt me." Her eyes glowed icy blue as she spoke.

Blanche looked back to the water's edge and saw the hermit crabs lurking. "You said it wouldn't hurt, and it didn't, but wow, Harmony, couldn't you have told us about those creepy claws? I'm not even gonna ask how they worked!"

"Would you have trusted me if I'd told you the crab claws were going to snatch you from the shore?"

Blanche smirked and shook her head.

"I say we take them by surprise. Just walk in with something like this hidden in our clothes," Sharon picked up a knife-shaped shell from a pile of beautiful and broken ones near the water, "and tell them we're in on whatever they're doing." She slid the shell up her sleeve. "We can stand around and wonder how they'll react for the rest of our lives, or we can go find out now. What are we waiting for?"

Blanche found a shell similar to Sharon's, walked slowly to where the hermits waited, turned her back to them and closed her eyes. "Let's go, then."

~ **24** ~

[The Village / Orville]

ORVILLE SENSED NICK'S ANGUISH. Never having had a child or a brother, he wasn't sure what to say, but knew he had to say something. "I want to thank you, Nick."

Nick looked confused. "For what? I haven't found her yet. I haven't really done anything that's helped."

"Ah, but you are wrong. You helped Celeste when she rescued Chimney and me from the fissures. Just knowing you were there when she departed to rescue those from the other side gave me the strength to hang on longer. And you helped her when the Shifter held my life in her hideous grip."

Nick seemed to study the wavy blood stain on the emerald scarf from when the villagers had knocked Celeste on the head before delivering her to the Overleader.

"She returned to you before, Nick, and I believe she will return to you again."

Nick lowered his head and smiled. "I hope so. I don't know where else to look for her."

Orville nodded and patted him on the shoulder. "I could really use your help now, if you are willing."

"Yeah, sure. But if you need me to stop time, I don't know if I'll be able to control when and where I do it. I feel, I don't know, weird. Not like before. Right now I almost feel like—" he stopped and looked down at the scarf again.

"Like what? You can talk to me," said Orville. "I do not believe you could tell me anything that would surprise me."

"Well," Nick continued, "my eyes just felt weird and I thought I might hop, you know, like a frog. You know what I mean?"

"Indeed. Yes, I do. You are not alone, though. Several of us have experienced, hmm, how do I say this? Urges. Yes, we have felt the urges of those around us. The fluxes seem to be distributing powers haphazardly since the water changed."

"So how can I help? I'll keep hunting, if that's what you're talking about."

"Yes, with more mouths to feed, we still need hunters, but even more than that, it would help to have your friendship. Because I made some suggestions recently, the people now look to me with growing expectations though there are others in the village who surely know more about life here than I. And I fear I am no natural leader, but here we are."

Nick smiled again. "Why wouldn't I be your friend? You know more about Celeste than any of us, and I . . . I think . . . I think I love her." He shook his head as if to convince himself he'd just said something ridiculous, and stuffed the green scarf back into his pocket. "But how will being your friend help?"

Noting the boy's obvious embarrassment, Orville decided to move past the comment about love.

"No one knows where Sharon and her sister are, and Blanche has disappeared. Chimney believes Blanche is with the girls and is searching for her now with Ranger and the horse-peacock, but I feel no confidence she will be found. The Overleader is, or was, just a girl, but we must assume she remains a danger. We know nothing of the little sister."

Just then, Mason walked past shaking his head and babbling to his feet. "Falling, falling, feathers and falling, clouds and clouds and clouds are calling, falling faster, danger approaching, feathers and fire and clouds encroaching. And they're watching, you know."

"*Monsieur* Mason!" Orville called to him, but the man didn't acknowledge the summons.

"What do you think's wrong with him?" asked Nick.

"I do not know, Nick, but something is telling me he is not as daft as he seems."

"Daft? What's that mean?"

"Hmm, daft. I believe you might say foolish. There is something about him that makes me think he knows more than he may be willing to share."

"So you think the Overleader—or whoever she is—might still hurt us? I should've stopped them. Why would Celeste come back to me after I couldn't stop them from dragging her there?" Anger flashed across Nick's face.

"Because she knows you could not stop the mob. You must not blame yourself for the actions of others."

"But I could've stopped time then. It wouldn't have affected her, and she could've flown away! Why didn't I stop time then? See? Being my friend won't help you at all. It won't help anyone." Nick ran away from Orville toward where the water once threatened the town.

Orville saw Riku on the porch and when their eyes met, she joined him.

"Again. Still. Something new troubles you." Her voice was soft. She took his hand.

"The boy, Nick. He takes responsibility for Celeste's disappearance. His feelings for her are strong, and I want to believe her feelings for him will bring her back. She was told to stop the destructive water and she did, but there is more for her to do, I fear."

"Why so much burden on one young woman?" Riku looked for an answer in Orville's eyes.

"If I knew why, perhaps I would feel worthy of these survivors' expectations. Celeste is strong. Perhaps she is being tested for something even she does not understand." He pulled Riku into a gentle embrace and watched as Nick disappeared beyond the village. "Will you stay by my side and help me make some sense of our new world?"

Riku's shy smile told him what he needed to know.

A commotion behind them captured their attention. It was the returning search party, and Chimney looked dejected.

"We walked and walked and walked all over the place and didn't see anybody." Chimney twitched and found a stone to kick. "Layla let me ride her after a while, and that was cool, but it was hard to hold on sometimes cuz her back's really slippery, but she slowed down whenever I started to slide off, right, Layla?"

The horse bowed her metal head toward the boy's outstretched hand and he patted her muzzle.

"Aww, ain't that sweet," Lou interrupted. "Now, do you think I can get a little shut-eye anytime soon? None of youz got any idea how tiring it is being bounced all over tarnation and back."

"But first I need to tell them about something weird," said Chimney.

Orville raised his eyebrows in anticipation, but lowered them quickly when he sensed his eyes might bulge out. He dropped Riku's hand and hopped in a small circle before apologizing awkwardly.

"The fluxes are disturbing, but I believe I will still be capable of communicating with you should I suddenly become a frog again. Tell me, Chimney, what did you see?"

"Well, I'm not really sure I saw anything, but I'm pretty sure there was something following us. I didn't say anything to Ranger and Layla cuz I didn't want to stop looking, but every once in a while it was like something moved up high in the trees, but it was all blurry when I looked up. And when we were outta the trees, I kept feeling like there was someone, well, someone like me following us."

"Like you?" Orville placed his hands gently on the bewildered boy's shoulders.

"Yeah, like how I can sorta be invisible if I don't want anybody to see me. Or, like I used to be able to do that."

Ranger looked over his shoulder before speaking. "There is nothing to fear, boy. You felt the presence of Merts. Perhaps they will tell us why they follow."

Trees at the edge of the forest shook subtly and Orville squinted, trying to focus on an amorphous object moving their way.

"Yeah. That's the thing," whispered Chimney.

~ 25 ~

[Celeste]

CELESTE WAS OBLIVIOUS to the threat from above, and a loud cry from far below startled her. It sounded like someone screamed the word "hurry." The voice seemed familiar, and a vague sensation of fear clouded her vision for a moment.

Nevertheless, she shook off the foreboding feeling and refocused on her journey. Giddy with excitement at the thought of being with people again, she shot faster and faster through the atmosphere. But her joy didn't last long. As the planet below grew more formidable with her rapid descent, so did worries about her ability to make it back to the village safely.

How will I find it again? she wondered. The planet was in the process of significant change since the watery ooze had receded. *And what will I find there when I arrive? Will Nick even remember me? How long have I been gone?*

She had lost all track of time, and other fleeting thoughts plagued her tiny brain as well. She wondered what would happen when Odin discovered she had betrayed him. Would he understand or be angry? Would he beseech her to return, force her to, or worse, punish those she had grown to love?

A strange tingling in her wingtips reminded her that if she focused her thoughts too strongly she'd precipitate a flux, and she still had far to go before she'd feel confident transforming into her girl form. She'd find out soon enough how her escape would affect the sky god, the god who lived in a realm of breathtaking beauty.

He called me "buddy." He's just as lonely as I am. Celeste felt guilty.

The idea of returning to the forlorn god tempted her. The world below was filled with challenges, uncertainty, cruel people, and mud. Life in Oblivia with its colorful ribbons of clouds would be predictable and safe. She would never be hungry and she'd have Odin as a friend forever.

But a deeper instinct told her she should not trust thoughts that flitted through her bird brain.

A friend forever? "Never forever," Orville once told me. Orville! I've got to get back to Orville and my friends below.

Celeste's mind was made up.

But what was happening? How was it that time and motion suddenly seemed to stop? Celeste hovered in mid-fall.

Warm winds rising from below? she wondered, *or was it possible that Nick had stopped time on the planet and in the sky? Can't think about Nick now.* She tried to shake his image from her mind.

Floating in the space between worlds, her beautiful white feathers glowing in the reflective atmosphere, Celeste lost herself in a blissful reverie.

A bouncy bed of swirling clouds . . . more food than I've ever seen . . . a good and powerful buddy . . . shaggy wolves who remind me of . . . of . . .

Visions of Ranger and his motley pack broke through her beautiful trance and flooded her tiny brain with more serious issues.

My friends! Why didn't I get answers from Odin about my family and friends? Does Odin even know the truth about The Event and the strange water?

Her wings tingled again and panic seized her feathered body. It wasn't time to flux yet.

A magnetic force seemed to pull at her from above, and it was enough to fill her with a desire to break free of it. She didn't know how long she'd been suspended between worlds and didn't like the feeling.

Still uncertain about her power to fly once she became a girl again, she aimed for a place over an ocean below and flapped her wings hard. If she failed to fly after her transformation, a splash into the water would be far more forgiving than a crash onto hard land. At least, that's what she thought.

Focus! Hurry! she told herself, but as hard as she tried to reach the planet below, her progress was slow. *Didn't I fly to Oblivia in a heartbeat?* she wondered, remembering the joy and power she'd felt when Odin's ravens had locked her wingtips between theirs and delivered her to the realm of beauty.

Just as she remembered the ravens . . .

"KRAA! KRAACAW!"

Celeste was startled from her efforts by the raucous screeches of Odin's approaching birds. In a moment of panic, she realized she was falling from the sky. The intensity of her desire to return home mixed with an intense fear she'd never make it, completing her transformation back into a girl before she was ready for it.

Sensing the imminent threat from both the birds and from the suddenly looming planet below, terrified, she lost her focus.

Tumbling through the atmosphere, she couldn't tell up from down, sky from water. Heavy rolling clouds reflected twin images onto the surface of a gently undulating ocean below, and Celeste couldn't distinguish one from the other. Clouds above and clouds below seemed to beckon her to hide in their silky, rolling layers, to camouflage herself against Odin's relentlessly approaching informants.

"AWAY! AWAY!" she screamed.

But the birds continued their approach as she spun out of control catching glimpses of the black creatures with each rotation of her body.

"Holy-moly-NO! Help! Help me!" Celeste screamed into the swirling, buffeting atmosphere, suddenly wanting the huge birds to save her from certain death as the planet's rotation had changed her impact zone from water to land.

Something glittered between her and the birds then, something with two pairs of diaphanous wings far larger than those of the ravens, longer even than the longest sea creature she'd ever seen from the captivity of her bubble bedroom beneath the sandcastle, and with a long, slender body stretching far behind its wings.

An enormous blast of fire shot from the creature's jaws and even as Celeste continued to plummet from the sky, she felt its heat and caught glimpses of the ravens' wings burning as they ceased their pursuit and fluttered away back to the heavens.

The glittering creature then flew in a graceful arc, swooping beneath Celeste and catching her gently on a box-like flat surface between its wings and saving her from slamming into the earth below.

Celeste's heart caught in her throat and she gasped. Holding firmly onto ridges along the creature's back—ridges that reminded her of Orville's rebar-like back ridges—she peered ahead and watched as the land they flew over became water again.

"What . . . who are you?" she whispered, not sure of her own voice or even if the creature could understand her.

"I am Noor. And I am sorry, small one, but it is time for you to learn more." The magnificent dragonfly's voice was peaceful, but her message was perplexing.

"What do you mean, learn more? More of what? And where are you taking me? Thank you for rescuing me, but would you please turn around? I'd like to return to a village with people like me!"

"I cannot," said the dragonfly. "You must go back, but not yet back to your people. You must return to the water. You must learn what they are doing and help the other to release the tortured creature."

"The other? Wait!" Celeste yelled. But it was too late.

~ ~ ~ ~ ~

Faltering in flight from wing feathers scorched and lost, Odin's ravens returned to Oblivia, frightened by what had just happened—and what they would have to tell their master.

Their feathers floated to a forest floor below where the three-headed archer stood squinting at all the commotion in the heavens.

~ 26 ~

[Harmony]

WHILE SHARON AND BLANCHE slid over the ocean floor in their water tunnels, Harmony swam alongside them. There was no need to put them to sleep this time. Unfamiliar flutters in her stomach left her with an emotion she couldn't quite name. Was it excitement? Fear? In any case, she didn't like the uncertainty she felt.

These were just people she was going to meet. The fact that they were her biological parents meant nothing to her, though she couldn't deny her curiosity. She wondered if they'd recognize her. Yes, she could name the fear she was feeling when she thought they might recognize her, even though she couldn't imagine what power they might hold over her after so many years lost.

"Almost there. Are you ready?" Harmony's voice carried to the girls in word bubbles. Both girls nodded, and Harmony detected fear in their eyes too.

She wouldn't let them know of her own fear when she noticed the silvery-pink water surrounding the poor creature. She closed one membrane tightly over her eyes to protect from the sting.

"I will approach the octopus—Zoya—first to let her know of our intentions. I will bring you to her then."

The girls nodded again, their progress in the tunnels temporarily halted, and Harmony swam slowly toward the enormous creature who had kept her parents and their submarine laboratory hidden for so long.

From what she knew about the intelligent, eight-limbed masters of camouflage, octopuses had very short lifespans. She didn't understand how Zoya could still be alive, especially in the unnatural water with a foreign object lodged within her.

The thought made her shudder.

Zoya's enormous body blended with its surroundings. Several of the creature's powerful arms seemed to be losing their ability to adapt to the undulating and peculiar changes in the water. Kumugwe had taught Harmony how to spot sea mimics—the subtle outlines of their attempts to disappear, the barely disturbed bits of sea life and detritus surrounding them—and despite the color of the water, Harmony could see her clearly.

A strange thought struck her. She too had become a mimic, her appearance changing from a hideous little sharp-toothed sea urchin of a child to the beautiful young woman preparing to meet her creators.

Her heart ached at the sight of the creature, for Zoya was well beyond her time for living a healthy existence.

Not wanting to startle her, Harmony approached one of her long arms, touching it gently and giggling in a way she'd communicated with other sea life. Abruptly, the arm lifted high above the pink-haired girl, revealing suckers the size of kitchen tables and causing the water tunnels to bounce. She could hear Sharon and Blanche gasp, but she didn't fear Zoya.

The arm floated back down to Harmony, who held her own arms above her to receive it.

"Zoya, I am Harmony, daughter of Kumugwe. I am here with two others from topside to learn of the foreign activity you hide, but we are no threat to you."

"No threat, daughter of Kumugwe, god of my world?" Zoya's voice came to her in weary thought waves. "I have heard your name and sense a kindness within. Help me, then. Rid me of my excruciating pain and agonizing exhaustion. Liberate me from the monsters who keep me alive."

This was not what Harmony had expected to hear.

"But how?" she asked. "Can you show me what's happening inside before we enter?"

Harmony closed her eyes and allowed the tip of Zoya's great arm to touch the center of her forehead. Visions and voices flooded her senses. A man, a woman, both appearing agitated as they studied dials on a dim dashboard, each seeming to accuse the other of incompetence.

"This stupid beast is resisting us. We have to increase the power of the ionic field."

"But if you increase it any more, Lilith, couldn't we lose it all? And we don't want to kill it, do we? Look at the water."

"Oh, shut up, will you, Thurston? I'm so sick of your childish blubbering I could spit. If I hadn't tried it before, we never would have known just how powerful it was."

"Well, I suppose you're right—"

"Of course I'm right. I'm always right. Now stop your sniveling and man up, man. This is what we've been waiting for, isn't it?"

"Yes, yes it is. But it's . . . it's . . . wait a minute! Something's out there!"

In a moment of panic, Harmony realized the people inside the lab could sense she was outside.

"I do not know how they do it," Zoya relayed her thought after disengaging her arm, "but now they know you are here. You must help me, girl. Do what you must."

"I will," Harmony promised. "Can they hear you?"

"No. I do not speak to them, though I listen. These are not good creatures. They have done outrageous things. Prepare yourself now. They will see you soon."

Harmony hurriedly swam to Sharon's water tunnel and entering it, much to Sharon's surprise.

"Play along with me, Sharon. They're watching. Those people inside cannot know about my abilities." Harmony would never again call them her parents.

Slowly, the two tunnels merged into one and moved through the putrid water toward a metal door at the junction of Zoya's eight arms. Through a small window in the door, the three girls, now together, could see another door beyond it and two people staring wide-eyed through its window.

"This is it," Harmony whispered. "We will say that we lost our way. We took a wrong turn in the tunnels. We were exploring the changes since the water turned blue and came across this strange new water."

"That's not a total lie." Blanche snickered, but Harmony sensed it wasn't a happy sound.

"We cannot threaten them. And whatever you do, do not trust them for a moment." Harmony waved at the couple behind the doors and gestured for them to open the entrance to the laboratory.

"They're so . . . white," whispered Sharon. "They look just like they did when they left me, but maybe a little bit crazier."

The girls watched as the two adults appeared to bicker at length behind the doors until the man reached over the woman's head and pushed something. The outside door opened and a strong stream of air kept water from flooding the enclosure. The man waved the girls into the outside compartment with vigorous hand gestures and when they were inside, the outside door closed.

The woman forced a horrible smile. Opening the inner door slowly, she said, "We're sorry, girls, but we don't allow solicitors in this neighborhood."

The woman then cackled, sending shivers down Harmony's spine.

"Oh, now, Lilith, let's see what news our surprise visitors have brought us, shall we?" He pushed Lilith aside and ushered the girls into a small chamber beyond the entrance.

"We didn't mean to disturb you," said Sharon. "Honestly, we don't even know how we got here." She looked at Harmony in a way that said, *they don't even recognize me.*

"Well, perhaps we can help get you back on your way home now." Lilith's impatience—or was it fear, Harmony wondered—was abrupt.

"Nonsense, my lily pad. Can't you see these critters are lost and hungry? Where are our manners? Come to the dining room, lovelies. Oh! What pretty pink locks the two of you have. Pity the third is so dull. And your skin!"

Lilith smacked Thurston in a way not meant to be seen, but Harmony noticed. She also noticed a silent interaction between the two that made her question whether she and the girls should follow the bizarre couple any farther into the laboratory.

But Harmony had said she'd help the poor creature whose life was being painfully extended by these monsters. She grabbed the other girls' hands and followed them into a spacious chamber.

Thud-thud-clink, thud-thud-clink, thud-thud-clink . . .

Zoya's three hearts—kept pumping by an elaborate mechanical device—echoed in the cold metal room.

~ **27** ~

[The Village / Orville]

MERTS PICKED UP several of the unscorched raven feathers scattered on the forest floor and spoke to themselves.

"Unusual find / Our arrows will fly true now / Sturdy as these are."

All three heads turned to see Orville and the others looking their way, and after carefully replacing their frayed fletchings with the shiny new black feathers, they slid slowly toward the expectant group.

~ ~ ~ ~ ~

Though he didn't sense the archer was a threat, its bow held low and arrows un-nocked, Orville moved between the bizarre being and the others as he spoke.

"You have been following my search party. If you understand my language, explain your actions. We mean you no harm and wish to hear the same from you."

"They understand," said Ranger.

Merts responded as they always did, in haiku and in unison with perfect harmony.

"Message from within / With you we will be made whole / Protect your people."

Orville stared at the most unusual creation he'd seen yet and was stunned by the beauty of their combined voices.

"Are you telling me to protect my people?" Orville was confused. "And, forgive me for being so very blunt, but this message from within is, ah, from within what?"

The three heads turned inward and Merts appeared to be communicating with one another, though Orville could hear no voices. Finally, they turned back to the group.

"We cannot answer / This mystery is ours too / We will help you live."

"Hey, did you see my sister while you were following us? Are you the ones who dumped all that meat by the trees? And can I see your bow?" When Chimney reached out toward the bow, Orville noted how Merts retreated a distance without making a sound.

It looked as if they'd floated over the ground.

Orville put an arm around the curious boy's shoulder, pulling him back gently. "Forgive my enthusiastic friend. Chimney has been gathering for his community since The Event. His sister, Blanche, has led these survivors for years. She left the village, and now the people look to me for direction. Like many others here, and perhaps like you as well, I have undergone physical changes since the great shaking of the planet."

Merts nodded their heads and moved closer while Orville continued.

"Blanche has been, ah, shall we say, forceful in her approach to leadership, and for a while, allied herself with a wicked old woman who now, we believe, is just a girl. This sounds nonsensical, I know, but we all have witnessed absurdities these past years."

"I know youz ain't lookin' at me with those words, mister hoppity." Orville knew Lou was jesting, and laughed.

"No, Lou and Layla . . . you know we're all not what we once were. But wait a moment. Here comes Nick. Perhaps he brings news."

Nick walked toward the group hastily, his forehead furrowed. He looked from the group to a place in the sky over his shoulder several times before reaching them.

"Did you see that? Did anyone see that?" Nick's breathing sounded shallow. "Anyone?" He stared at Merts—Orville couldn't blame him for that—while waiting for a response. Merts' three heads stared back before speaking.

"Skyward commotion / Two black birds in flames / Swooping, falling things." They pointed to the new feathers on their arrow and several others stowed in their braid.

Nick raised his eyebrows. "Yes! What was that? I was on my way back to apologize to you, Orville. I was acting like a selfish brat. You've known her longer than I have, and I know you're as worried as I am."

"So?" Nick returned his attention to Merts, and Orville did too. "What was all that about? It was too far away for me to make out, but that thing had to be enormous for those flames to catch my attention—and I felt the heat. It looked like it caught something falling from the sky."

Orville held Riku and Chimney a little tighter. *Could it be Celeste*, he wondered. It would explain his visions of her surrounded by ethereal beauty and his recent gut feeling that she was heading for danger.

"Raven messengers / A fire-breathing dragonfly / And a girl, we think."

"A girl? What did she look like? Did she have long black hair? Is she all right? Where is she now? Was she flying? Is the dragonfly dangerous?" Nick's rapid-fire questions had Orville holding his breath for answers.

Chimney shrugged away from Orville's protective grasp. "But my sister." His plaintive little voice broke the atmosphere of anticipation. "What about her? Did you see her too?" He twitched and dug his toe into the dirt, and Orville knew the boy wanted to disappear.

He then watched Merts—as if they sensed the child's distress—lay down their bow, slide over to him, and place their two hands gently on his head. Chimney visibly relaxed beneath their touch.

"Three girls disappeared / Two sisters, one yours, we think / Blanche went willingly."

Orville frowned. He'd just learned that three girls with questionable intentions had disappeared. Merts didn't seem to know where—only that they were beyond the forest—and one girl, possibly Celeste, had fallen from the sky and was possibly saved, or captured, by a gigantic fire-breathing dragonfly. It was too much to wrap his tired brain around.

"Chim," he said gently, "you know your sister can take care of herself, right?"

Chimney nodded, still digging with his toe.

"And we know you want her to come back, and I'll bet she will, so perhaps now we focus on trying to find out where Celeste is, *oui?*"

"Yeah, I guess. Maybe she can find my sister and we can be a family again. Maybe she's looking for her right now." Chimney leaned against Layla, and Orville was grateful that Lou didn't offer a wisecrack.

"But how do we even begin to look for Celeste if that thing took her?" Nick asked. "She could be anywhere. Bridger's little boats wouldn't get us very far, and none of us can fly."

Orville smiled. "We may not be able to fly, but there are still two doves in our village, and they found her once before."

"I'll find Teresa!" Nick ran from the group and shouted over his shoulder, "Wait right there!"

~ ~ ~ ~ ~

Noor scanned the ocean until she saw the perfect cloud reflection near the edge of the slowly expanding pink ooze. The magnificent dragonfly didn't like what she was about to do, but knew it was necessary.

~ **28** ~

[Celeste]

"FIND AND RELEASE HER," Celeste heard Noor announce as they drifted low over a perfect reflection of a cumulous cloud. The creature apologized once more to Celeste and with no other warning, tipped her into the watery apparition before vanishing.

Celeste had tried to hold on, but the swiftness with which Noor rolled was too sudden. Holding her breath and falling backward through the deep water, Celeste reached up toward the water's surface, hoping to beckon the dragonfly back to her, but all she could see was a wavy, fluffy white cloud drifting farther and farther away.

A memory startled her as she sank. The shape of the giant dragonfly recalled an image—*Where did I see that?*—and with sudden clarity she remembered the great door to Odin's dining hall. The image at the top of the door, a fire-breathing, winged creature with someone riding atop it, looked like Noor.

Everything was upside-down, and Celeste was tired of it all. Ever since her family and friends had been taken away from her, her life had been a battle. She'd been both rescuer and rescued in a world that no longer played by reasonably predictable rules. Since leaving the children's home, nothing she'd done had truly fixed anything. *Just breathe in the water and let it all go*, she told herself.

But a vision of Orville fighting for his life against the wicked Shifter startled her from her self-pity. She had to live. She had to know if he'd somehow survived. The last thing he'd done for her was to sacrifice himself again by plunging with the Shifter—trapped inside his transformed mechanical body—into the ocean, the very ocean in which she was now sinking.

But she could hold her breath no longer, and in a final sobbing exhale, she lost consciousness.

~ ~ ~ ~ ~

When a raft of sea lions saw the dragonfly drop a girl into the undulating cloud, they alerted a powerful black crab, which hastily opened a water tunnel beneath the limp human. The crab caught her just in time, for if it had been a moment later, the girl would have inhaled a great amount of water.

The sea lions and the crab had heard stories of weak-fleshed humans who could not breathe underwater, and though they didn't know if the stories were true, they didn't want to be responsible for killing this one. They fancied themselves better than sharks.

Not knowing who she was or why such an exotic creature would deliver her to their realm, the sea lions suggested transport to their king's dwelling. That is where the crab opened the end of his tunnel, depositing the unconscious—but breathing—girl inside Kumugwe's great chambers.

~ ~ ~ ~ ~

"Where am I? And who are you?" Celeste sat up and scampered backward from the intimidating bearded face that greeted hers when she awoke. Fins encircled his enormous head and from his back, tentacles appeared to float. His muscular torso merged into a wide fluke that spread onto the ground behind him.

"Did not my little Harmony tell you about me— Kumugwe, King of the seas, maker of copper and many good things? And where is my sweet girl? I knew she would not let me down. But tell me first your name, child."

"I'm Celeste Araia Nolan, and I don't know who you're talking about. How did I get here? Last thing I remember was trying to hold my breath—"

"But why? Surely the girl who recovered my spear and returned it to me would be powerful enough to survive in my world!"

Celeste didn't pick up on the implications of the water god's last words. "Your spear? Do you mean the Spear of Sorrow, that horrible thing the Overleader used to torment the villagers?"

"And now it is I who do not know what you are talking about, child! My spear, inlaid with waves of powerful orichalcum, contains wonderful magic! But ah, now I see how in the wrong hands it could be used for dark purposes. This makes me sad. But alas! It has found its home and so, now, have you."

"Wait, what?" Celeste stood and for the first time, took in her surroundings. Beyond the large room to which she'd somehow been delivered, she could see an enormous hall made of and filled with copper and sea creatures and—"Are those sea lion columns holding up your ceilings?"

"Yes! They love me and serve me well! In turn, they are well cared for. Note their size and strength! Yes, you will find your new home has many wonders. Now, where is my Harmony? Surely you know my child with the lilting voice! I charged her with bringing to me the girl who returned my spear, and here you are! We were both distraught when the mechanical frog took you away, but I blame my greedy brother Odin for that mischief."

Celeste felt faint when she heard Odin's name and slumped back onto the bed. And now she knew the name of the child who'd lulled her with sweet tunes into a cruel sandcastle world, teasing her with replicas of her parents and puppy. Such a cruel joke. And for what purpose?

She wondered what she'd done to deserve such a fate— escaping from one god's realm only to be trapped in another.

"Please don't tell him I'm here," Celeste implored. "His world is beautiful, but I want to return to my people. He wanted to keep me there in Oblivia, but—"

"So, he wanted to keep you for himself? Shame on him. He must have seen great power in you. And that is what I see, for no one else could have escaped his realm if he had wanted to keep them there. Hmmm." Kumugwe stroked his broad chin and appeared concerned.

Celeste had to think fast. She was no longer the naïve little girl who'd long ago run away from the children's home. *How long ago?* It didn't matter anymore.

"A god more powerful than you or your brother has sent me here to perform a secret mission," she announced, "and you would be wise not to keep me here against my will."

Kumugwe at first appeared alarmed, but then a smile spread across his great face.

"Tell me, Celeste Araia Nolan. Who is this more powerful god?"

She'd hoped he wouldn't call her bluff, but she couldn't back down. "Noor, god of fire and light." She waited. Was it a look of fear that flashed across his face? Of recognition? She waited longer.

"Noor," he repeated. "I do not know this Noor, so tell me something to make me believe there is a god greater than I."

Celeste finally felt she was in a position of power with the sea god. Knowledge of something unknown to her potential adversary appeared to give her the upper hand. And he believed she was powerful. She was beginning to believe it herself. The teardrop marking Odin had discovered on the back of her head tingled.

"The next time you talk to your brother, you might ask him about his ravens' feathers. Then have him tell you the truth about your waters." Celeste remembered Odin pointing out the growing patch of sickly pink water from her vantage point in the heavens.

Kumugwe seemed to consider her words before turning toward the doorway. "You say you have not seen my Harmony?" He sounded concerned.

"No. But let me accomplish my mission and I'll help you find her. Please leave now and let me rest. I've had quite a long day."

She was pushing her luck and she knew it, but figured she had nothing more to lose. Someone or something wanted to keep her alive, and she needed time to think.

Kumugwe left her alone to wonder who she was supposed to release, and where she was supposed to find her.

~ 29 ~

[Harmony]

"SQUID SOUFFLÉ, GIRLS?" Harmony heard Lilith's offer, but had no idea what a soufflé was. "We were just about to eat when you dropped in. Thurston, set out a few more utensils, would you, darling?"

Lilith's act of playing the welcoming host felt unnatural to Harmony, and it was evident to her that she'd long ago emasculated her husband. He jumped to a counter and returned with several spoons and forks.

As there were only two chairs at the small metal table, the five stood around it in uncomfortable silence. Harmony tried not to stare at the people who had discarded her as an infant. She glanced at Sharon and Blanche, who looked with disgust at the pallid, horrible-smelling casserole.

"Don't be shy, now. Dig in!" Thurston plunged his fork into the steaming dish and pulled out something gelatinous and still slightly squirming.

"Thank you for your generosity," Harmony spoke when she saw the other girls' eyes widen, "but we ate . . . at the beach, just before we traveled. Really, we didn't mean to disturb you. But my! What a wonderful laboratory this is!"

"Yes," Sharon jumped in, "we'd love to see what you're working on. I love doing experiments."

"We'll see about that, dearie," said Lilith.

Harmony shot Sharon a look of warning while Thurston, seemingly oblivious to the comment, continued to stuff his mouth with the soufflé. Harmony noted a certain vacancy in the man's eyes.

She saw Lilith, on the other hand, narrowing her eyes and studying each girl, lingering on Sharon. Harmony hoped she wouldn't identify the older child they'd abandoned just before The Event that shattered the planet. She saw no indication of recognition.

"Thurston, wipe your chin! You've got suckers all stuck to it."

The man did as he was told, pulling on a dismembered rubbery arm that had escaped his mouth and attached itself to his chin. It made a squishy sucking sound when it released, and Thurston popped the piece back into his mouth. Harmony thought Blanche might throw up.

"Do excuse us a moment, girls." Lilith grabbed Thurston by the sleeve and pulled him away from the table. "We have something to discuss. We won't be long. Help yourselves to whatever's left of the soufflé, and please, don't touch anything else." The bizarre couple shuffled down a narrow hallway and closed a metal door behind them.

"Oh, I swear, I'm going to be sick." Blanche clapped a hand over her mouth and turned from the table.

"Oh, grow up," said Sharon, sounding very much like her mother. "Can you believe this place? Look at these sketches of . . . whatever these monsters are."

"Don't touch them," Harmony reminded her. Sharon's comment felt personal. She had once been seen as a monster too, and a deep ache welled inside. Her sea-green eyes turned an icy blue.

"Increase that ache a thousandfold, child, and know how I feel," Zoya's voice sounded inside Harmony's mind. "No one will hear us. You made a promise to help me. Do not be led astray."

"Seriously, though," Sharon continued to search the room for clues as to what her parents were doing. "This is brilliant! Look. They're changing particles to be able to morph into, well, lots of things."

"How do you know all this?" Blanche had stopped retching and moved to where Sharon studied scattered schematics on a long countertop.

"They kept me out of the house most of the time, but I'd sneak into their room at night and take a book or a folder—there were stacks of them—and read them. I'd spy on them too when they thought I was asleep. I remember them talking in the living room about making more land and things they could control—"

"Beware the two whose energies imitate that of the woman," Zoya warned Harmony just as Lilith and Thurston shuffled back.

"Get back here," Harmony ordered the girls in a harsh whisper. The two girls hurried back to the table and Sharon stuck a fork into the soufflé.

Thurston stared at Harmony, and she thought his foolish grin emphasized the vapid look in his eyes. But there was something else there too.

"Funny you should arrive just as we were discussing the need to hire some help." Harmony saw Lilith take a quick visual inventory of the room. "I see potential here. Call it potential energy, if you will." She laughed at the pun she'd made and jabbed Thurston with her elbow. He laughed with her, though it was clear to Harmony he had no idea why he was laughing.

"Help? What kind of help do you need?" Harmony sensed the pending offer was too hasty. After all, Lilith had practically refused them entry at the door. But once she realized the woman was truly working alone—her husband was in a world of his own, and for who knows how long—she understood why Lilith might seize the chance to solicit assistance.

She pitied the woman for a moment before remembering what she had done to her children.

"Before we talk specifics, tell me something about the world on land. Seems we've lost track of time since moving our work to a more hospitable environment, isn't that right, Thurstie?" She elbowed him again.

"Yes, topside, time, um—"

"Topside? Oh, I do quite like that expression. Do excuse my husband as he has grown tired of late. Now, topside?"

Harmony felt the girls' hesitation to speak and gave Sharon a subtle nod. Having lived her life in Kumugwe's realm, she was no expert on things topside. She was also curious to hear what her sister would say.

"Well, right after you both let us in, I wondered how long you've been down here. Were you up top when the water turned bad and started to expand?"

"Yes, yes, we know about that." Harmony didn't believe Lilith. "Tell us about others like you, and the land. Who survived that . . . horrible event?"

"Oh, but it wasn't horrible at all!"

When Sharon spoke those words, Harmony could see Lilith stifle a smile and remembered Zoya's warning about the other girls being a threat.

"Not horrible? Tell me more, girl, ah, what did you say your name was?"

Harmony held her breath and shook her head slightly, but she could feel the momentum building in her sister and could feel the girl's desire to be just like her mother.

"It's Sharon, mother and father. Don't you recognize me? It's your daughter Sharon."

Lilith fell back against her husband, who looked more confused than ever.

"Tell me, mother, whose brilliant idea was it to hide your lab in an octopus!"

Harmony stifled a gasp, and then quickly drained all color from her hair and body.

~ 30 ~

[The Village / Orville]

ORVILLE WATCHED TERESA SMILE as she walked with Nick toward the group, her doves shadowing her from above. Having regained her vision, hearing, and speech after the enormous spear of water had crashed down upon the Overleader, the young woman's confidence seemed to radiate like the essence of gardenias on a soft summer breeze.

Orville remembered gardenias.

He held out an arm and the birds lit upon it. "Hello, my friends. How I wish I had my wings now."

"Do you really want to be a frog again?" Chimney smiled. "You were the coolest frog on the planet."

"I was likely the only frog on the planet, Chim. Certainly the only flying frog." Orville's bond with Chimney was strong. He thought about all they had endured together, and still blamed himself for the time they almost died in the fissures. "But no, I am happy to be back in the body I was born into."

"Nick told me my beautiful birds could help to find Celeste," said Teresa. "She is a good person and has sacrificed much for us already. Please tell me any news you might have about her. Something about a dragonfly and flames? And who are our new friends?" Teresa smiled at Merts.

"They're even more bizarro than me and this clanker. Come on, kiddo, let's us grab some grub. Feeling mighty peckish again." Lou cocked his head toward the boy, and the giant horse nudged him gently.

"Go ahead, Chim. We'll join you soon," said Orville, and the peacock-horse and boy sauntered away. "Teresa, this is Merts. They are here to help us in this newly strange world."

"I don't think I'll ever get used to seeing that incredible tail," said Nick, and Orville laughed when Lou fanned his feathers, shaking them in a way that reflected their brilliant iridescence. "Show-off!" Nick called after the retreating creature.

When they all stopped laughing, Orville told Teresa about the visions both Nick and Merts had seen, and the birds flew back to perch on the girl's shoulders.

"I will talk to them," she said. "I know they will do what they can to find her."

Teresa walked a short way down the road, paused, and her doves flew from her toward the water. When she turned back toward the group, Orville saw her point to a place in the forest behind them, an expression of fear clearly visible on her face.

He turned to see figures crouching in the trees, and as soon as he spotted the strangers, they charged, whooping and barking in unearthly tones and wielding sticks and sundry metal objects.

"Ranger! Thunder!" Orville shouted, and the two appeared quickly. Without hesitation, they charged headlong toward the attackers, frightening several of them back into the trees.

Orville heard the WOOSH—WOOSH—WOOSH of Merts' arrows and knew the THWACK of each direct hit was lethal. Chaos reigned and his attention was divided. He saw several of Merts' arrows fly back to the archers, seemingly on their own.

"There are too many!" Orville shouted over the ruckus. He saw at least twenty and didn't know how many more might be hiding. There were humans and animals and creatures that made no sense at all to him. Several of the humans had copper-colored skin.

"Get inside!" he yelled to Teresa, searching frantically for anything he might use as a weapon and finding only a small stick and several rocks.

Just then, Layla galloped from around the houses toward the attackers, frightening more back into the trees and stomping on several of those less quick to run. "Go back to where youz came from, youz turd-munchin' ne'er-do-wells!" Lou's brash voice traveled across the field.

"Nick! Nick! Are you all right?" Orville almost forgot about Nick, who stood behind him with eyes tightly closed and fists clenched.

"I can't do it! I'm trying, Orville, but I can't make it stop!"

"That's okay, Nick! Run and get help from the other houses." Orville needn't have directed that, for many of the older residents were already on their way with weapons and heavy tools.

"What magic is this? / We never miss our target / Whose feathers are these?"

Orville had no time for Merts' questions. Their arrows continued to fly, though not every one hit an attacker.

"Some spared by arrows / That they may warn enemies / We are protected." Merts nodded their heads in unison as if satisfied with their own explanation.

With the arrival of more defenders from the village, Orville watched as the remaining attackers either fled or dropped to their knees with their hands in the air as a signal of surrender. It appeared that none of the bizarre creatures lived, though one emaciated dog lay whimpering behind those fallen, her left front leg broken during the attackers' hasty retreat.

While Ranger circled the fallen dog, Orville spoke to him and approached the strangers slowly.

"Ranger, perhaps Ryder can help."

Ranger ran toward the house and soon, Ryder followed him to the fallen dog. He knelt by her side while Ranger paced in a circle around them. Orville glanced their way and took another moment to survey the carnage on the battlefield.

"You three," Orville pointed to the three remaining humans, "stand and follow Thunder back to town. And wait."

He didn't tell the attackers who Thunder was because he didn't find it necessary. When the giant swirling-color-spotted jaguar turned toward town, he knew they'd figured it out.

He saw Ryder reach out a tentative hand toward the injured dog and pull it back when she snarled at him. Ranger stopped his pacing.

"Be still, you. The boy is here to help." Ranger's voice sounded harsh, and the emaciated dog collapsed back into a whimper.

"I won't hurt you," Ryder whispered, slowly extending his hand again until he laid it on her hind leg. He petted her gently while staring at the broken leg, and Orville watched her relax under his touch.

Ryder turned to Ranger then. "I . . . I can't see it. There was a flash, it's a clean break, but it's gone now. It's been on and off all day. I'm sorry!" Tears dripped from his wet lashes as he continued to pet the dog.

Orville put his hand on Ryder's shoulder and spoke to Ranger. "Bring her something to eat. She will need strength to heal." He then spoke to Ryder. "The fluxes have been strong today. Stay with her and perhaps in a moment you will regain your powers. In the meantime, I will bring a litter and we will carry her to a safe place. You are a fine young man. Do not despair."

As Orville turned back to town, Mason walked past him as if he were invisible, a shovel in his hand.

"Bury the dead, bury the dead, sticks and stones have broken bones and names, names, names can hurt you too. Bury the dead, bury the dead, can't have little ones playing in the pig-pile. This little piggy went to market, this little piggy never made it home." Mason wandered past Orville and the dead bodies to a spot at the far end of the field and began to dig.

Nick, Mac, and several others looked around them in disbelief, and Orville addressed them quietly. "Mason is right. This is not a sight for the little ones. Will you help him?" When they nodded without hesitation, he continued. "There may be more to come, so remain alert, and keep your weapons with you."

"But why?" Mac spoke for the group. "Why would anyone attack us? What have we done?"

"Perhaps it is not what we have done, but what we have," said Orville. "These houses, though battered, provide shelter. In my travels before finding this place, I saw nothing but water and devastation. This neighborhood, this unlikely neighborhood, may be one of very few remaining."

"But why attack?" Nick asked. "Why not come in peace, like you and . . . and Celeste?"

"Not everyone believes in the goodness of others, Nick. I will question the three who surrendered. Thank you for helping Mason with this unpleasant chore. And do stay alert near the forest. Holler at the first sign of danger."

Orville patted Nick on the shoulder as he passed him and walked toward the three held hostage by Thunder, who sauntered around them and kept them huddled in fear. He could see Riku standing on the porch and was happy when her eyes met his and her strained expression softened into a smile.

As he was about to greet her, however, the sky darkened. He looked up just in time to see what appeared to be an enormous dragonfly hovering over the entire village, its wings glittering much like his had when he'd been a flying frog, its needle-like body armored as his had been when his next transformation trapped him in a metallic wind-up toy.

And then, silence filled his senses.

~ 31 ~

[Celeste]

THUD-THUD-CLINK, *thud-thud-clink, thud-thud-clink,* the monotonous rhythm of a bizarre heartbeat drifted across her subconscious as Celeste dreamt and slept more soundly than she had in days or weeks or months.

Swirling water, first crystal blue then sickly pink, buffeted a dark-curled girl toward a looming creature, blurry in the undulating distance. Snake-like limbs, one, two, three, more, rose and fell softly, coming in and out of focus as if by magic. Thud-thud-clink, thud-thud-"help me," thud-thud-clink.

"Where are you? Who are you?" the girl asked, great bubbles floating away from her mouth as she spoke. Panic crossed her face, and then she did what her body demanded. She breathed in deeply. The salty pink water stung her nose and burned her lungs, but only for a moment.

"I am here. You see me. I am Zoya. You must help her. Tell her what she must do." The voice was soft and strained, as if the speaker were about to cry.

Were tears possible for those who dwelt in the sea? the girl wondered.

Something tingled on the back of the girl's head.

"Help her? Or help you?" she asked. "Tell me what to do! I'm just a girl!"

"No, Celeste, you are not just a girl," the creature whispered. "You are more. You must help the daughter of—"

BOOM! BOOM! BOOM! Celeste was jolted from her dream and bed by a pounding on Kumugwe's door that rocked the entire living structure. Wide-eyed and breathless, she watched the columns of sea lions slip and regroup with each deafening percussion.

"Let me in! You have betrayed me, brother!"

Celeste trembled at the sound of Odin's voice and searched for a place to hide. How was he able to breathe underwater? And how had he found her so quickly? Did he even know she was there? Could there be another reason for his aggressive arrival? Questions flooded her brain, and a vision of a wizard—she knew now it had been Odin—delivering a package to her pretend-home in the sandcastle made her wonder even more.

She decided not to hide.

Instead, she strode from her room and stood with her head held high in the center of the great room, noticing for the first time the thickness of moisture in the air, and within moments Kumugwe appeared, flustered and surprised to see her there.

"Over there, girl, behind the drapery! Hide!" He gestured toward an enormous sheet of waving seaweed against a glistening wall.

"No," she said. "Let him in. If this is about me, then we will put an end to it right now."

"I did not tell him you were here. There is still time, Celeste. Hide now and I will send him on his way. He is powerful, my brother, though less so in my realm. Now go!"

But Celeste planted herself more firmly on the squishy floor and put her hands on her hips. She nodded toward the door. "Open it."

"—in let me in let me in!" Odin's booming continued while Celeste stared down Kumugwe.

"You are a brave and foolish girl," said Kumugwe, and finally, he gestured toward the punished door and it opened.

Odin, in mid-knock, tumbled into the room and slid a distance across the floor on a gush of turbulent water that pushed him in. Kumugwe closed the door and looked down at his old brother.

Celeste noticed how he had aged in the flash of time since she had escaped from Oblivia. She considered helping him to his feet, but stopped herself. If she was to break free from not one god but two, she would have to remain strong. She would need to convince them, and herself, that she was their equal, if not better.

Odin rose slowly to his feet, and Celeste felt him judging her with his squinting eye.

"Buddy—"

"Buddies don't imprison their friends." Celeste cut him off, surprised by the volume of her response. She could feel his distress. *Don't budge*, she told herself.

"You! You did this!" Odin pointed his finger at Kumugwe and little jolts of electricity crackled in the air around it. "You stole my buddy, and you will pay!" He turned his eye toward one of the sea lion columns and out from it shot a lightning bolt that singed one of the creatures.

The sea lion barked, and when it fell from the column, the others hustled to keep their section of the roof from collapsing.

"How dare you come into my castle and strike an innocent!" Kumugwe howled. "Do not make me show you who is the stronger of us in my realm!" With a swipe of his hand, a riptide washed across the floor and swept Odin off his feet again.

Celeste was frightened by the dangerous escalation of emotions and yelled, "Stop it! Stop it!" But the gods ignored her.

"You and your copper skin, you think you are the mightiest god remaining with your slimy hordes of sea creatures, but you forget!" Odin taunted Kumugwe as he rose once more from the floor. "You forget that I, god of the skies, can still challenge you here in your realm! Can you say the same, *brother*?"

Celeste looked to the younger, handsomer god and saw his brow furrow, but then Kumugwe straightened to his full height, seeming to grow taller as he did, and spoke.

"You are envious, *brother*, and it does not become you! Yes, it is true, I am bound to my sea, and I would want for nothing more!" He looked concerned then, and continued. "The girl tells me you know some truth about my world. Tell me what it is, brother, and I will keep you on your feet."

"Admit I am the more powerful one, brother, and perhaps I will tell you!"

Celeste was tired of the childish one-upmanship. "Tell him, Odin! Tell him about the ooze."

Odin looked at her then with great fatigue in his one eye and swept her aside with a flick of his hand. She slid across the floor until she bumped into a column of sea lions, and the one at the base of the column caught her. Odin then pinched his fingers together and Celeste found her mouth bound closed. Her eyes grew wide, and once again, frightened, she questioned what she was doing.

"The imp knows nothing, but she was to be my connection with those like her. She was to be my bud—I mean, she was the one who would keep me, keep *us*, alive, Kumugwe." Sparks from Odin's eye flickered in the heavy atmosphere. "Have you not felt it? Have you not felt the disbelief, the disregard, the disrespect toward us from those on the planet?"

"No, brother, I have not, for I do not care to meddle with such underlings, nor do I crave their adulation. That will be your downfall, not mine. I have plenty to keep me well exercised down here in my musical realm, so you must now fly back to the place where minions no longer need you!" Kumugwe flexed his muscles, and the great room flexed perceptibly with him. "Perhaps it is time for you to realize you truly are no longer needed."

Celeste struggled to open her mouth, working hard to keep panic from welling within.

"Fool!" Odin's face grew red and when he flung his hands out to his sides, lightning bolts shot from them and ricocheted around the great room.

Celeste ducked to avoid getting hit, but Kumugwe seemed to gather strength from the electricity. He grabbed several of the bolts from their flight and pointed them back at Odin.

"Not in my realm, brother. Don't you remember what your little zappers do for me?"

Celeste watched as Kumugwe grew even larger, his muscles bulging as he advanced on the older god, and her jaw dropped. Odin's spell on her was broken and so, apparently, was he. She opened her mouth.

"Fine, then, I will go," said Odin as he backed away from the copper god. But Kumugwe grabbed the shoulder of Odin's cloak and lifted him off his feet.

"No. Too late. You will stay here as my . . . guest, until we finish this discussion. Until we are both perfectly clear on where we go from here. Until we discover what this girl knows, and until you concede to me." Kumugwe dragged the defeated god down a hallway and Celeste heard what sounded like an enormous metal door slamming closed.

Realizing she was way out of her league and frightened by the battle between the two gods, a battle she believed would only grow more fierce once Odin regained his strength, she needed to escape—and fast.

~ 32 ~

[Harmony]

ON THE HEELS of Sharon's confession, Harmony felt a jolt to the chamber that nearly knocked them all off their feet.

"What was that?" Blanche's fear was palpable, and Harmony found some comfort in the idea that the brash girl could be shaken. She may have been a leader in her little village topside, Harmony mused, but she was no match for the powers of the other personalities within the submarine.

When she noted alarm in Lilith's face, Harmony knew the jolt was more than a normal ocean current buffeting the octopus lair.

"It's just this cranky old beast, right dear?" Despite her cheerful tone, Lilith appeared flustered.

"Cranky beast, indeed! She wants us to do a little jig," said Thurston, who then giggled and lurched around in what Harmony presumed was some kind of dance. Lilith elbowed him and snarled something under breath, and the man became somber.

Harmony had a strong feeling the turmoil emanated from Kumugwe's chambers, and she suddenly missed her sea-god father horribly. Was he in danger? But she had more immediate concerns. Her sister had just exposed her true identity to parents who were clearly insane, and at any moment she could expose Harmony as their offspring as well.

She caught her sister's eye and was afraid of Sharon's next move. No one had yet commented on Harmony's color change, and she planned to remain as different from her sister as she could. She grew herself an inch or two, and now appeared to be closer to Blanche's age, clearly taller and older than Sharon. No one seemed to notice her subtle transformation either, and she credited both the shake-up and the dreary light within the chamber for their inattention.

"So, girl," Lilith sneered at Sharon, "I'm afraid your sudden plunge in the ocean, however you got here, has played a little tricky-trick with your brain." She looked at Thurston then. "Our daughter, she says! Ha! Can you imagine the two of us having a child?"

Sharon looked confused and hurt, and when she looked to Harmony for support, Harmony shook her head no and did her best to relay a warning. But Sharon persisted.

"But it's true! Remember? It's Sharon. You'd send me out to play in the morning and wouldn't let me back in till dark, remember? And I'd be really quiet when I came home so I wouldn't disturb you and father, and remember when I'd bring home those dead animals? Remember how you screamed that first time you found one? And then you left me. Why did you leave me? And Harmony—"

"Our friend is a storyteller!" Harmony broke in. She saw Blanche's jaw drop—the girl looked stunned—but Lilith remained stone-faced. "Let me apologize for her as she has recently endured a tragic loss and her judgment is impaired."

She moved to where Sharon stood and, wrapping a powerful arm around her sister's shoulder, asked, "May I talk with my two friends for a moment before we continue our conversation?"

Sharon struggled against her sister's hold but stopped when Harmony made it clear her strength was superior.

"Well, I suppose you might sit in our sleeping chamber for a few moments, but do be quick about it. I'll need an answer soon about whether you're here to help, or if it's time to send you back . . . home." Lilith's eyes conveyed her suspicion of the three intruders. Thurston grinned stupidly. "Second chamber on the left," she said.

Harmony pushed Sharon in front of her, grabbed Blanche by the arm and led the two into a tiny bedroom. She wasted no time.

"Stop it, Sharon. Can't you see they've both forgotten about you? They never wanted either of us, so get over it. Maybe we can help them, but not if you keep trying to tell them something they don't want to hear."

Harmony would have to be clever with her words. She was still learning about the subtleties of topsiders' speech and didn't want them to discover her true intentions. She hoped Zoya would continue to guide her efforts toward freeing the octopus from the intruders and stopping her pain.

"I agree," said Blanche. "Your father, ah, Thurston, seems not to know, well, anything right now. I'm sorry." She looked at Harmony then as if for the first time. "What happened to your hair? And your skin? You look like a ghost."

"It's just something I've learned to do—it's not important—but listen, you two, let's get back out there and see what we can do to help them with whatever they're working on. Thurston is ill, yes? But I think Lilith is still quite intelligent. Let's see what we can learn. No more talk now about parents. Or sisters. Got it?"

Sharon looked contrite and nodded her assent, but Harmony felt a rage growing within her shrinking sister.

She had a growing sense that her sister was a threat even as she witnessed Sharon's subtle yet apparent age regression. She would play along with the idea that she was there to help the demented scientists, and she wouldn't give Sharon any indication that she was anything other than on her side.

She needed to learn more about the submarine and its inhabitants' routines before she could do what Zoya asked of her. She knew nothing about machines and metal hearts.

As for Blanche, Harmony felt she was just a wayward young woman, though it was clear she harbored darkness within too.

"Let's go," Harmony told the girls, but Blanche held her back.

"What if . . . what if we wanted to leave? How could we? I mean, those people don't seem very stable, and we're way under water. Could you get us back to land?"

"You already had your chance to stay behind, Blanche, now stop being such a baby." Sharon sneered at her, and Harmony avoided the question.

"Come on, then. Let's tell them we're ready to help." As Harmony followed the girls back to the adults, she heard Zoya's voice in her head.

"A brave sea creature has risked this foul water to tell me a girl has fallen from the sky. She has been delivered to your father's home and is in danger. Another god comes for her." Zoya's voice was weak. "From what I have been told, I sense that she, like you, is more than what she appears to be."

Harmony froze in the hallway, vaguely aware that the other girls were already making small talk with Lilith.

"I connected with her in her dream," the octopus continued. "She will help you."

"Harmony, come on!" Sharon startled her back to the group. "They're going to show us what they're working on."

"Wonderful." She refocused on her sister and Blanche, who looked at her quizzically. "Sorry. I think I'm finally feeling fatigue from our travels here."

Harmony found it odd that the suspicious woman would share their work so quickly. She didn't trust her at all, and worked hard to camouflage her loathing.

"So before we go any further," Lilith narrowed her eyes, "tell me more about you. I must say I do find it coincidental that you should lose yourselves and discover our laboratory. There's a reason we work inside this great beast, you know, though I fear its ability to camouflage is waning. Tell me of this tragic loss, girl who jokes at being my daughter."

Sharon appeared flustered. "I, ah, I lost my parents recently, in an accident, and I was about to run away—I don't know where to—but these friends from the village found me by the water and brought me along on their, ah, their day trip to help me feel better. They told me we could maybe find a way to make a living from things we find down here."

"Yes," said Blanche. "Maybe you've seen the underwater tunnel slides that have appeared since the ooze stopped spreading. They're really fun, but they're hard to steer. I think that's how we got lost." She looked at Harmony, who nodded subtly. "And we did find some really cool things down here, and now that we've found you and you're already working on something—"

"Yes, yes, of course," Lilith replied, but something in her manner let Harmony know the woman was clueless. The woman returned her attention to Sharon.

"So you are an orphan, then. Poor dearie." Her words fell flat. "And your friends, who suddenly appear so ready and eager to stay here and to offer help, as you say, in our confined quarters? What are your stories? Do forgive my curiosity, but after having no visitors for . . . a time, your arrival raises questions."

Harmony took the lead. "Of course it would. You see, we're orphans too."

She was making up a story she hoped she could sell, and Blanche nodded while she spoke.

"I've been through the tunnels more than both my friends, and one day I saw the pink water around here. I guess I got curious. I tricked them by pretending to be lost. I really wanted to check out what was here with friends, so, here we are. We were really surprised when we saw your window from our tunnels."

She could see Lilith considering her story.

"I see. So, you're looking for a way to make a living, you say? Could you not do so on land?" Lilith seemed to be softening.

"Sure, we could," Sharon asserted herself back into the conversation, "but how much more awesome is it down here? We'd be lucky to work in a lab instead of back up on the muddy land. And we're smart too." She looked at Harmony warily. "And strong. And we're willing to do whatever you need, right?" She looked at the two girls and they nodded.

"So, Thurston," Lilith smiled awkwardly, "should we show these dearies what we're working on below?"

Thurston smiled and nodded.

"I sure hope they can handle it. Not sure what we'll do with them if they can't." She laughed horribly then, and a shiver ran down Harmony's spine.

"Steel yourself, child," Zoya's kind voice echoed in Harmony's mind. "It will bring back terrible memories."

"Follow me, recruits. Welcome to your new home." Lilith pulled open a small metal hatch and stepped through. Sharon pushed aside the others and was the first to follow.

~ 33 ~

[The Village / Orville]

ORVILLE COULDN'T MOVE. Trapped in time with eyes upturned to the dragonfly, he was vaguely aware that everyone around him was in the same situation. The dragonfly, looming over the entire village, seemed to be flapping its four expansive wings in slow motion. Stifling his fear, Orville studied how each wing moved independently from the others and was mesmerized by their ability to keep the colossal creature hovering overhead.

"Do not fear me, Orville, for I am Noor, and I bring tidings of great import." Noor's voice echoed in Orville's head. "A great wave threatens your village once more, the result of two quarreling deities in the sea."

Orville tried to speak. He remained frozen.

"You have questions I am not at liberty to answer," Noor continued. "The girl, Celeste, has been challenged with a mission. Your ultimate survival and that of those remaining will depend on her success. When I depart, your powers will be restored. For how long, I cannot say. Use them decisively, for your immediate survival rests in your own hands."

Orville struggled to say something, anything, to the creature, but his mouth remained closed. A tingling pain in his shoulder blades startled him as he watched Noor rise into the heavens, and as soon as she shot out of sight, he let out a scream of pain.

"Orville!" Riku's alarmed voice grabbed his attention and filled him with trepidation.

He scrunched his shoulders to his ears, aware of an unusual weight pulling him from behind, and when he raised his arms to regain his balance, he gasped at the sight of familiar, though larger, emerald wings spreading out to reveal their full glory. He longed to run to Riku and take her in his arms—he was still a man, at least for the moment—but Noor's grim message of an approaching wave left him no time.

"Gather the villagers together, quickly," he called to her before taking flight. "I will return shortly." He needed to know what was coming.

Awkwardly at first, never having flown as a winged man before, and then with a quick confidence spurred by fear, he flew toward the muddy beach beyond the hill closest to the village. It didn't take much time for him to spot a menacing swell far from shore and growing in magnitude as it churned relentlessly southward.

He could tell that by the time the swell came ashore and crested, its ultimate crash could easily destroy his village—and everyone in it.

"Your powers will be restored," Noor had told him. *"Use them decisively."* But how could his beautiful wings and his ability to fly stop a tsunami?

"Think, Orville, think!" he told himself on his return flight. "Think of Riku and the others."

The others. When Noor had said "powers," did she mean all with powers would have them restored? If so, there might be a chance.

He landed lightly just outside the gathered crowd of awe-struck villagers. The animals formed a half-circle behind them, the injured dog hanging limp, but alive, in Ryder's arms. Riku ran to him, threw her arms around him and tentatively stroked the emerald feathers he held tucked behind.

"What was that thing?" someone from the crowd shouted. "It looked like . . . like a dragonfly."

"What happened to us? Why couldn't we move?" said another.

"We're in immediate danger." Orville worked to keep his voice calm and realized that although the entire village had been immobilized, only he had heard Noor's message. "Ryder, can you see? Bridger, do you sense your power? Tell me quickly."

Ryder looked at the dog's paw and nodded yes. Bridger stirred up a small whirlwind and smiled.

"Listen, everyone, a wave the size of none other is on its way here right now. We don't have much time. Nick, do you believe you can stop time just beyond the hill? Could you stop it long enough for Bridger to build a wall high and long enough to stop it—to turn it back on itself?"

Nick and Bridger exchanged frightened glances and nodded unconvincingly.

"Come then, now, I will bring you there. The rest of you get to the highest rooftops, just in case—" Orville didn't finish.

What could he say? Just in case we fail? Just in case the sea seeps around a wall he wasn't confident could be built? Just in case the dragonfly would swoop back down to rescue them all?

Holding Nick and Bridger firmly on either side of him, Orville spread his glittering wings, lifted the two from the ground and flew them to the hillside. The wave had grown in magnitude significantly, its deep turquoise waters blending kaleidoscopically. The three gasped at how close it was to the shore below.

"Now, Nick!" Orville's voice cracked.

Nick closed his eyes and held both hands toward the threat. Sweat dripped from his forehead.

"I'll use mud! I can build with lotsa stuff!" Bridger announced, and in a sudden moment of empty silence, Nick opened his eyes and the three stared seaward at what looked like a massive still life painting. Ominous storm clouds dotted the horizon and created a sharp contrast to the wall of water that seemed to glow from deep within.

Orville remembered Noor's comment that the gods were quarreling and wondered briefly about the storm clouds, but shook his attention back to the imminent danger. He had no idea how long any of their powers would hold.

Bridger was already swirling up materials from the shore and his wall expanded rapidly in height and width along the hillside with great globs of mud splattering them all as it grew.

"Yo, dudes, we came to help." Thunder startled them all from their focus and an errant spray of mud coated the newcomers. Katie sat perched upon his back and wiped the mess from her eyes.

"Whoa! That was unnecessarily refreshing. Hey, the little one here said she has an idea." Thunder knelt and Katie slid from his back.

"Can I see it?" she asked Orville.

The wall was so tall and wide that it completely obliterated their view beyond.

"Beautiful work, Bridger," Orville whispered to the boy, "keep it up for as long as you can." He then turned his attention to Katie. "It's good that we cannot see it, child. We want to make sure it stays on the other side of this great wall."

"But we could see it if you took me up there." Katie pointed to the top of the wall, a top that continued to rise as Bridger kept summoning glop from the other side. "You know, the way you took Nick and Bridger."

In the insanity of the crisis, Orville had forgotten about his wings. He was also afraid of what he might see on the other side. He knelt in front of Katie and took her little hands in his.

"Tell me your idea, Katie," he said softly.

"Well, I was thinkin' it's just water, right? So I'll just freeze it. That'll stop it!"

Orville considered her words and his heart beat faster. It just might work, though he'd never known salt water to freeze. And if it didn't, well, there was still the wall.

Use the powers decisively, Noor had said.

"Let's go then. I've got you, child." Orville lifted Katie into the air above the growing wall and those below smiled when they heard her exclaim, "Oh! How pretty!"

"Can you do it, Katie? Can you freeze the big wave?" Orville compared the enormity of the threat to the tiny bundle he held in his arms and felt foolish asking the question. How could she possibly freeze an ocean?

"'Course I can, silly! Watch." The red birthmark on the girl's forehead glowed brightly and she swept her eyes across the width of the wall of water.

Orville couldn't believe his eyes.

It started slowly, but from left to right, the wall lost its turquoise glow and a web of white ice crystals spread across it. Within moments, the entire wall looked like a glacier.

"Should I keep going?" Bridger called from below. "I'm gettin' tired."

"No, Bridger, you can stop now," Orville called as he brought Katie back to the group. "Katie froze the wave."

"So, what now?" Nick brushed dried mud from Thunder's fur. Thunder stood and shook, and dust flew in all directions.

Orville hadn't considered his next decision.

"I think we should release time on the other side of this wall. Wouldn't we rather know now what will happen to the water once your power wears off? The wall is strong; thank you, Bridger."

The boy smiled and fell back onto Thunder's soft side.

"And the water is, quite incredibly, frozen. At least what we can see of it. Thank you, Katie."

"Yeah, I guess." Nick sounded worried. "But—"

Orville cut him off. "Up we go, then." He lifted Nick far above the top of the wall and Nick's eyes grew wide when he saw the ice beyond.

"But, shouldn't we send them back to town in case this doesn't work?"

"If this does not work, Nick, then there will be nothing—and no one—remaining. I fear we will not have our powers for long."

Nick gazed along the expanse of wall and ice once more and made his decision. "I'm tired too," he said, and when he squeezed his eyes closed, Orville felt the air shift, as if a vacuum far away was trying to pull his breath from him.

The ground rumbled and Orville saw fear in the eyes of those below.

"No," he whispered, his eyes drawn back to the forces beyond the wall.

The expanse of ice shook and started to crumble, large chunks of it crashing into water that seeped from behind it, and within moments, the entire glacier collapsed, the force of the ocean on the other side bursting through and sending huge chunks of ice up the front of the wall and into the air, each surge pulling away a layer of mud from the bottom of it again and again before surging up and falling back onto itself, crash after crash after crash while the frightened group held their breath . . .

And the wall held.

~ **34** ~

[Celeste]

"**YOU CANNOT KEEP ME** locked in here forever, you waterlogged warthog!" Celeste heard Odin pound once on his locked chamber door.

"Now, now, old man, there is no need for vulgarity. Mustn't insult your host. I know you will soon be hungry, and that you have no stomach for eyeballs. More for me, then." He popped a handful of round objects into his mouth.

Celeste had only glanced at an open vat by the main door filled with what looked like small, gooey globes of different colors, and bile rose from her stomach. She hoped he was joking.

She would have to pretend she didn't care about the older god. But he was tired and alone, other than for his ravens and wolves, and must have been desperate for the friendship of someone he could laugh with, share his knowledge with, dine and fly and make rain with.

Yes, Odin had attempted to trap her in his celestial kingdom, but she understood his motives.

Still, she remained firm in her conviction that buddies shouldn't imprison their friends. Evidently, rules for imprisoning brothers were different, at least in the realms of gods.

She cleared her throat and spit out the sourness as Kumugwe lumbered back from where he had just confined his brother.

"My brother grows weak in my kingdom. He was a fool to think he could barge in and take you away from me."

"No one gets to *take me*, do you understand?" Celeste was proud of herself for her brazen act of confidence.

Kumugwe raised an eyebrow. "Now, then, since he would not tell me and you clearly know the answer, what is this pink ooze you say threatens my world? Out with it, girl."

But she didn't know the answer. She knew only that the sickly shade of pink ooze had been deadly the first time it had spread across the land.

"All I can tell you is that when I threw your spear back into the water, the ooze stopped, the water turned from silvery-pink to turquoise, and it moved away from the shore. How could you never have noticed it? Or did you?"

"Pink, turquoise, green, black, gray, my waters have been many colors, my inhabitants many species. My sea world is in constant flux. What is to fear with change?"

Although Kumugwe's words indicated he had nothing to fear, Celeste thought the expression on his face contradicted his statement. *He's afraid of something down here,* she thought. *I wonder if it has anything to do with my mission.*

"Well, maybe you don't have anything to be afraid of, but after The Event—you know about that, right? The thing that shook the planet and swallowed everything?—the pink ooze was growing onto the land and killing things in its path."

"Oh, my. Yes, I am aware of a shaking greater than in ages past, but not of its effect topside. That would be my brother's realm."

So the gods are not omniscient, Celeste realized.

"You should release him and send him home. He is . . . needed," she said. She was suddenly worried about what would happen to the atmosphere and her people on land with Odin trapped and powerless.

"Not so fast, young one. You do not know my brother. I think there are many things you do not know."

And things you don't know either, she thought.

Kumugwe continued. "Whatever this pinkness is, to my knowledge, it has not harmed my creatures."

Celeste saw the concern on his face again.

"When you returned my spear, I saw you on a hillside, and a horrible old woman was about to attack you. I gathered my waters into a great tower then and dropped them upon her—you must remember that—and she cried. That is all."

Celeste's brain hurt. Could Kumugwe's spear, back in the hands of its rightful owner, have cured the ooze? Could his punishing tower of water have sucked up all of the silvery-pink sorrow before dropping it onto the Overleader? Perhaps in her pitiful wail, the Overleader had absorbed all of the horror she'd inflicted on others. Perhaps her suffering had purged the sickly spread that day.

With all of the factors at play that confusing moment, Celeste had to believe her act of returning the spear had been the key to curing the water.

Something else, then, was turning it again.

"But how would you know your creatures haven't been harmed? Do you know about everything and every living being in your world?" She was not yet ready to tell him of the dream she'd had about Zoya, an octopus in distress.

"I know all I need to know," he pouted, "and my creatures would tell me if something was amiss."

"Fine, then. If you don't care about this new poison I saw growing again for the sake of your world, would you agree that I'm justified in wanting to protect those in my world? Few survived, and I don't believe they'd make it through another disgusting ooze."

Celeste pouted too. "And even if you think your world is safe," she continued, "Noor sent me here with a task to perform." Her task was still nebulous, but she would figure it out.

"This task. What does it entail?" Kumugwe raised one bushy eyebrow. "Was there any mention of a foreign threat?"

"She will tell me the details when I'm ready," she said, and then Celeste made up a story. "Actually, she said something like, 'great consequences shall befall the sea should its master not do everything possible to assist my efforts and honor my requests.'"

I'll keep him on guard, she thought. She would use the story of Noor for as long as it worked on the gullible god. She wondered about his foreign threat comment.

Kumugwe looked appropriately thoughtful.

"And what might you now request?" He paced his words carefully.

Celeste closed her eyes and extended her hands out to her sides, as if trying to feel the atmosphere. She would pretend to channel instructions from the mysterious god of fire and light.

"Noor says you must feed your brother now," she spoke with eyes still closed, "after which you will release him." She opened her eyes and put her hand to her head dramatically. The thought of her friends suffering in an unstable atmosphere plagued her.

"But if I release him, he will find a way to take you back with him. If Noor tries to stop him, or if I do, you may be in danger as well. Tell her. Tell the god of fire and light that you will be safer, that you will be able to complete your task faster with him in captivity. And I will feed him well."

Her charade backfired, but now she knew that Kumugwe did have a heart for his sea and its creatures. He may have acted like a monster, and as for the eyeballs, well, she would just have to avoid looking more carefully into the vat, but he was willing to put aside his immediate wishes for the good of his domain.

And maybe Kumugwe was right. Maybe Odin should remain in confinement and kept from potentially interfering with what she had to learn and do. Maybe he wasn't necessary at all for ensuring the atmosphere was balanced for those on land.

Maybe he wasn't necessary at all.

"Let me see if I can sway her," Celeste replied, assuming her channeling stance once more. She held it for longer than before, until she sensed Kumugwe fidgeting around her. "Yes, all right. She sends praise to you for thinking of others before yourself."

Kumugwe smiled.

"And when the time is right, you will release your brother and end your foolish competition."

Kumugwe frowned.

"And now, Noor tells me I must eat well and rest undisturbed in anticipation of instructions she will deliver when she feels I am prepared."

"I will send a feast to your room, and to my brother, and will not disturb you. Here is a summoning shell should you need attention. Harmony gave it to me after that flying metal contraption took you away. Pretty little thing, isn't it?"

Kumugwe handed her a turritella, and at the sight of it, Celeste fainted.

She awoke to the unusual aromas of more food than she could possibly eat, and the shell—a reminder of her make-believe home and her make-believe parents in the sandcastle—resting next to her water bubble pillow.

Who and where was this Harmony who had lured her to a fake home? Did she have anything to do with the bizarre heartbeat that still echoed in Celeste's head? And where, oh where were her real parents?

~ 35 ~

[Harmony]

"WATCH YOUR STEPS, now, dearies." Harmony heard Lilith's voice echo from the other side of the metal hatch. She squinted against a powerful presence of sterile alcohol in the air. "It can be a bit slip-slidy down here."

"Slip-slidy," Thurston mumbled, and then giggled.

They wound their way down a spiral metal staircase until Harmony wondered if they'd ever reach the bottom. When they were finally crammed together at the base of the stairs in what looked like an anteroom outside another metal hatch, Lilith spoke again.

"One at a time and wait for a count of five, that's five full counts, after each one. Otherwise you'll be stepping on heads, and no one wants your feet in their hair. I'll go first. Thurston, you close the hatch after the last girl, will you please? And have a nice warm beverage for us when we return." She pushed several buttons above the doorway.

"Nice warm beverage. In you go, now." Thurston opened the hatch and held Lilith's hand as she stepped across the threshold and sat on what appeared to be some sort of slide. "Off you go, now," he said, and gave her a little push. She disappeared and he began to count.

"One thousand one, next in, one thousand two, who's next?"

"I'll go next," Sharon pushed Blanche aside and stepped onto the platform with no help from Thurston. She waited for him to finish his count.

"One thousand three, one thousand four one thousand five, and off you go!" He reached across to give her a push, but she had already started on her way. "Flighty, that one." He spoke more to himself than to anyone else. "Too bad. Reminds me of someone."

"I'll go next," Blanche offered, prepping herself on the seat while Thurston finished his countdown. She sat until he pushed her.

"I guess that just leaves you, ghost." He indicated the way for Harmony, and she searched the man's eyes—for what, she didn't know—before taking her seat. His lips smiled, but not his eyes, and she got a shiver.

"Won't you come along too?" she asked the man. For some reason she felt sad for him, and without realizing it was happening, a blue-green teardrop slipped from one eye.

"No, little baby, little cry-baby, little ghost baby who came back. Your mother's a funny old broad and wouldn't like it." With his last statement, he pushed her down the slide and slammed the hatch behind her.

What did he just say? Harmony wondered, but before she could process the man's words, she was swept feet-first through a dark, narrow tube that felt slick to the touch and . . . alive.

"It is I," Zoya's voice spoke to her. "You will see."

With a gentle nudge, Harmony was deposited into a vast cavern at the end of the tube, similar to the one in which the three girls had made their hasty plan to walk in on the scientists unannounced. The others were waiting for her. She turned back around just in time to see the tip of an enormous tentacle sliding beneath the murky water at the edge of the chamber.

It was one of Zoya's arms.

Not only had Harmony's birth parents invaded the creature's body with their cramped submarine, they'd also used this arm, and perhaps more, as passageways to other places.

It was barbaric.

Harmony's heart ached for the abused creature.

"One more door and quiet as you enter." Lilith's harsh voice was magnified by the slimy cavern walls. "They should all be asleep right now."

The girls exchanged uncertain glances before following Lilith through yet another door. On the other side was a cavern so expansive they could see neither its height nor its depth. What they could see in the yellow-green ambient light were row upon row of makeshift tables on which squirming, unidentifiable shapes were chained. The place smelled of dank decay.

Harmony's skin crawled when she scanned the ghastly chamber.

"What *are* these?" Sharon whispered. She was glued to Lilith's side.

"These, my dear, are what we're working on. These will repopulate the planet. These will be our new friends, and there will be nothing to stop me, to stop . . . us, from doing as we please when we return."

There was no longer any question in Harmony's mind that the woman was insane.

"When you and fath—I mean, when we all return? Sorry, Lilith, but you two remind me of the parents I just lost." Sharon gave Harmony a sinister look and stroked the bony woman's arm.

"Yes, why yes, of course, when we all return," said Lilith, subtly stepping away from Sharon.

"But they're so . . . so . . . jiggly," said Blanche. "How will they be able to do anything?"

"Well, dearie, this is where we could use a few more nimble hands. Follow me." Lilith walked to the end of one row where a table of shiny metal pieces lay in neat order from small to large. "These will provide the skeletons for our soldiers. We've been collecting and polishing pieces for years, and we do believe it's time now to start building."

"Let me see if I understand." Harmony felt it was time to show some interest in the despicable project. "You would have us insert these metal pieces into those . . . sleeping things, like making stick figures?"

"Yes, why yes, you understand." Lilith's lips smiled.

"But what about their brains?" Harmony wasn't sure she wanted the answer. "How will you make them do the things you will need them to do when they're back up topside?"

"Another good question. You girlies *are* clever, aren't you? You see, we have planted devices inside every creature we've created, and programmed them to respond to a number of basic commands. Still rudimentary, of course, but allow me to demonstrate."

Lilith turned her back to the girls and faced the rows of tables. "This first command is to raise a right arm, and when their metal arms are inserted, this will look more impressive. Watch."

Lilith turned a dial and pressed a button on a device she took from a pocket, and while Sharon and Blanche giggled at the gelatinous masses' attempt at complying with the motion, Harmony stifled a gasp when a jolt of pain zapped in her head and her right arm began to lift.

She checked to see if any of them had witnessed her reaction, but saw no indication they had.

"It's unbelievable," Sharon gushed. "We're ready to start whenever you give the order, Lilith.

"That's enough for today, girlies. We will return for a warm beverage and sleep and begin in the new day."

"How do we get back?" asked Blanche.

"This button summons the beast." Lilith pushed another button. Harmony flinched, and soon the tentacle rose from the water and opened.

"How, though. I really want to know how you were able to navigate your laboratory inside this octopus. It's such a brilliant idea."

Sharon's excitement was wearing on Harmony's patience.

"It was easy," said Lilith. "It had just spawned a huge batch of vile babies when we spotted it. It would have died soon anyway, weakened as it was, so we just made ourselves at home."

Harmony's heart pounded in her chest and she struggled to breathe.

"Of course, we had to keep its three hearts going so it could stay camouflaged, but that was easy. Thurston was good for something."

"How did he do it?" asked Sharon.

"Easy. He made the main one a mechanical heart. It'll keep the others going for as long as we need."

Thud-thud-clink, thud-thud-clink, thud-thud-clink.

Harmony vomited onto the cavern floor.

~ 36 ~

[The Village / Orville]

"IT APPEARS WE DID IT, my friends, we turned the wave." Orville took a deep breath and controlled the shaking in his hands. "You did it. The village is in your debt."

"I'm hungry. Tired too." Bridger climbed to the top of Thunder's back and promptly fell asleep. Katie climbed up after him, snuggled up next to him and did the same.

"I think the wall should stay," said Nick. "Who knows what caused the wave or how many more might come. I sure wish we could feel like things are gonna get better soon, but without Celeste . . ."

"Yes. What more does this planet want from us? But let's return to the others now, shall we?" Orville examined the great wall the tiny child had built and shook his head. "Hard to believe, is it not?"

"Little dudes don't even know what they're doin'. It's mind-blowing," said Thunder. "I'll get 'em home safe now." He sauntered toward town, careful not to dislodge his precious cargo.

"Ready?" Orville asked Nick, his arm extended to hold him.

"Nah. Think I'll stay here just a little while longer if you don't mind. Would you drop me on top of the wall before you go?"

Orville glanced to the top of the wall. "How will you get down?" He didn't want to patronize the young man, but he had legitimate concerns about his safety. The wall was well over thirty feet high and extended as far down the shoreline as he could see.

"See down there? Where it slopes? It's like a slide. I'll be fine, really. I just need some time to think, okay?"

"Of course, Nick. Come back when you're ready." Orville sensed Nick would probably spend more time searching the sky and beyond for signs of Celeste. He couldn't blame him. And he just might find her. Stranger things had certainly happened since The Event years ago.

Orville flew him to the top of the wall and the two gazed out at the water, in retreat once more, this time with enormous chunks of ice bobbing in it. At least it was still blue.

"I was really afraid Jack would die with me in that underwater box," Nick whispered. "Crazy kid. Crazy *strong* kid. And then I saw that horrible spear sinking in the water and saw the water change, and I knew it must've been her. How'd she do it, Orville?"

"How indeed, Nick. I suppose it was that same moment when I was transformed back into my true body. The memory is jumbled in my brain, but there was a one-eyed wizard who gave me Celeste's scarf while I sped through a tunnel beneath the surface of the water. When the metal wings tore from my back, I swam to shore, probably just as you were carrying Jack to safety."

"Can I?" Nick reached a hand out to touch Orville's wings, and he nodded yes. "What's it feel like?"

"I will not lie. It hurt when they, how to say this, sprouted? But now I feel as if they have been a part of me forever." He stretched his wings behind him and they glistened in the setting rays of sun that escaped from behind passing storm clouds.

"Flying, though. What's that feel like? With you and Celeste, I've felt safe, but I've just been hanging on."

"Exhilarating, I must say. And joyful. Free and light. It is like nothing you will experience on feet."

Nick smiled.

"One more thing, Nick. The dragonfly has a name. It is Noor. She told me that Celeste is alive."

Nick grabbed him by the shoulders. "Where? Where is she? Is she all right? Is she coming back?"

"So many questions. Celeste must do something important. What? I do not know. Her success, however, will be ours as well. You know as well as I the power of her convictions. She will succeed. Of that, and little else, I am certain. I will leave you now, and thank you, Nick. What you and the others did here is, well, I do not have the words to say."

Orville took Nick's hand and shook it before flying back to the village. He understood the boy's longing to be with the one he loved, and smiled in anticipation of seeing Riku.

He landed in the village just as Riku and Mac were lifting the children from Thunder's back. Riku smiled at him, and for the first time in years he believed everything would work out just fine.

"Her leg's fixed," Ryder looked up at him from where he sat softly stroking the new dog's fur, "but she's awful skinny."

Ranger was sitting beside the boy with healing powers and asked about Nick.

"He'll be back soon. And now I must visit with our three guests." He looked to Thunder. "Where might I find them?"

"They're just fine, boss. Out back in the cage. Even gave 'em some snoodles before lockin' the gate."

Orville chuckled when he remembered Celeste's reaction to Chimney's bag of snoodles when they'd first met. The long black objects had looked like snakes, though they were actually flavorful roots.

He walked around to the back of the house to a place he was all too familiar with. It was the place the villagers had kept him locked when he and Celeste had first arrived, both outcasts, he in the body of an enormous flying frog, she in the body of a confused young teen just looking for a new home.

It was the place they'd dragged him to once more after the shapeshifter—the Overleader in her vulture body—had nearly consumed his final breath. The memory horrified him. Possessed or not, he had nearly caused Celeste's death with his last wish to be pushed out into the water, the horrible water that had already killed so many.

And the Overleader was really just a girl. None of it made sense to him.

He shook off a chill, his beautiful wings fluttering out to his sides, as he approached the cage where two young men and one young woman huddled on the ground. They appeared frightened.

"Where did you come from, how did you find our village, and why did you attack us?" Orville assumed an authoritative stance and waited.

"Where'd *you* come from?" the woman spoke first. "Where'd any of us come from?"

Orville had to admit, her question was a good answer.

"The caves, where else?" said one of the men. "We were starving, we were lost, we were sucked from the underworld by these crazy black crabs and spit out on a beach with other people and things not too far from here."

"Let us out, wouldja, fella?" the other spoke. "We didn't do nothin' wrong."

"Nothing wrong? You attacked our village." Orville's voice was calm but firm.

"Yeah, well, looks like you got the better of us, didn'tcha."

"Yes, I suppose we did. Tell me how many more are in the trees? How many more will we need to defend against tonight, or tomorrow?"

"You killed most of us," said the girl. "Not many others, and they wouldn't be crazy enough to come back here knowing the likes of your villagers."

Orville had a decision to make. Would he release them or keep them confined, caged unjustly as he had been when the villagers saw him as a threat?

"I will send blankets and food. If you are telling the truth, we will reassess our arrangements tomorrow." He had to consider the others. Like it or not, he had to make decisions that would affect everyone and everything in the village.

As he rounded the corner of the house, he heard Mason returning from his ugly task.

"Little Bo-Peep has lost her sheep and doesn't know where to find them. Leave them alone and they'll come home, wagging their tails behind them. Little Bo-Peep fell fast asleep and dreamt she heard them bleating, bleeding, one-two-three, one-two-three, one-two-three beating, why won't they ever stop beating, bleeding, bleating? Oh, hey boss. Dirty deed's done." The man continued his nursery rhyme until Orville could no longer hear him.

Lost sheep, he thought. *That's what we all are now.*

Orville made good on his promise to deliver blankets and food to the three newcomers, and when all was quiet in the neighborhood, he found Riku in the house. Wrapping his arms and wings around her, he held her in an embrace he never wanted to break.

They held one another silently for a long time. Finally, Orville spoke.

"There will be more challenges. The great dragonfly, Noor, told me Celeste must do something for the sake of us all. You will stay by my side?"

"Why must you ask such a question?" Riku bowed her head, and then rested it on his chest.

"We will need guards tonight. Let me see who I can find. And then, we may sleep." Orville kissed the top of her head and went outside.

Mac and Teresa were sitting on a porch, hand in hand, when Orville approached them. He noticed Teresa's doves had returned. He looked at her with anticipation, but Teresa shook her head slowly.

"The newcomers are secure. Mac, will you find others you trust and establish a guard throughout the night?"

Mac stood without hesitation. "Of course. What you did today—"

"I did little, but thank you. Please have your guards wake me if they fear another attack."

"You can count on me, Orville."

~ ~ ~ ~ ~

Late that night, fast asleep entwined with the woman he loved, Orville dreamt.

Thud-thud-clink, thud-thud-clink, thud-thud-clink.

"She will need help. She does not yet believe." A pained voice spoke to him, and when he opened his eyes to find her, he saw vague shapes drifting in and out of focus.

"Who will need help? How do I help? What help, help, help?" When he questioned the shifting shapes, bubbles rose from his mouth.

"Celeste," the voice answered. "Find her as you have before."

Thud-thud-clink, thud-thud-clink, thud-thud-clink.

~ **37** ~

[Celeste]

CELESTE ATE HASTILY, though the food was quite good. *But was it real?* she wondered. Memories of what turned out to be illusions of bacon and lobster and peanut butter sandwiches and parents and her puppy—poor little Ranger—reminded her to question everything she was experiencing.

Surprised she was still alone—it seemed like people and creatures and gods were always barging in on her—she considered her next move.

Someone named Zoya had come to her in a dream with a request for help. She'd also said something about her being "more than just a girl," but what did that mean? And what was there to trust in a dream anyway? Sure, she had heard Orville's voice in a dream back at the children's home and his advice had been real and true, but she'd also had plenty of crazy nightmares that never amounted to anything. So many nightmares.

She wondered what might have happened had she never run away that lonely night so very long ago. Or had it been long at all?

And then there was Noor, who had unceremoniously plopped her into the water to help someone, another "her," and to learn more.

"Is it possible I'm still in a dream?" She said the words aloud and pinched herself, but trusted neither her voice nor the pain.

With the tip of the turritella she cut her leg. "Ouch!" She didn't remember ever bleeding in a dream before, and finally decided her surroundings, food and all, were real.

"Great. Now what?" she whispered as she tore a small piece of seaweed from the wall to stop the bleed. Her blood seeped from the wound and oddly merged with the atmosphere in the room. She was surprised by its bluish hue.

"What now, did I hear you say?" Kumugwe peeked through a crack in her door with one eye. "I was beginning to worry your faint might be permanent. I have not been waiting here all this time, of course."

"Of course you haven't," Celeste responded flatly. "Come in. The food was excellent. Thank you."

Keeping the door open after entering her chamber, Kumugwe fidgeted. "You are welcome, Celeste. You are welcome to stay here for as long as you need. And yet I would ask one thing of you."

"What's that?" Celeste's response showed her growing fatigue at everyone's mounting expectations of her.

"I would ask you to find my little Harmony. I sent her topside to find you, and yet here you are, delivered by another, and my Harmony is still away. She is just a child. Never should I have sent her on such a quest."

"And why do you think I'd be able to find her? You're a god in control of most of the planet, aren't you?

"You returned my spear, and it is clear that you have special powers." Kumugwe stroked his beard absentmindedly. "I am perplexed, however. In every fiber I feel she is no longer topside, but if she were back in my realm, why has she not returned home? As for being in control of most of the planet, well—"

"Even if I could find her," Celeste interrupted, "why would I want to? Why would I want to help the person who almost killed me and my friend? Why did she trap me like that, and why'd you let her? And while I'm asking questions, where is my family? Did you—or she—have anything to do with their disappearance? That was really awful, you know, tricking me like that."

Kumugwe looked contrite; he avoided her piercing green eyes.

Good, she thought.

"My Harmony is a special being," he whispered. "Such a beautiful voice for such a tiny, misshapen thing. She just wanted a playmate. I am sorry I did not check on her after she brought you to her playhouse. She seemed so happy, and I, with the tides and the creatures and the expanse of my domain, I did not think it necessary to supervise. You must understand. But yes, I am sorry."

"And my parents? My puppy? My friends? Where are they? You want me to find one girl, but where are all the others?" She was not about to relent.

"I know of many places where topsiders fell below when the planet shook. In those many places, some survived. They were rescued, much like you were rescued and brought here, by my sea creatures. Unlike your drop into the sea, theirs was violent and tragic. Many did not survive. Those who could be saved were kept in a state of suspension in caverns throughout my seas."

"And now? Where are they now, the ones who survived?"

"This I do not know. When my waters turned and receded from the shores after you returned my spear and I punished the old woman, my followers brought as many as they could to where they would find ground, and woke them. I believe there are many now returned to topside."

Celeste's heart skipped a beat, or added one. Perhaps her parents had survived. Perhaps her puppy and her friends would be there when she returned home.

Home. Where was that now?

Her heartbeat. It felt different. Should she tell Kumugwe now about her dream and the strange heartbeat of the creature who called to her for help? Perhaps it was time.

"Does the name Zoya mean anything to you? One of your followers, maybe?"

"No. If I were to name all the creatures in my seas, there would be time for little else."

"Do any of them have hearts that echo with three distinct beats?"

"You ask curious questions, Celeste, but yes, certainly. Many in my domain have more than one heart. My wonderful octopuses, for example, have three hearts. Why do you ask? Are you feeling all right? Perhaps what I have told you has given you the vapors."

"The vapors? No, no, never mind." Celeste had no idea what he was talking about, but was excited to learn something that seemed to fit her dream like the final piece of a mysterious puzzle.

Zoya was an octopus.

"So if I agree to search for Harmony, you will get me back to topside as soon as I am ready, right?" She wouldn't tell him how long it would be before she was ready to go. She was dropped into the sea with a purpose, and the purpose had something to so with an octopus named Zoya.

She longed to return to the village as fast as she could, to find Nick and possibly, just possibly, her family. But she knew there were greater powers influencing her destiny. She would be patient.

"Certainly. When my Harmony returns to me, and after you find a way to stop the unnatural changes cracking and shaking the planet—"

"Wait a minute! No, no, NO! My task has nothing to do with the planet shaking, and yes, I'll do my best to find your little girl, but after that, I'm going home." She paused then, wondering about her task and its possible implications in stabilizing the planet. The thought frightened her.

"Can't you and Odin figure out what's happening?" She wanted him to tell her they would, they'd find what was causing the fluxes and repair the cracks, but she had already questioned the need for any gods at all.

As if summoned by Celeste saying his name, Odin resumed his banging on the door at the end of the hall.

"Let me out, brother. You'll have to sooner or later, and my sentinels need me. Have a heart, you crusty old sea urchin!"

"In time, Odin, in time," Kumugwe answered, and then turned his attentions back to Celeste.

"All right then, young one. Your mission first, then my child—she is somewhere in my waters, I am certain of that—and then I will see to it you have safe passage back to your dry home. Is there something I might do to help? Anything at all, just ask."

Celeste wasn't sure what to ask for. And then it hit her.

"When I was in Odin's realm—"

"Oh, do let me out of here!" Odin interrupted. "I cannot abide your talking about me as if I do not exist!"

Celeste rolled her eyes just as Kumugwe did the same, and she thought she might laugh.

"As I was saying, when I was in Odin's realm, I could fly without effort in air too thin to breathe. You must empower me with the ability to swim and survive in water too thick for me to breathe." She knew it was a mighty request, but he did say "anything at all."

"Oh, but do you not know?" he looked surprised. "You already have that ability. Do you not see? You surely would have perished already if you had not adapted to my realm.

Hahaha! You were breathing the entire time my lions transported you to my door, and even now, do you not see how you speak and breathe and eat in my waters?"

It was true. Though the great halls and rooms of Kumugwe's castle appeared to be filled with moisture-thick thick, she could see it now. They were filled with water. That explained the odd seeping of her blood into what she had thought was air. Only the walls kept the sensation of movement at bay.

For a moment, panic set in and she coughed, but when she breathed in again, her copper skin tingled, as did the water drop marking—or was it a tear drop?—on the back of her head. She could feel an unseen pressure holding things in their right places, which explained why they didn't float off.

She regained her composure, not wanting to appear silly, and made her second request.

"I would ask then that you tell all of your sea creatures to assist if I should need help, and to do me no harm. That is all. I will leave shortly."

"It will be done, Celeste. In no time at all they shall know of a dark-haired sea girl who will find our Harmony."

"*After* I complete Noor's directive," she reminded him. She wished she were as certain as the powerful sea god was of her abilities.

~ 38 ~

[Harmony]

"HE KNOWS WHO I AM," Harmony told Zoya wordlessly as she slid back through the creature's long tentacle. "The way he spoke to me before sending me to that horrible cave was strange, but I'm sure of it. He knows I'm the child they abandoned to the sea. "

"Do not worry, child. He fears the woman. I feel your secret is safe with him. It is the others you must guard against, for they now cleave to the woman whose cruelty knows no bounds. Please, when the time is right—and how I wish it were now—find a way to dislodge them all and stop this abominable heart. Let me die in peace."

Zoya's words were heartbreaking. Harmony could feel her pain.

"I will. And this girl you say who was dropped from the sky? How will she help me?"

Before Zoya could answer, the hatch into the lower chamber of the submarine opened and Thurston was there to help her to her feet.

"Pretty little girl," he whispered, stroking her long hair like a child would stroke a soft blanket. "Guess we were wrong about you."

Harmony shushed him, but relaxed when she saw the others were already to the top of the stairs and making their noisy way into the upper chamber.

"Thurston, stop saying these foolish things." Harmony would deny being his child just as Lilith had denied Sharon. "You don't know me, and I certainly don't know you. If you say anything more about this, Lilith will punish us both. Do you understand?"

A flash of fear lit Thurston's milky gray eyes for a moment and then he smiled. "Secrets. So many secrets. You can be my secret buddy."

Harmony had no experience with someone like Thurston. What was the appropriate way to respond to the man who had spawned her, had aided in performing horrible experiments on her, had abandoned her ruthlessly, and had lost touch with reality? He couldn't be trusted.

"No. I'm not your secret buddy. I'm not your secret anything. Now listen to me. We're going back up to join the others, and not a word of what you've said to me. I'm just someone looking for a job, and it looks like there's much to do in the cave at the other end."

Thurston's face grew somber. "It's icky over there. But you're here now and you can do the work."

"Yes. Sharon and Blanche and I can do the work. Now let's get that warm beverage. It's cold down here." Harmony's body was used to adapting to the ambient temperature, but visions of the disgusting creatures in the cave and her sudden realization that she was somehow linked to the horrible project made the copper in her blood run cold.

And she was feeling horribly dehydrated. She grabbed Thurston's exposed forearm before heading up the long ladder, startling him. "Remember, no secret anything. Just work, right?"

Thurston nodded and frowned, then stumbled briefly before grabbing the handrail. Harmony felt better. She didn't take much from the man, but it was enough to stop the queasy sensation in her stomach.

"What took you so long?" Lilith's voice made all but Sharon flinch. It was unnecessarily loud. "Did you get trapped in the tacky-tacky-tentacle? Do we need to flush it with hot oil again, Thurstie?"

Thurston smiled at the pet name, and Harmony shouted, "No! No, I didn't get stuck at all, it was really slippery. I was just talking with Thurston about the groundbreaking work you two are doing. Right, Thurston?"

The man nodded, but said nothing. Harmony ached at the idea of hot oil being poured through Zoya's arm.

Something was steaming in a pot on the stove, presumably their warm beverage, and as much as she mistrusted the criminal couple, her cells craved more liquid.

"That smells delicious," she lied. "May I serve everyone?"

Thurston had set out two mugs and three beakers, and Harmony poured the opaque liquid into them. She didn't care how it tasted and drained hers quickly. Sharon and Blanche were more cautious in drinking theirs, and after obviously forcing themselves to take a first sip, couldn't hide their disgust.

"What's wrong, dearies? Too strong? You'll get used to it. Everything tastes stronger down here, but soon it will all just taste the same. Now, where shall we put them for the night, Thurstie?"

The man shrugged his sagging shoulders and looked at Lilith like a lost dog. She met his weak eyes with contempt in hers.

"I suppose they could stay in the unfinished wing." Lilith chuckled to herself. "Not a wing at all, really, more like another slimy appendage. Yes, yes, that will work. Follow me now, if you've finished your beverage."

Without looking back, Lilith left the room and headed for her sleeping chamber. Sharon and Blanche jumped up to follow her, and Harmony stayed back a moment to finish off their drinks. She didn't like the sound of what Lilith had just proposed.

"No secrets, Thurston. Where is she taking us?" With one finger, Harmony raised Thurston's chin until he looked at her with sorrow in his eyes.

"Another tentacle. Another tunnel. I could hear her cry when we were digging. I want it to stop. I just want it to stop." A teardrop fell from one eye.

"Thank you, Thurston. You're a good . . . man." Harmony felt suffocated by conflicting emotions. "Get some sleep now and I'll think about what you've told me. We're here to help now, and that's all you need to remember."

She rushed after the girls, catching them just after they entered the chamber.

"Why are you always so far behind?" Blanche whispered.

"I was really thirsty. I just finished your drinks. We don't want to insult our hosts, do we?"

"Yeah, whatever. Hey, check it out. Another secret door!"

Lilith pushed back a curtain on the far side of her sleeping chamber to expose a metal hatch like the one they had entered to go to the cave.

"In you go. Just nestle in there anywhere, I guess. We'll keep the air pumping through so you won't suffocate, but don't go too far in or you'll find yourselves in trouble. There's nothing at the other end yet. Nothing but water."

"I'll go in first this time." Harmony pushed past the other girls. "How will we know when to return?"

"Oh, I'll make sure you know, don't you worry your pretty little head about that," Lilith replied. "Sleep well, dearies. Tomorrow, we start building our stick people."

Harmony climbed through the hatch and felt Zoya's pain as she crawled as carefully as she could down the tentacle.

When Sharon and Blanche were behind her, the hatch slammed shut and they were thrown into darkness.

"Hey, that's my foot, get off of me!" said Sharon, and when Harmony increased the power of her glowing eyes and looked behind her, she saw Sharon kicking at Blanche.

"Ouch! Not cool, Sharon. I can hardly see anything in here. This is seriously giving me the creeps. What the heck have we gotten ourselves into?"

"Listen, you two, we're safe in here. So could we please just settle down and stop kicking and get some sleep? I have a feeling they're going to work us pretty hard tomorrow."

"Making stick slimeballs," said Blanche. "Can't wait."

Harmony couldn't tolerate any further talk about the horrid cave and its repulsive blobs. She blew a steady stream of air out over the girls as she had when they were in the tunnels, and their chatter ceased. They were asleep before they knew what hit them.

Zoya, are you there? she thought.

"Of course I am here. Thank you for your gentle movement and for silencing the rough ones."

Harmony nestled against the living creature.

"Why . . . why do I feel like I could sleep now too? I've never needed to sleep."

"Perhaps because you are becoming more like the others? More human? The body you have evolved has needs unlike those in Kumugwe's world and in his castle, where the girl from the sky now stays. I sense you have been looking for her, this girl who is more than a girl. She is called Celeste."

"What are you saying? Celeste is the girl I was sent to find? And she's with my father? How can that be?" Despite her excitement over the news, Harmony yawned and struggled to keep her eyes open.

"Let yourself sleep. You will find a way to work with her. I will keep you safe now."

"I know that." Harmony yawned for the first time in her short, young life. "I know." She stopped fighting her fatigue and fell into a dark, deep sleep while Zoya moved her damaged appendage slowly up and down in a hypnotic rhythm.

Thud-thud-clink, thud-thud-clink, thud-thud-clink.

~ 39 ~

[The Village / Orville]

DAY BROKE AS SILENTLY as night had passed and Orville stretched luxuriously. Unfolding his wings, he gazed at the still-sleeping woman—recently cocooned in his embrace—who believed in him. She opened her eyes after several moments and pulled one outstretched wing back over her.

"I slept a sleep of ages," she said. "And you, my treasure?"

"Yes. How could I not? No noise to wake us, no dreams to startle us, could anything be more peaceful?"

Orville couldn't remember a time since The Event when he'd felt so certain he was in the right place at the right time with the right woman. That she had once been a gigantic lizard meant no more to him than his once being a frog meant to her. It actually made their pairing feel more harmonic.

"May we stay like this until the end of time?" Riku's soft voice lulled him back into a light doze, his lips upon her forehead.

When they woke again minutes or hours or days later, it was still quiet except for the rumblings of hunger in their bellies. Orville paused for a moment. A snippet of a fleeting dream from when he fell back to sleep lingered in a corner of his mind, and he tried to make sense of it. A vague sense of unease gripped him when he remembered seeing Celeste.

"Shall we see how the others are doing? Perhaps see if Chimney has found something new for us to eat?" Orville sat up awkwardly, his long wings making an easy task difficult. "I wonder how long these will last." He stood and shook them out. Light from a window reflected off his feathers, sending sparkling flashes of light around the room. Riku eyed him appreciatively.

"They are glorious, like you. Yes, I am hungry. The little ones must be starving as well. I will go to them."

"The children are lucky to have you watching over them. You will take a great burden from Maddie with your help. She and Teresa now have someone to look up to."

Orville hesitated and a look of concern spread across his face. "Riku, do you have . . . did you lose—"

"No, my dear man. I have had no children of my own. Come now. I will see to the young ones and you to the ones confined. Those, I do not trust."

As they walked down the hallway, Orville was surprised to find everyone still nestled under bedcovers.

"Seems we were not alone in our 'sleep of ages,' as you put it. I'll be right back." Orville kissed her and walked toward the back of the house, but before he reached the corner, Layla and Lou stopped him.

"Well whaddaya know? Birdman finally leaves his nest, and I'm guessing, his little chickie!" Lou's snarky voice caught Orville off guard. It was hard for him to imagine such an incongruous matching of the crass bird with Layla, a gentle horse despite her obvious power.

"Yes, we slept quite well. Amazing what one good night can do to recharge one's energy." Orville stroked Layla's metallic muzzle when she leaned in to nudge him. He wondered if she could feel his hand.

"One good night? Ha! You're a real comedian!"

"What are you saying, Lou? If there is one thing I have never been called, it would be comedian. I have made no joke."

"Well, from my perspective, and I got a good one way up here, youz all been asleep now for comin' up on three days. Haven't had a home-cooked meal for that long, anyways, and the grub's been slim pickins."

"Three days? You jest, Lou." Suddenly agitated, Orville ruffled his wings. He couldn't believe he'd been asleep for that long, and yet . . .

"Oh, so now I'm the comedian? Eh. I've been called worse. Nice feathers, by the way. Almost nice as mine. Yup. Sun's been up and down three times already. Pretty sure this is the fourth. Tried to wake youz all, but I guess my hollerin' ain't that loud. That big ol' bug must have some kinda plans for ya seein' as she found it necessary to have youz all asleep for so long. Guess me and Laya and Merts is just chopped liver, but Layla here don't need no sleep anywho."

"Big ol' bug?"

"Yeah, you know, that big ol' four-winged thing that came by the other day and darn near blocked out the sky? That one."

"Did she say anything?" Orville was eager to know if she had delivered another message, though he believed he would have heard it.

"She? So big ol' bug's a dame? Go figure. Nah. She just kinda hovered there for a while after youz all went to bed and then left. I felt kinda weird for a while, but it passed."

Orville remembered his task. "Any word from our guests yet, or are they still asleep?"

"Oh, yeah, well, ya see, that first night while youz were all sleepin' and before the bug came by—hey, she got a name?"

"Noor."

"Yeah, well, they kinda dug their way out under the gate. Guess they wasn't feelin' the hospitality."

"Where are they?" Orville scanned the forest for any signs of movement.

"Cool yer jets, boss. Merts caught 'em tryin' to lift stuff from some of the houses. Let's just say, shall we, that youz all don't need to worry about those three bad apples no more. Merts is pretty swift with them magic arrows."

Orville wasn't sure how he felt about what Lou had told him. Any of it. On the one hand, he felt responsible for the safety of everyone in the village, even uninvited guests. He too had once been uninvited. On the other hand, the three in the cage had clearly harbored nefarious intentions. Perhaps it was best to cross them off his list of concerns.

"Morning, Orville." Nick approached, his hair a mess from his long slumber. "What a night, huh? Hope you slept as well as I did."

Orville shared what he'd learned from Lou. "We'll let the others know too, and perhaps things will make sense after we've all cleared our minds."

"Three days of sleep? My head feels pretty clear already, except for a strange dream I had." Nick smiled, and Orville noticed him fidgeting with the emerald scarf.

"Hey, this might sound a little crazy, but while I was up on that wall last night—or, I guess, whatever night that was— I was thinking about how Celeste always used to write in that diary. Some weird things happened with it, like Eenie's poem—still not sure how she wrote it—and the Shifter's. I wrote in it too, after she was dragged to the Overleader's house, and I don't know, I just kind of have this feeling like if I write to her, she'll get the message. So I did. I wrote to her before I fell asleep. Stupid, right?"

"Not stupid at all, Nick. Do you have the diary?"

"No, it was buried in the cave when it collapsed. That must have been horrible, Orville. I'm sorry."

Orville remembered the terrible scene as they had tried to escape the collapsing cave. He would never forget Ranger's mournful howl and Eenie's tears when they realized their friend Floyd and two of Eenie's babies hadn't made it out.

"Yes. It was horrible. And I thought I had rid the world of the Overleader forever, but here I am once more transformed, and she? A mere girl? Where is she now? But your letter, yes. What did you write? Oh, never mind. That is for you to know. Look. The others are waking."

People from each house yawned and squinted on porches, looking into the too-bright day with bewilderment.

Completely disheveled, Mason brushed past Orville and Nick toward the adobe huts he and several other workers had been building.

"Fire and ice, fire and ice, everything's nice about fire and ice. Where is the girl, the girl with a curl, where is the girl, my girl, my girl?" Mason looked to the sky and shook his head.

So he has lost someone too, Orville thought.

He followed Nick back into the house and watched him disappear into the common room. He wondered what guidance he would receive next and hoped it would come soon, for he was out of ideas. He also hoped Nick might share his dream.

~ **40** ~

[Celeste]

"I'M HEADING OUT NOW and I don't know when I'll be back," Celeste told Kumugwe. "Maybe you could give me a few tips on travel down here that'll help me get back sooner so I can start looking for your precious Harmony. If you remember, the last time I was down here I wasn't exactly comfortable."

Celeste was more than ready to escape the drama between Kumugwe and Odin, but still felt awkward underwater. It was time to find an octopus named Zoya. How hard could it be?

"Let your arms relax by your sides as you swim and move your tail—ah, your legs—together like the dolphins. And stay away from the sharks, the box jellyfish, some of my sea snakes, and certainly my blue-ringed octopuses. Those are my naughty children."

Celeste's heart skipped a beat at the mention of octopuses. Could the message from Zoya be a trap? What if Zoya had blue rings? Who would have any reason to hurt her, other than Harmony and the Overleader? And Harmony had evidently been unaware of the harm she'd inflicted on her playmate.

"Where would those octopuses be, and how big are they?"

"You would have to swim for days near the other side of the ocean to find them, and they are quite small. Sharks will be your biggest nuisance."

Celeste had never felt so unprepared for a journey in her life. She recalled her decision to run away from the children's home that chilly night with no other plan than to discover why her family had disappeared, and she still had no solid answer. She had witnessed their fall into the great fissure that had opened in their house, but according to Kumugwe, they and many others could have been saved and kept alive in undersea caverns.

She had to believe in the possibility.

"Thank you. I guess I'll be on my way, then." For a fleeting moment she thought she might hug the concerned-looking copper god.

"I might provide more guidance if you would give me a hint about your task." He sounded sincere, and Celeste didn't want to spend any more time than necessary away from land and the people and animals she'd grown fond of before her ascent into Odin's magnificent realm.

"So, remember when I asked you about the name Zoya? I think she's an octopus, and I think she's probably pretty large, and important." Celeste felt confident, finally, that Noor's intention was for her to find Zoya, for whatever reason. It was the only lead she had. "How would I narrow my search to find someone like that?"

Kumugwe's brow furrowed. "There are countless octopuses in my waters, many who guard against interlopers, and they are quite prolific. Sadly, they are not long-lived. Once mated, their days are numbered. I cannot imagine one so large or important that I would not know its whereabouts."

"But if you had to guess, where would she be?"

"I would point you to my deepest places where caverns abound in the mountains that plunge from topside. But beware. My waters grow darker in the depths."

A chill ran though Celeste.

"And you've told your creatures about me?"

"Yes. They will watch for you and do their best to keep you from danger. Now, make haste so we may both soon reunite with those we love. And if you should find anything unnatural—"

"Just my mission. Nothing extra." Celeste cut him off.

She walked to the door and when it opened, a dizzying sensation of unbalance washed over her. The movement of water outside Kumugwe's castle walls swept her off her feet until she remembered she should be swimming.

Moving her body like a dolphin, she swam around the enormous castle several times until she felt confident in her ability to navigate where she wanted.

"Holy moly!" she exclaimed. Her voice sounded muted as it dispersed in the current surrounding her, and it felt like she was in a dream. She couldn't believe how slick and weightless she felt. It felt much like when she'd flown.

And free. She was free of Kumugwe and Odin and her first thought was to swim to shore as fast as she could and run, or fly, to the village. She hoped she still could fly, and that Nick would be happy to see her when she arrived.

But the great dragonfly was in the air too, and had made it clear to her that she wasn't to emerge until she had learned more and saved someone, or something. She had to find Zoya.

Skimming the sea floor, she searched for darker, cooler depths and wondered briefly how she would find her way back to Kumugwe's castle. Soon, though, the gentle undulations of water currents lulled her into a trance and a sense of tranquility filled her being. She spun and rolled, marveling at her long black curls as they straightened and swirled around her. She felt like a mermaid and wished she had a real tail instead of slender legs.

Deeper and deeper she dove, startled occasionally by passing schools of fluorescent fish that studied her briefly before darting away. Glorious vegetation rose all around her, swaying gently and tickling her as she passed. Several times she felt her heart grip within her chest when a long dark shadow lurked nearby, but as if the sea were sentient, thick strands of slippery kelp surrounded her then, camouflaging her from apparent danger.

"Thank you," she said, and then laughed at the idea of talking to seaweed.

She lost track of time and space and who she was, and it didn't matter. Her new world was filled with mystery and beauty and she never wanted to leave it. Why would she? Why would the idea of leaving even enter her mind? She was an odd fish in a magical realm without a care in the world.

"Celeste," a voice echoed in her mind after what may have been hours or days of swimming. "You are close. Please hurry."

Her trance broken, Celeste recognized the voice from her dream.

"Where are you?" She strained her eyes in the darkness for signs of an octopus.

"Not far. You will feel the change."

Wondering how far she had come from Kumugwe's castle and how long she'd been away, she felt a pang of guilt. Shaken back to her senses, she swam purposefully. When a wave of foul water choked her, though, she panicked. Below her and not far off was a wall of silvery-pink ooze.

"I am here," the pained voice spoke, and Celeste could hear the odd beating of Zoya's hearts.

Several times Celeste attempted to swim into the poisoned water to find the creature, but each time she was repelled, gasping, her eyes and throat burning. On one attempt she saw the shadowy outline of the enormous octopus, but feared for her own life.

"I'm sorry," she called to the creature after retreating to clear water. "I can't get through!" And then she realized she would need the help of someone with more knowledge of the sea to complete her task. "Kumugwe can help you. I'll return with him! Hold on!"

"Wait!" Zoya stopped her.

Celeste turned and watched as one of Zoya's immense tentacles crept along the sea floor toward her. She suppressed her fear as it broke through the poisoned water and stretched upward.

"I must show you something. Please. Allow me to touch your head. I will not hurt you."

Celeste bent toward the tip of Zoya's over-stretched arm and gasped when she made contact. She saw a vision of the submarine laboratory inside the octopus and the unnatural heart, the metal heart with a beat that had haunted her dreams.

She pulled away, and the tentacle slumped into the silt.

"Who's in there? What can I do?" Celeste's mission suddenly seemed impossible.

"They must go, and I must die," said Zoya. "The scientists continue to damage the planet. Two others are led astray. You must guide the daughter of Kumugwe, for she is still a child in years. You must show her the key to stopping my hearts."

"Harmony? Harmony's in there?" Celeste wasn't sure whether to be angry or excited. She could fulfill Noor's directive and deliver Harmony back to her home and father.

As for the scientists, she would tell Kumugwe about them too. He would know what to do with them. His words about finding something unnatural replayed in her mind.

"Hold on, Zoya. I'll be back quickly!" She sped away without waiting for an answer.

After swimming for what seemed like forever, she remembered the last thing Zoya had said. In her haste to return to Kumugwe, she hadn't thought to ask the octopus about the key to stopping her hearts. *Another key*, she thought.

Celeste wondered how Zoya had survived in the toxic water. She would find a way to end the creature's suffering.

Without knowing how—though she suspected several schools of fish that surrounded and swept her along with them at times—she found her way back to Kumugwe's castle.

Knowing how pleased he would be to see her again, she squeezed through the main door noiselessly to surprise him and motioned to his sea lions to hush. Everything was quiet, and she thought the god might be out patrolling his domain when she heard his voice down the hallway near Odin's door.

"So, we take our chances with this Noor character?" Kumugwe's voice was clear.

"I told you, as soon as she can, she will betray you as she betrayed me." Odin spoke to him from the other side of the door. "Celeste has powerful gifts, yes, but she is not to be trusted. When . . . if she returns, we must ensure she cannot leave again until we know more."

"And I suppose my Harmony will find her way back to me without the girl's help . . ."

Celeste was horrified by what she heard and started back toward the door, but was stopped by several barking sea lions that drew Kumugwe's attention. She was trapped.

Pretending she hadn't heard the gods' conversation, she announced, "I'm back, and I need your help!"

Kumugwe looked delighted to see her, but Celeste could see that Odin's warning had influenced his welcome. "How long you have been gone!" he announced. "I thought perhaps you would not return. But you would not betray me, now, would you, child?" There was a hint of threat in his question.

"Of course not! Why would you say such a thing? Your world is more beautiful than any I've seen, and my task from the god of fire and light is within my reach. But I need your help." Celeste held off telling him about Harmony. She would free Zoya from her burden first.

"Ask for my help on the morrow, for I have matters to attend, and you, you are a frightful sight. Eat and sleep and we will discuss when I return and you are rested."

"But—"

"To your chamber. Now." He waved his hand toward her and she was brushed backward into her room without a chance for further protest. Several of Kumugwe's creatures delivered trays of food and the door closed, shutting her off from any chance of escape. She felt a disturbance in the water when Kumugwe left his castle, and knew his sea lions guarded the other side of her door.

Despite the fear she sensed knowing that her situation had changed drastically, she devoured the food. She hadn't eaten since she'd left his castle and fallen under the trance of his sea. And despite her best efforts to stay awake after she filled her stomach, she fell into a deep sleep and had a startling dream.

In this dream, she felt connected to Orville and Nick and all of her friends from the village, and she sensed the presence of Harmony, though she couldn't quite make out the girl's face.

She dreamt she was talking to them, telling them where she was and that she was trapped. She could see her friends' faces clearly and believed they were listening to her intently. She recognized Orville in a winged man's body and then she saw Nick bent over a piece of paper. She walked up behind him and peered over his shoulder as he wrote:

Dear Pip-squeak,

Where are you? I don't understand why you disappeared that day the water turned normal again and neither does anyone else. I've been looking for you, but maybe you don't want to come back. If I knew that, I might stop looking, but I don't believe that. I think you're still out there somewhere trying to come back to us. I want you to come back to me. Orville said you would if you could, so I have to believe you are in trouble and can't get here on your own.

I just wish I knew where to begin to look for you. I've searched the skies every day. Someone new in the village—there are more unusual beings here now—told us they saw a huge dragonfly drop a girl into the water far away. Could that be you? Could you be trapped in a sandcastle again?

You need to know that the Overleader is just a girl named Sharon now, and a really odd little girl named Harmony came out of the water that day you disappeared, and it's Sharon's little sister. They left the village after we returned, but we've been too busy to look for them. We don't trust either of them, and if you get this message, neither should you.

This sounds crazy, I know, but crazy is our new normal now. Anyway, if you can hear me, if you can feel me, if you're still out there somewhere, please come back. And if you're in trouble, please find a way to let me know. Because, well, we need you. I need you. Love, Nick

Celeste woke with a start and suddenly believed her dream world was more real than her waking world under the influence of the gods. Sensing that she had somehow made actual contact with the people in her dream, she feared for her friends' lives.

~ **41** ~

[Harmony]

HARMONY STRUGGLED to make sense of her new experience. Never having slept deeply or dreamt before, both her body and mind felt disoriented. With the soft glow from her sea-green eyes, she could see everything clearly inside the dark protuberance that was one of Zoya's eight arms, and noted the other girls were still fast asleep.

"Zoya?" she whispered.

"Here," the creature spoke wordlessly.

Harmony remembered she didn't have to speak aloud. "I think I was sleeping, but I saw things that seemed real to me. How can that be?"

"You were dreaming, child. Dreams are fitful, fanciful dances in your brain that try to make sense of all you have experienced and wondered during your waking hours. I dream of the times before my captivity."

"I'm not sure if that's true, though. I saw her. I saw Celeste. She was swimming all through Kumugwe's waters and she was near. I felt like she was trying to come here, like she wanted to help release you, but something repelled her— it was the water around you!—and she swam away."

"You saw the truth, then." Zoya sounded perplexed. "You have not moved from my folds until just now, and she came and went long ago."

"So she truly is nearby and will help me free you of these monsters?" Not only was Harmony thinking of the two mean-spirited girls resting peacefully nearby, she was thinking of Lilith too. She was still unsure of how to characterize Thurston. He had been in cahoots with Lilith when they had deposited their helpless child into the sea, but something in him had changed since then.

As for the other monsters, those vile blobs in the cavern, they would have to be destroyed.

"She could not breathe in the abominable water spreading from where I linger on. The scientists, with their probes and calculations and painful electrical currents, have altered what was once pure and beautiful in my world. Every breath I take is vile, but they will not let me die. No other creature has been successful in finding me, not even the little ones I released into the sea so long ago, for once they encounter the perimeter of this horrid substance, like Celeste, they flee."

"But she will find a way to help." Harmony said this with certainty. "I saw other things too. I saw some of the beings from the village. I was there only briefly before Sharon pulled me away, but I recognized many of them. They were in my dream too. One attractive boy was making shapes on paper with a yellow stick."

Though she had recognized the drawings in the schematics back in the subterranean laboratory of Sharon's sunken house, Harmony had never been taught to read. There was no need for such a frivolous skill in Kumugwe's realm.

"I too have made contact with Celeste in her dream state, and I have summoned her. She does not yet believe in her own powers and has returned to Kumugwe's castle for help. What else did you see in your dream, Harmony?"

"I didn't see much more, I'm afraid, but I do feel strongly that my father may try to detain her. Another power is interfering. And those villagers from topside? I believe they will try to find her, and that will put them in danger. How do you explain these feeling that are not dreams?"

"Those feelings come from a special place deep within you. Intuition is a gift. Let it guide you in your decisions, for it can protect you from darkness."

Harmony thought for a moment, and then examined her right arm. "Zoya? Do you know about the horrible things in the cavern beyond your other arm?"

"I know only what I have heard in conversations. I know what the man and woman are doing in there is as atrocious as everything they have already done. They have ripped our world open with their shock devices and destructive beams of light and released abominations."

"But why hasn't Kumugwe stopped them? How does he not know about this?"

"His burdens are vast and abundant, as you should know, and he has existed throughout the eons. He has experienced shakes and shifts and anomalies too numerous to imagine. This most recent one is just another. And as I have told you, those who might inform him of my condition are repelled by my surroundings and quickly distracted by their own needs. It was not until I linked into Celeste's dream that I had any hope at all of ridding these demons from my shattered body."

"And now I am here as well." Harmony noticed the girls stirring. "What more can I do to help? We will be adding skeletons to the monsters they've created in the cavern, and I'm afraid I may be forced to do something I don't want to do. Lilith has a contraption to control the creatures, and it affects me as well. She demonstrated a simple command yesterday, and my arm moved without my control. What if she makes me do something horrible? How will I be able to stop her?"

"Now that you know what she is doing, you must take control of your own mind and your own body. You must fight to remain free of their control or you will become like me, a victim of those with ghastly intentions. And since you felt the presence of others and their possible attempt to find Celeste, you must watch for them as well."

A powerful gust of air swept past her and she instinctively closed a membrane over her eyes. She could see the outline of a stick-like figure in the hatchway.

"Time for work, girlies." Lilith's harsh voice startled the two awake and as they tried to jump to their feet, they slipped and fell again and again against the scarred flesh inside Zoya's arm.

Harmony cringed with each violent movement and before they could fall again, grabbed them each by an arm and escorted them to the door.

With distasteful tasks awaiting her, she would work on controlling more than just her own body and mind. She would use what she knew of her own powers over humans to exert some control over them as well.

~ **42** ~

[The Village / Orville]

"DO YOU THINK she'll come back, Orv?" Orville helped Chimney unload his bag of snoodles on a table with other new food items from Teresa's garden. "I miss her."

Chimney's question was vague, so Orville decided to play it safe. "Yes, Chim, I believe your sister will return to you. How could she stay away from such a wonderful young man much longer?" He ruffled the boy's hair, and Chimney smiled.

"Yeah, I kinda miss her too, but I was thinkin' about Celeste. Had a weird dream about her last night. Lots of us were in it."

Orville interest in Nick's dream suddenly became more urgent.

"How much do you remember about your dream? But wait just a moment. Let's get everyone fed and then we'll talk. I dreamt about her too."

As was becoming their custom, people from each of the houses gathered around several tables in the center of the village and shared food their hunters had gathered. Merts drifted nearby with their share of small game and, having previously expressed discomfort in the open, summoned Orville aside.

"Girl needs assistance / Strange visions in our heads warn / Water trap below."

Mesmerized by the sight and sound of Merts, Orville was oblivious to a growing commotion back at the tables.

"Strange visions? Do you mean dreams? Did you all dream of a dark-haired, green-eyed girl named Celeste?" Orville's excitement was growing. "Is she all right?"

"Gods interfering / Bad people in octopus / Evil intentions."

Although Orville wished Merts would speak more clearly, their comment about gods interfering brought back a scene from his dream. For a dizzying moment he felt he was looking through Celeste's eyes. He also felt hands holding him up and realized Merts were steadying him until his vision passed.

"I saw him," he told Merts. "A huge, copper man with a beard and bulging eyes and strange legs—no, a tail, like an enormous fish, and he has Celeste trapped in a water-filled room. How can she still be alive? But I feel it. She is." He searched the three pairs of eyes staring at him. "You said 'gods,' but I saw only one, if that was indeed a god."

"Sky brother joins him / Causing suspicion, jealous / He may keep the girl."

"Hey, Orv?" Chimney called from the tables. "You might want to hear this."

Orville stared at the melodious archers for a moment longer before returning to the tables. Visions, traps, water-filled rooms, gods, bad people, and an octopus. Bad people *in* an octopus. None of it made any sense, but he knew it all to be true.

"What is it, buddy?" Orville returned to the group and stood by Chimney and was instantly aware of everyone's eyes on him. He looked around the crowd and noted expressions of hopefulness, confusion, and fear, and addressed the group.

"What has happened?"

"The dream," Nick spoke. "We've all had the same dream."

Without any need for explanation, Orville knew Nick's words to be true too. "How is everyone feeling?" He still hadn't fully processed the idea that he, and apparently everyone but Merts and Layla and Lou, had been asleep for several days.

"Like, crazy, dude." Thunder's voice rose from behind the group. "Like I've been drugged."

Orville noted several people nodding. "Okay, so it would appear that we have all experienced an unusual flux in our atmosphere, perhaps, and have been asleep for longer than necessary. May I hear what you remember from some of your dreams?"

The villagers all seemed eager to talk about what they had seen while they slumbered, and each one provided a detail or two to add to the one just described. When they all finished sharing their dream, they looked back to Orville with expectation in their eyes.

"What does it mean?" someone asked.

Orville weighed his words carefully. "I believe Celeste is trying to help us. I know many of you did things you may now regret from when she and I first arrived in your village, but it is time to move forward. I have shared her dreams many times. It does not make me special, but each dream turned out to be significant. Now we all have shared a dream, and I believe that is no coincidence."

"But what are we supposed to do about it? It made no sense!" someone protested, and those around her shushed her.

"They often do not make sense, you are right," Orville acknowledged the young woman's frustration, "but we know several things now. Celeste disappeared after saving us all from the encroaching ooze. The Overleader and her sister and
. . ." he looked at Chimney to gauge his response, "Blanche have disappeared too."

"She better not come back!" someone shouted.

Chimney frowned and started to disappear.

"Something is happening in the water again—that tidal wave could have washed us all away—but another creature, Noor, told me that Celeste was still alive and had an important task. Somehow, we were all put to sleep and given the ability to share Celeste's dream, so we must believe it is because she needs our help."

"I'll help." Katie's little voice rose from the silence that followed Orville's interpretation.

"I'll help too," said Chimney, who reappeared.

Soon Orville couldn't keep up with the offers of help from the crowd.

Mason pushed his way to a place beyond the group and walked in a circle around them, and for the first time since he'd arrived, they all watched and listened.

"Fire and ice, fire and ice, sugar and spice and everything nice, bacon and books in slippery nooks, nooks and cooks and everything shook, everything swirling and waterlogged crooks, boys and dogs and girl with curls, find the girl and save the world, Zoya Zoya secret lair, evil girl with long pink hair, not the one you think she is, parents have a shady biz, gods compete to stay alive, using her they will connive to keep her there, the one you seek, save her or our future's bleak."

He stopped circling and returned to his masonry work beyond the pond.

Orville addressed the dumbfounded group. "I think we also need to start thinking about what all that might mean."

He was growing tired of riddles.

~ 43 ~

[Celeste]

CELESTE PACED AROUND her expansive room, occasionally pushing off to swim its perimeter once she remembered it was actually filled with quiet water. She was too angry at herself, however, to enjoy the weightless feeling of floating.

"Now what, genius?" It was a question she'd asked herself long ago.

Celeste knew she had made the right decision to leave the children's home, especially in light of its demise in a deluge not long after, but for all the challenges she'd faced and overcome since then, she'd grown no more clever when it came to avoiding traps.

And now her friends could be in greater danger too.

She swam over to check the door again, but found it still immovable. "Kumugwe, please, I've got to tell you what I found! I think it's why the water is turning deadly again." She peeked through a tiny crack in the doorframe and was startled when several round eyes stared back at her.

"Come on, guys," she whispered, "let me out, please? Wouldn't you rather be free too? When was the last time you swam and twirled and frolicked outside these walls?"

But the sea lions just grunted and turned away.

"I found Zoya, and she's in trouble!" She tried again to get the god's attention, and was surprised to hear Odin's voice instead.

"Why, my buddy? Why would you leave me, only to fall into the crabby clutches of my inferior brother? And now here we both are, growing weaker in our salty cells with no one to stabilize the atmosphere around the mortals!"

Celeste remembered how Odin had toyed with the weather and taught her how to make rain, and also knew he was powerless against the ooze following The Event.

"Don't pretend that you're just a good guy, Odin. You told and showed me things that have convinced me otherwise. Now, where's Kumugwe?"

"Most likely out looking for that horrible humming thing that almost killed you. You were to find her after your super-secret mission, but now it appears you will accomplish neither. Pity, really. I was growing curious. I miss being able to hear your thoughts. Tell me, Celeste, where is the god more powerful than I? Were it true, this Noor should be able to free us both."

Celeste knew less about Noor than she knew about Odin and Kumugwe, but they didn't need to know that.

"She will, in time. But come on, Odin, don't you know anything about your brother's castle that could help us escape?"

"Slender as you, you could probably find an opening among the living layers of this bedrizzled dump. As for me, I am too large, too old, too weakened, and too sad to try."

Celeste's heart squeezed tightly and she fought back tears. It was true. He had shared his fear of death with her and had found hope in her companionship.

"Are you crying, child? Would you even know you were, immersed as you are in this salty wet sludge?"

The water drop on the back of Celeste's head tingled and her entire body felt unsettled. She tried to speak to Odin, to tell him everything would be all right, but her words dissolved as she spoke them.

In a moment of disbelief, like the words unspoken, her body dissolved too into a gelatinous, amorphous substance. She wanted to scream, but had no mouth.

"Not even an acknowledgment? Done with me just like that, then." Odin continued his discourse and then became quiet.

Celeste's shapeless form floated to the far side of her room and slid through thick layers of sea kelp curtains. Behind the curtains, slivers of water from outside the castle sifted gently in and out of the room, and in no time at all, she eased her way through one of the cracks.

Yikes! she thought, having no way to scream. She wondered what to do next, and as she floated away from the castle walls, she remembered Zoya telling her she was more than just a girl. She also recalled a booming old mountain spirit telling her to remember who she was.

Old Man Massive had been her first guileless father figure since she had lost her own father, and in retrospect, her short time with him had seemed so easy.

Who am I? More like what am I? She floated on aimlessly until an enormous rush of water buffeted her, threatening to disperse her more widely than she could imagine, and behind the sudden flow loomed Kumugwe on a fast approach toward his castle.

Celeste sensed he was about to burst right through her, and in her terror, she felt a *SNAP* and there she was, back in her own body.

"Blood and thunder!" Kumugwe roared as he stopped just short of slamming into her. He grabbed her hand and pulled her the rest of the way back into his castle. Both of them were wide-eyed.

"What? How? Why? Balderdash!" He stumbled around his great hall staring at her all the while, and his sea lions barked their bewilderment.

"What trepidation toils in your mud-drenched mind, brother?" Odin called from behind his door. "The girl has chosen not to speak to me, so let me hear a friendly voice!"

Celeste could tell Odin was trying to sound upbeat, but his lonesomeness came through more clearly.

"Tell me how you did it, Odin, and why." Kumugwe's nostrils flared. "Were you not the one who told me she would try to escape? Why, then, would you help her?"

"You speak nonsense. Let me out and we can talk like the brothers we once were."

"He didn't do it," Celeste blurted. "At least, I don't think he did."

"Oh, so now you release the girl and blame me for her escape?" Odin banged the door once without vigor.

"Talk, girl." The threat in Kumugwe's voice was real.

"I don't know what to say. I think maybe being in the sea for so long has made me . . . soggy? I couldn't help it. One minute I was talking with Odin—it gets pretty boring down here locked in a room all day, you know—and the next thing I knew, I melted and slipped through a crack in the wall. If it's anyone's fault, it's yours." Celeste was badly shaken by the experience, but stood her ground.

"Melted? HAhaha. Now, there is a new incarnation." Odin sounded genuinely amused.

Kumugwe flipped his tail and was inside Celeste's chamber in a flash, swiping away the kelp from the walls and exposing the tiny cracks. "*Melted*?" she heard him mumble.

"The door shall remain opened, lions, and four of you shall remain inside with her. She will not escape again, do you understand?" Kumugwe's sea lions barked appropriately.

"But *you* don't seem to understand." Celeste stomped her foot and silt swirled all around it. It didn't have the effect she'd hoped for. "I found Zoya, this enormous octopus, and all around her the water is poisonous. And it's spreading. I couldn't even breathe there."

She had the god's attention.

"So I'll tell you now. Noor's instructions are that I help Zoya, and I can't do that without *your* help. There's something very, very wrong where she's trapped, and if I couldn't breathe there, your other creatures probably can't either. There are scientists working in a metal laboratory *inside* of her, keeping her alive, and they're still damaging the planet and your waters. You wanted me to find something unnatural, and I did. Now, do you want the poison to spread and kill all of your followers like it killed those topside? And maybe even you? Are you ready to die, Kumugwe?"

A long silence followed.

"Well, brother? Are you going to answer the girl sent by a god more powerful than us both? I have contemplated death for eons. Not until the girl flew into my realm did I entertain thoughts of retaining my immortality."

Celeste wished Odin would stop making his sorrowful comments. With each one, he made her feel more and more like a heartless daughter.

"But she is deceitful, Odin. You have told me so yourself. Tell me where this Zoya is, girl, and I will find her myself. You will not leave my castle again. Not until I am prepared to release you, if ever I am."

"I can't tell you. I swam like I was in a dream and could only do it again if you set me free." She was still unwilling to tell him about Harmony, and wouldn't. Not until Zoya's request was fulfilled.

"Take her to her room, then, lions, and perhaps time without food will jar her memory."

"You are foolish, you fish-finned freak." Odin sounded defeated.

Celeste sat in her chamber and had a staring contest with her whiskered guards until her eyelids drooped. The thrill and fear of her most recent transformation had left her exhausted and hungry. She flopped back onto her bed and dreamt as clearly as she had during her last sleep.

Her friends all gathered in the village center. Many offered help. They mentioned her name. In the distance through the trees, a great ball of fire rose and spread, backlighting the spindly trees in the forest.

"Celeste, Celeste, come back!" Zoya's voice drowned out her friends' commotion and suddenly, she could see a cramped, cold room with a man, a woman, Blanche, and two other girls, one with long pink hair, another who appeared ghostly.

"Harmony. She is here, and you must help," Zoya whispered, and the girl with white skin, white hair, and warm sea-green eyes turned then and looked straight through her dream and into Celeste's eyes.

~ 44 ~

[Harmony]

HARMONY REPRESSED ANOTHER wave of sickness in her stomach when she thought of returning to the cave of monsters. She'd have to play along with the plan until she could find a way out.

Or would she?

Maybe I could change their minds, she thought. *Thurston is already frightened. He knows what they're doing is wrong. But the others?* She believed the others would not be swayed so easily.

"I trust you slept like sleepy little cave bats." Lilith fluttered her hands like wings and chortled.

"Feels like I've been sleeping forever." Blanche rubbed her eyes and looked around the room for something to eat. "Do you have anything to eat that's not . . . beige?"

"Picky-picky girl, isn't she, Thurstie?"

Harmony found the pet name insulting, and then decided she shouldn't care. She needed to remember they were not her real parents. They were horrible people who did unthinkable things to their own offspring and to the suffering creature they had invaded. They were working on creating a force of creatures to carry out their bidding on what remained of a planet their experiments had nearly destroyed.

"Picky-picky girl," Thurston echoed. He picked up another nondescript casserole from a counter, moved it onto the table and passed around utensils.

"How should we start today?" Sharon looked eager for the day's work. "Do you have a plan for building the inside frames for those . . . what should we call them?"

"We call them our children, don't we, dear?" Lilith elbowed her husband. "Yes, since we never had any children of our own, these will be our kiddiwinks, our pride and joy." Harmony saw the woman staring into Sharon's eyes as she spoke, and Sharon frowned.

Something jolted the submarine, throwing them all off balance and causing the casserole to crash to the floor. Harmony watched as small things slithered away from the mess.

"That better not have been you, beast!" Lilith screeched at the ceiling. "You know what happens when you're not careful!"

Thurston's eyes grew wide and it looked like he might cry.

"What happens?" A crooked smile spread across Sharon's face.

"This one," Lilith pointed to Sharon, "this one I like. Shall we show her what happens when the beast misbehaves?"

Harmony knew she had to divert the conversation quickly. She couldn't bear to witness what more the wicked woman might do to Zoya.

"Our work! We have so much to learn today if we're to be any help to you. That was probably just a current shift. I've noticed lots of those lately in the water tunnels."

Sharon glared at her.

"Yes, yes," Lilith replied dully. "Let's get to it then. Here," she grabbed a few squishy bags of something and tossed one to each girl, "this should fill your bellies until dinner."

On their way through Zoya's arm to the disgusting cavern, Harmony concentrated on how she might stop the scientists and dislodge them from Zoya's body. She felt another jolt just as she was nearing the end of the tentacle, and being too far away from the edge of the cavern, slipped into the water near the edge of the work space. She knew Zoya wasn't causing the disruption, and also wondered if the octopus had dunked her purposefully, knowing the strong need she had for hydration.

She thanked the creature silently and swam easily to the cavern where the others waited. Another surge of water lifted her into the open space. It spilled across the floor and sent the others scurrying back from the edge. A blast of wind from far back in the cavern pushed the water back out and over the edge.

Blanche appeared frightened, and Harmony wondered if there might be an opportunity to convince the wayward teen not to partner with the demented woman and her ill husband.

When the mini-crisis abated, Harmony spoke. "Lilith, have you considered returning to topside to continue your work? It's a lot more stable up there, and—"

"Stable? We're not looking for stable, my dear pale thing. After all, it was our idea to shake the planet and everything on it. Lesson number one: When people are fearful and ignorant, they're as easy to control as . . . as these blobs!" Lilith pushed a random button and when the blobs jiggled, she cackled.

Harmony winced and fought the urge to march forward. *"Take control of your own mind and your own body."*

"We've worked down here for years uninterrupted until you three barged in. There'd be too many nosy-nosy bodies anywhere else." Lilith narrowed her eyes at Harmony. "I'm getting the feeling you're having second thoughts about your employment."

"No second thoughts at all, really." Harmony had to be more cautious. "I guess I was just thinking that if the sea becomes more turbulent, it could endanger your work. What if this cave flooded?"

A flash of uncertainty on Lilith's face let Harmony know she was on the right track, and before Lilith could speak again, there was another rumble followed by another splash of water across the cavern floor. The powerful air jets kicked on again, but Harmony noticed a look of surprise replacing the former uncertainty.

"You may have a point. I will discuss this with my partner. For now, however, come with me and I'll show you the schematics for today's work."

The three girls followed Lilith to a side table, and Sharon jabbed Harmony as they walked. It was clear her sister was annoyed. Harmony ignored her.

The schematics were surprisingly straightforward. The array of metal components they'd been shown the day before were all meticulously numbered to align with matching components to make up a complete set for each blob. There were hundreds of sets.

"We've worked quite diligently on these. Aren't they magnificent? And once assembled, our kiddiwinks will be ready for action. They won't need food or sleep and they'll frighten anyone they come across just because they're so hideous!" She cackled.

"If there are no questions, I'll leave you to your work. The beast will know when to bring you back for dinner. Just watch for the nasty tip rising above the water, like this—" Lilith pushed another button and Zoya's arm rose to take her back to the submarine.

In a moment, she was gone.

"What the heck, Harmony? What do you think you're doing?" Sharon sounded furious.

"I'm just trying to keep us all safe. You remember that day years ago when everything shook and you changed? When I came out of the water, you were a horrible old woman. They did that, you know. They broke apart the planet and somehow changed the composition of so many things."

"I know that!" Sharon shivered visibly. "And that's why we're going to be so awesome when we go home. I was checking out some of their other schematics and they're manipulating ionic fields. The salt water probably helps. Maybe they cracked the planet by mistake, but if they can give people powers, then maybe I can get mine back, and maybe you can get some too, Blanche. They're absolutely brilliant! Well, our mother is, anyway."

Harmony controlled her desire to scream "She's not my mother!" Instead, she said, "Brilliant, yes. But to what end?" She turned to Blanche. "And Blanche, don't you want to be with your family again and know that they'll be safe?"

Blanche looked thoughtful. Harmony could see she was struggling with how to respond. She finally looked at Sharon and said, "This is my family now."

Sharon smiled like a Cheshire cat, but Harmony didn't believe Blanche was being truthful to herself.

"Okay then. We should get to work while Lilith talks to Thurston about a possible move topside." Harmony was the first one to pick up a set of metal parts and move to the same numbered specimen.

"Ooo, gross," said Blanche when she inserted the first piece into her blob far away from Harmony. Sharon laughed.

Harmony knew the girls probably believed she couldn't hear them whispering, but they were wrong.

"There's something fishy about your sister."

"Oh, you think so? What was your first hint, Miss Obvious?"

"You know what I mean. I don't trust her. But what do you think? Maybe it would be safer on land."

"Maybe. My mother will make the right decision. I'm sure of it. And someday, she'll know I'm her daughter."

"But what if Harmony, I don't know, stops them somehow? What if she has friends we don't know about down here?"

There was a pause.

"Don't worry about Harmony. I'll take care of her."

Harmony noted something cruel in her sister's last words.

~ 45 ~

[The Village / Orville]

"MAN'S JUST LOOSE in the noodle," Orville heard someone mumble as the villagers watched Mason return to his task. Several in the group chuckled uncomfortably.

"Perhaps, or perhaps not." Orville made a mental note to spend more time with the man. Some of his babbling was beginning to make sense in a roundabout way.

"In any case, can any of you say you have worked as hard as he has since his arrival? Let us not make fun. Our wisdom as a village comes from us all. If we are to survive in this new world, we must work together and share our knowledge in whatever way our words may come out."

"Sorry, Orville," the mumbler spoke up, "I didn't mean no harm. You gotta admit, he says some funny things. We all gotta laugh sometime."

The group appeared agitated. Riku walked to Orville's side and took his hand.

"Yes, indeed we do, and forgive me for my hasty censure. It would appear I need to heed my own advice and think for a moment about my own words before speaking."

He chuckled and the group relaxed, laughing more freely with him.

"Now, knowing or believing that Celeste is being held against her will somewhere underwater, do any of you have an idea of how we might find her? I have saved her from a fall into the ooze before I first came to you as a fleshy flying frog," Orville shook his head at the absurd memory, "and a one-eyed wizard delivered me in the body of a wind-up toy to rescue her from a deadly sandcastle. We both nearly drowned, and I cannot imagine surviving underwater in my current configuration." He spread his wings and indicated his human body.

"Bridger could make a bigger boat, big enough so lots of us could fit in, and we could head toward where that dragonfly dropped her," Chimney suggested.

"I can do that, Orv." Bridger nodded. "Now I got my power back, I can make anything you want." As if to demonstrate, he pointed to where Mason was stacking mud bricks and finished the work for him with a swirl of his hand, leaving the man scratching his head and the villagers chuckling.

"I can freeze the water again and then maybe the dragonfly can burn a fire hole down to where she is and we can fish her outta there," Katie suggested to more chucklers.

"Yeah, and I could push that boat over the ice till we get there!" Jack added, flexing his skinny arms to get a laugh.

"I'd help," said Ryder, but I think I should stay here and make sure Penelope's okay, and anyone else who might get hurt." He had named the dog after healing her, and she hadn't left his side since.

Orville had noticed how Ranger stayed close by too.

"If I stopped time again," Nick paused, his eyes narrowed in deep concentration, "maybe I could—"

Before he could finish his thought, the village was thrown into shadow as Noor swooped over it and continued to fly over the forest. Despite all of the anomalies he and the villagers were growing accustomed to seeing, Orville gasped at the sight.

"Where's she going?"

"Did she hear us?"

"Maybe she'll tell you more, Orville!"

"Let's call to her! Maybe if we yell her name all together, she'll hear us!"

Orville listened to their comments and before he could respond, a ball of fire rose from beyond the forest in a place they knew once belonged to the Overleader. They watched as Noor rose above the forest and the flames and disappeared into the sky.

"Where'd she go?"

"What's it mean?"

"Hope we're not next!"

"What do we do, Orville?"

"Why burn an empty field?"

The last question caught Orville's attention. "Why, indeed? Who wants to go find out?" He looked around the group and saw several hands raised.

Riku squeezed his hand more tightly then. "Do wait until the flames subside, yes?"

He wrapped one wing around her and smiled. "Yes, my patient beauty. We will wait."

Many of those who didn't raise their hands dispersed to where Mason continued to labor, to the gardens to help Teresa, or back to the endless tasks of preparing and storing food and repairing structure damage. When the smoke stopped rising above the forest, Orville and his small crew headed toward the scorched field on the other side.

Merts greeted them when they entered the forest.

"Fireball unveils / Hidden passageway below / Proceed with caution."

"Thank you, Merts," said Orville. "I was hoping you'd tell me something I wanted to hear, and perhaps you have. Would you consider being our guides? There have been no more intruders and I thank you for that as well. There may be others lurking in the shadows."

"Safe passage is yours / We'll move ahead quietly / Answers are within."

Merts flung their braid toward the highest limb in a tree far from them and disappeared.

"A mystery hunt awaits us, friends. Our guides may have disappeared, but I believe we will have nothing to fear in the forest." Orville led the way, and soon they were standing at the edge of a charred field.

Chimney twitched, and Orville could see he was distraught. "Looks like a big ol' mess. My sister came this way to find Sharon. You don't think—"

"No, Chim, I do not believe Noor would harm the girls. I believe she cleared the field so we would find something. Merts said something about a passageway."

Nick and Mac searched around the perimeter of where the Overleader's house had once stood, and the others spread out around the field.

"Look! Something sparkly in the middle!" Katie ran to where a crystal doorknob lay on the ground and the others soon surrounded her. "It's still warm." She pulled her hand away.

"It's still attached to a door," said Mac, brushing off the ash around the knob.

"Open it." The command came out of Orville's mouth before he realized what he was saying. "Please."

They stood back while Mac pulled and pulled, but he was unable to lift the singed door from the ground.

"Can I try?" Jack had come along on the mystery hunt. Orville had seen how proud the boy had been to help in the past, and his strength was a source of amazement to anyone who would otherwise dismiss the scrawny child.

Mac stepped back.

With an easy grip on the doorknob, Jack flung the door open, tearing it from the ground and flinging it into the field behind them. "Oops!" he shrugged.

"Nice work, kiddo," Mac ruffled the boy's dark hair. "If I weren't so secure in my manhood, I think I might be pretty embarrassed right now."

They laughed, and then peered down the dark stairway.

"A secret passageway!" Katie's eyes grew wide.

"I will enter first," said Orville, "and when I see it is safe, I will call." He disappeared into the hole in the ground and was gone for several moments before he beckoned the others. "Come down slowly. There are many obstacles, but I believe it is safe."

Nick, Chimney, Jack, Katie and Mac descended into the dark, damaged rooms and rummaged around.

"What exactly are we looking for? This is just an old destroyed house," said Nick. "But wait, they were here! Look at those cans!" He pointed to the empty food cans in what appeared to have been a kitchen.

"Over here!" yelled Katie. "Look at the mirror! It's off the wall, and look, there's another door!"

Without being asked, Jack pulled the secret door open and started down the stairway to the underground laboratory. The others followed.

"Hidden doorways everywhere," said Orville as he gazed around at the tools and schematics. "And where might this one lead?" The top was off of the surgical table, and Orville could smell the salty water far below.

"This is scary," said Jack. He grabbed Katie's hand.

Orville knelt down in front of the children and wrapped his wings gently around them. "You two have been very brave. We never would have found these passageways without you. Would you like to go back to the village now and tell the others what we've discovered and let them know not to worry?"

The children nodded their heads and Katie asked, "Mac? Can you bring us home?"

Mac looked at Orville, who nodded his approval, and led the children away.

"Nick? Chim? I will be fine if you return as well."

Both boys shook their heads no.

"All right, then. Down we go." Orville descended first, and when the three reached the bottom of the ladder, there was only one way to go from there.

When they got to the end of the tunnel and found the vast cave surrounding the water hole, they were speechless.

And before Orville could find the words he wanted to say to the boys, words of praise and thanks and encouragement, two shiny black crabs sprang from beneath the water's surface, their claws expanding to an impossible size, and snatched them from the edge.

"NOOOOOOO!" Orville's cry echoed again and again as he flailed wildly in the water in a futile search for Nick and Chimney.

~ **46** ~

[Celeste]

"NOOOOOOO!" **CELESTE HEARD** Orville's voice echo in her dream and experienced his fear. Weak from physical transformations and hunger, she nevertheless forced herself to open her eyes. When she did, she was staring into the attentive eyes of one of her big-bellied sentinels.

"Did you hear him too?" she asked the one whose nose was only inches from hers. "Something bad has happened. Get Kumugwe for me, would you, please?"

The animal barked, but it was Odin who answered.

"He believes he can solve this dilemma himself, foolish girl. And then what will become of us?"

Celeste didn't respond.

"Ah, but I was foolish too, thinking I could come down here and steal you back. I had forgotten how quickly this salty realm steals my strength. Is this what they call irony? I come to steal something and instead, become the victim of thievery myself?"

Celeste didn't understand irony and had nothing to say. The gods were both acting like petulant children and her most trusted friend was in trouble.

"I would have treated you more kindly, you know." His voice trailed off.

Celeste concentrated on what it had felt like when she'd melted. It was the only way she could think to escape again. She remembered the mark on her head tingling, but couldn't recall what had caused it. Was it something about crying? She had no energy left for tears.

She felt a rumbling all around her and even the sea lions looked disturbed.

"He is returning unsuccessful," Odin explained. "Just like a little child, he stomps his tail in frustration."

Celeste had done the same thing before being sent to her room again, but Kumugwe's demonstration was far more effective. After all, he was a god, a god with a powerful tail, and she was just a pip-squeak.

She missed Nick horribly.

"I'm not foolish and I'm *not* just a girl!" she shouted. "I am Celeste Araia Nolan and I've *done* things! There's more I need to do now, and you and your ancient old brother need to help me!"

She tried to stand, but her feet felt like butter. When she looked at them, they appeared blurry, as if they were about to melt. She willed the rest of her body to melt too, but to no avail.

Kumugwe burst through the main door and seaweed swirled everywhere. Celeste's feet rematerialized. The animated god appeared in her doorway, and her guardians seized the opportunity to squeeze past him into the main castle.

"Perhaps I have wasted my gift. Now I see how foolish I have been." When Kumugwe looked at Celeste, she felt as if he were looking at an injured baby bird. His rage had subsided.

"Gift? What gift?" Celeste stood, though she felt frail. "Did you hear him scream? Could you tell me if he's all right? Are my friends safe?"

"You talk in riddles, girl. A scream? I have heard nothing but the constant swirling and swishing of creatures and currents in my realm. I know nothing about a 'he' or your friends, only that my gift to them, and to you, has been wasted." He slumped down, filling the doorway with his massive body.

"What's this gift you keep talking about?" Celeste's frustration was as great as Kumugwe's.

"Look at your arms, girl, and tell me what you see."

Celeste complied. "I see, I don't know, my arms, my hands, my fingers." She wondered what he was seeing.

"And you see no gift? Nothing new since you ran away from my Harmony? Where, oh where is my funny little music maker?" Kumugwe squeezed his eyes closed and smacked his forehead with his fist.

She knew where.

"If you recall," Celeste interrupted his melodrama, "someone you know delivered a gift to me to help me escape from your funny-little-music-maker's sandcastle prison. I know you say she didn't mean to harm me, but she was killing me."

Odin shouted, "You are welcome, Celeste, and thank you for finally acknowledging my generosity."

Celeste rolled her eyes and continued. "That was a gift that helped save my life so I could stop the putrid water from killing my new friends."

"Ah, and I too have given you a life-saving gift. Look at the color of your skin, Celeste, and tell me you understand its meaning."

Copper. Her skin, and the skin of everyone now in the village, was copper. She was surrounded by copper in Kumugwe's realm and Odin had bragged about "borrowing" riches from his brother's world. But what was its meaning?

"I'm sorry, but I don't. We all started turning copper-color after I rescued a little boy from a tree back at the children's home. At first we were scared, but it doesn't hurt and it seems more durable than the skin we used to have, but other than that, it doesn't mean anything."

Kumugwe looked exasperated. "Think harder," he told her.

She thought back to when she'd first arrived in the village with her flying frog companion and remembered how the villagers housed people of different races separately, a practice she'd found abhorrent.

"Is it to show us that we're all the same under our skin? That we're all just people?" She scratched at the mark on the back of her head. Her attempt at making sense of their color transformation didn't really explain how the change would be life-saving. She heard Odin laughing quietly behind his locked door.

"Such a noble-minded being you are, Celeste. You have been deceitful, yes, though I see now why. Your ultimate intentions have been pure. But no. *My* intentions had nothing to do with your species' apparent silly squabbles over skin tone. The copper in your skin is now in your blood as well."

Suddenly fearful that at any moment the copper in her blood would somehow harden and choke her, Celeste grabbed her throat reflexively. And then she felt foolish.

"As you have discovered," said Kumugwe, "it will not hurt you. On the contrary. I have given the gift of copper skin to those who were strong enough to survive the breaking of the planet and what you call the ooze that followed. Though I honestly feel no affinity toward topsiders, I saw no reason for them to perish unjustly."

"I still don't get it." Drained again from the confrontation and from thinking too hard, Celeste plopped back onto the bed.

"Do you not see? Do you not breathe freely in my realm? It is the copper in your blood, my gift to you and to all who have survived. You see, I truly am not a monster."

"Are you saying we can all breathe underwater now?"

"In my clean waters, yes, but only those whose intentions are pure. Knowing how easily you adjusted to my realm after your fall into my sea, I should not have doubted you. I am, um, sorry."

Celeste felt dizzy. She had to get back to Zoya. She had to stop the scientists from shaking the planet. Her head felt heavy and she wanted Kumugwe to stop talking, but he continued.

"The layer of ooze that killed your kinsmen did not grow deep enough to affect those of us below, but you tell me now it spreads again in a form poisonous to my domain. I see that I must stop it, and I will accept your help. I fear for my Harmony and do not understand why she has not yet returned to me. I fear the poisoned waters—Celeste? Wake up, child. Celeste?"

Celeste heard him calling her name from a distance, but couldn't rouse herself to respond.

She was floating, floating, floating away, and in the distance she could see two figures. They were trapped in long water tunnels and looked frightened. It was Nick and Chimney!

But they were in grave danger. Silvery-pink water swirled just beyond them and a horrible old woman peered at them from behind a tiny window.

"Help them, Zoya!" she called to the undulating mass of blurry head and tentacles.

"Help me!" Zoya's request was mournful. "They must all go away, even the gods who have failed to protect those of us in the sea and you on the land and you, you, you . . ."

Thud-thud-clink, thud-thud . . . clink, thud-thud . . .

~ **47** ~

[Harmony]

HARMONY PRETENDED to work diligently. She never gave the other girls any indication that she could hear them whispering about her. The blobs were abominable, and the idea that each contained some sort of control mechanism inside them—the same kind that was implanted inside her—made her sick.

She intended to find where they were embedded and remove them, but didn't know how she could do it without being discovered. Perhaps if she found just one, she could figure out a way to disable it. She had to find a way to disable the one in her own body.

"I think I did it!" Sharon shouted, and Harmony noted something different in the way she sounded. "Look! I finished one!"

When Harmony looked, she could see that Sharon had, in fact, changed again. She was smaller and younger than she'd been just moments earlier. Blanche's eyes opened wide and she stepped away from her project. She looked at Harmony, startled.

"What? You two are just jealous that I finished one first. What? Why are you staring at me that way?"

"Sharon," said Blanche, "you're, ah, different."

Sharon looked herself over and pulled up sleeves that were suddenly too long. "What the heck? Knock it off, Harmony, or I'll tell our parents who you really are!"

"It's not me, Sharon. I may be able to breathe underwater, but what's happening to you is none of my doing. If you're looking for someone to blame, talk to Lilith, but I think she will deny responsibility just as she has denied you. And do not threaten me, sister." Harmony's eyes turned icy blue.

"You look like you're only about ten," Blanche told her. "How do you feel?"

"I don't know. Weird. And full of energy, like I could swim to shore and run around the planet. I've never felt this good. It's sure better than being an achy old lady."

"Do you think you have your powers back?" Harmony asked. She hoped not.

"Let's see! If I do, then I should be able to morph into that scary white tiger that Blanche named—what was it? Oh yeah—Cassius. What a stupid name."

Blanche looked embarrassed. Sharon closed her eyes and grunted, but nothing happened. "Rats. I was really hoping I could do it again. Maybe if I try something smaller." She grunted again, but still, no change.

Harmony noticed she'd been holding her breath and finally let it out.

"Maybe we should go back and tell them what's happened," said Blanche. "What if it happens again, or to the rest of us?"

"I agree," said Harmony, "but Lilith left us no way to contact her. She said we'd know it was dinner time when Z— when the octopus raised its arm." Only she knew the name of the octopus. Only she could feel her pain.

"Oh, but you could swim back over to the door, sister, or are you just a normal girl now too?"

Harmony had to give her sister credit. As small as she was, Sharon could still deliver a big insult.

Harmony could pretend to be "just a normal girl," but it didn't feel right. And if she did swim over to the door, they'd know she had special powers. Just as she was about to answer Sharon, she heard Zoya's voice.

"Tunnels approach. Topsiders, two of them. They will be here soon. I will bring you all back now. Come." She raised her tentacle tunnel.

"Whoa! Do you think it heard us?" Sharon ran to the opening and was the first one inside. Blanche followed, and before Harmony got in, she sent Zoya a message.

"Give me a little more time! Take them back slowly! I must find something." She ran to the closest blob and dug her hands inside it, trying to feel something other than goo. It had to be something very small, and there was so much goo to plunge through, but finally she found something solid.

"Okay, I'm ready," she told Zoya, and slid into the creature's arm. Before she reached the lower vestibule, she hid the tiny chip deep in a pocket.

Lilith and Thurston appeared startled when she entered the main room with Sharon and Blanche.

"Well, well, well. What have we here? Back before your work is done?" Harmony heard displeasure in Lilith's voice. "And who, may I ask, is this?"

"It's me, Sharon. Something really weird happened and I just got younger. Look!" As if to prove what was already obvious to the others, she lifted her arms and kicked out a leg to demonstrate how large her clothes were.

"Well isn't that just silly. Right, Thurston? A silly, silly thing. But have you made progress with our kiddiwinks?"

Sharon's jaw dropped, and Blanche spoke up for her. "Yes, well, a little, but look at her! She's just a little girl now! Why? And will it happen to us too?"

Harmony could hear the girl's voice tremble and felt bad for her. She'd obviously been pretending not to be frightened for a long time and her mask was slipping.

Thurston, who had been standing at the hatch door and looking through the small window, walked over to Lilith and tugged on her sleeve.

"What are you doing?" Lilith slapped at his hand, but he persisted in pulling her to the window. Without saying a word, he positioned her so she was looking out into the sickly pink water.

"And well, well, well," she said again. This time, Harmony noted a hint of fear. "What have we here now? Have you little girlies done something wicked?"

Harmony saw Blanche's confused expression before the girl pushed Lilith brusquely out of the way to look out the window. Sharon, too short to see out of the window, jumped up and down next to her repeatedly to catch a glimpse.

When Blanche turned back around, she was almost as pale as Harmony. "It's my brother. And Nick. How'd they get here?" She looked to Harmony for an answer.

Harmony peered outside and recognized the boys from her short visit in the village after she had pushed away the enormous sea-filled cloud. She'd been a twisted little thing then, and Sharon had pulled her away from the laughing people. She had wanted to stay with them.

"Brother?" Lilith snapped. "And another boy? What will be next? Flying sea horses and smiling sharks?"

"We tried that already, lily pad, don't you remember?" Thurston smiled goofily and turned to the girls. "Didn't work!"

"Tell them to go away. There's no room at the Inn. Ha! And you, missy, better watch how you treat your superiors." Lilith shoved Blanche against the door and returned to her warm beverage.

Harmony could see the boys were frightened inside the water tunnels, but she knew the crabs wouldn't harm them. They would be all right as long as they didn't try to leave the tunnels. The crabs would have had a good reason to deliver the boys to her, but what was it?

Zoya spoke to her. "They have come to rescue Celeste. You were right about your father Kumugwe. He detains the girl in his castle, too long, and she is dying. You must find a way to bring the boys to her, especially the one called Nick."

"Tell them to go away? That's my brother out there! We have to bring them in." Harmony could see tears threatening to spill from Blanche's startled eyes.

"I thought *this* was your new family, Blanche." Sharon sneered, and Blanche looked helpless.

"I will take them away and ensure they will never return again." Harmony was excited about her plan, especially since she would finally be reunited with Kumugwe again.

"And how do you intend to do that, ghost?" Lilith yawned as if she didn't care one way or the other.

"Well, I haven't shared this with you yet because I didn't know your intentions. Now that I do and am anxious to help, I'll tell you."

Harmony had to pretend she was excited about their plans to control the topsiders.

"I can swim for a very long time underwater. Don't ask me how. I'll pull the tunnel far, far away so we won't have to see or hear from them again. I don't imagine any topsiders will follow after these two don't return."

She saw a look of horror in Blanche's eyes.

"Now you're talking," said Sharon. "I was starting to wonder about you, sister."

Lilith sat up straight and her eyes darted between Sharon and Harmony.

"That's what good friends call each other topside," Harmony said quickly, and Lilith relaxed.

"Make it so, then, and until you return, your other two sisters will get back to work. Down the hatch you go, girlies. I'll bring you back when your pale sister returns."

"How about a hug before I go?" Harmony intended to relay information to Blanche. She planned to tell her she'd ensure Chimney's safety. But she'd have to touch foreheads with the girl for it to happen.

"Yeah, right!" Sharon pushed away Harmony's open arms as she walked by.

Blanche looked at Harmony as if she were insane. When Harmony grabbed her arm, doing her best to coax her into an embrace, Blanche pushed her away like she'd pushed Lilith earlier.

So, you actually have chosen a new family now, Harmony thought, *and left your only true blood to die.*

"Let her out, Thurstie," Lilith commanded her husband, and he joined Harmony at the door.

"You're a good girl," he whispered to her, and then pushed her into the outer chamber. Before he opened the outermost door, she looked back at him, searching for . . . something again.

Harmony noted the boys' fear when they saw her swimming toward them, and watched as they tried unsuccessfully to retreat back through the slippery tunnels. She grabbed the closest ends and pulled them away from Zoya and out of the putrid water.

It felt good to be home again.

~ 48 ~

[The Village / Orville]

AFTER DIVING AGAIN and again into the deep water beneath the cavern in search of Nick and Chimney, Orville dragged himself onto the muddy bank, his beautiful wings sodden and heavy upon his back.

"What have I done?" he wailed, but the cavern walls simply resounded his question.

He pulled himself to his feet, tears streaming from his eyes, and stood for moments longer scanning the surface of the water. He wondered how he would break the news to the villagers.

Why had Noor sent them to this gods-forsaken place? Was it a message that all was lost? That Celeste had failed? That they were all destined to become sacrificial lambs? But for what purpose? And if so, why hadn't the murderous crustaceans taken him too?

A deep rumbling sent ripples across the surface of the water. Odd rusty objects fell from where they'd been lodged in the cavern walls. Orville ran back through the tunnel and up the ladder into the cold laboratory where surgical instruments and glass beakers crashed onto the floor from the vibration.

Hastily he grabbed schematics from countertops and fled up through the crumbling house, making it out and onto the charred field just as the secret stairway collapsed onto itself. Running toward the forest, he remembered his wings, but they were too wet to lift him from the ground. He thought he'd never make it back to the village.

Merts met him shortly after he entered the forest and glided along with him just as the sky opened, sending pelting rain and hail and wind that rattled the trees.

"When gods are away / Children will play tricks on us / Sensing your sorrow."

"I am lost, Merts! The boys—they are gone. What will I tell the others? They look to me for answers to questions that are absurd!"

"Tell them all you know / Even if all appears lost / Someone will be found."

"But how do you know? Is it Celeste? Will she be found? And how do you know these things?" Panting from exertion, Orville had to shout over the blustery winds that whistled through the creaking trees.

"We three are but one / In tune with the universe / Seeking normalcy."

Orville was too tired and distraught to try to make sense of their answer.

The odd archers moved to a distance ahead of him as they hurried through the forest. At the halfway point, as quickly as the storm had started, it stopped. Bright sunlight flooded through the sparse foliage and the resultant rising steam from the sopping undergrowth turned everything into a mirage.

Orville slowed to a walk and shuddered. "Huge, hideous crabs plucked the boys from the edge of a deep water hole below the sunken house right before my eyes. It happened so quickly, they did not have a chance to defend themselves. What will I say? What will I do?"

"You will find the words / The flux has taken many / They will understand."

Orville wasn't convinced. Other than those who had died in their ill-planned attack on the village, he hadn't heard of any other deaths since the sea had receded. Then again, Merts seemed to have access to information no one else had, so he supposed the fluxes could have taken other lives.

Noor had given him hope. But how could he be sure of anyone's or anything's intentions anymore?

Despite his desire to return to Riku, each step he took brought him closer to having to explain the horrifying tragedy. He was grateful that Mac had taken Jack and Katie back to the village. The children had been right to be scared. Orville couldn't imagine if they too had been devoured.

There would be no clear message from Merts, though he believed they meant well, so he trudged onward in silence.

As Merts and Orville neared the far side of the forest they smelled smoke, and not the smoke from a cooking pit. Orville ran past Merts into the open and saw a house porch on fire. It was climbing up the front of the structure.

Was Noor on the attack?

Someone had already organized the villagers into a bucket line from the pond to the house with younger children running the empty buckets back, and Orville could hear Mason chanting as he filled each empty container.

"Ladybug ladybug fly away home, your house is on fire your children are gone, rock-a-bye baby in the treetop, when the wind blows, the cradle will rock, when the wind blows, the fire will rise, fire and ice and bug in the skies, where is the baby the baby who cries, look in her eyes, her sea-green eyes."

"Orville!" Riku ran to him. "Chaos has reigned since you left. Rumbling clouds, rain, biting cold, blistering sunshine, lightning bolts—one that struck the porch—Ryder tends to two injured children," she searched behind him, "where are the boys?"

So it wasn't Noor.

"First, the fire," he said, and as soon as he joined the effort, storm clouds came rolling back toward the village at an alarming pace.

"Hurry!" someone shouted, and Orville saw several people flinch after looking to the sky.

As if hitting an invisible wall far above the village, the clouds stopped overhead and billowed into one enormous towering threat. Everyone stopped their frantic firefighting efforts and stared at the bizarre sight. An ominous silence surrounded the scene. And then, snowflakes fell, softly at first, and then as if someone had popped a gossamer bubble surrounding the immense cloud.

The bulk of the snow dropped with a WHOOMP onto the flaming porch, extinguishing the flames and sizzling in the heat, and the rest spread into a slippery sheet between the houses and the pond.

Orville watched in awe as the children abandoned their buckets and—evidently—their fear and frolicked in the short-lived wonderland.

Empty of its load, the cloud disappeared and the sun returned, melting the snow and creating another steamy mirage. Orville heard sighs of relief and nervous laughter, and when the villagers had reverted to a state of stunned silence, Riku repeated her question.

"Where are the boys?"

The others gathered around the two. Orville looked at each of them before responding and could see anticipation heavy in their weary faces, their eyes surreptitiously scanning the sky for the next unpredictable flux.

"I wish I could tell you I knew where they were, but I cannot." He would not tell the overwrought crowd what he had told Merts about the black crabs. It was simply too awful. Holding Riku and looking into her eyes, he felt her horror and realized she was witnessing what he had witnessed on the muddy banks of the water hole. It was too much to bear.

"Noor!" he howled to the heavens. "Where are you! What have you done?"

When he looked back around at the faces in the group, he saw only their tears.

~ **49** ~

[Celeste]

. . . CLINK.

In her loss of consciousness, not only could Celeste hear the struggling octopus's three hearts beating, she also could hear what was happening inside the creature's body as if she were one with Zoya.

"Welcome back, Celeste." The octopus acknowledged the presence of her essence.

"Where am I?" she asked the beautiful creature. "And what are these horrible people planning?"

"It must end soon, though I fear they are not yet finished using me."

"There's so much noise. Who's that horrible woman and what is she screaming? I feel one of your arms—one of my arms?—growing heavy. It hurts."

"Yes, it hurts," Zoya agreed. "The woman you hear gave birth to two daughters as different from one another as you are to me. The woman and her husband plan an escape, for despite their cruel manipulation of my body, their experiments with the water have destabilized me and all surrounding me. I have hurt for too long now and welcome this new pain, for it cannot continue forever."

"Forever. Never forever," Celeste whispered in Zoya's consciousness. "And are you and I truly that different?"

"Ah, Celeste, you have knowledge still unknown to you. And now your mind must leave mine and return to your slumbering body, for Harmony will soon be reunited with her father, and you with—"

Like a diamond needle being lifted from a vinyl album in the middle of a rousing symphony, Zoya's voice disconnected from Celeste's subconscious and she felt herself snap back into her own immobile body. She tried to scream "With whom? I'll be reunited with whom?" but she remained trapped in her own head.

And then she heard something that both frightened and entranced her: the lilting giggle of a child mingled with an echo-vibration of a young woman.

"Can it be?" she heard Kumugwe say.

Celeste realized the god had been shaking her gently, trying in vain to waken her. She sensed his hasty departure from her side and felt the swirling of water as he threw open the massive door to his castle.

"Father!" she heard the young woman's voice, and felt herself buffeted gently on the bed when she sensed Kumugwe had flapped his great tail to greet the approaching visitor.

"Harmony! It is you! And still as beautiful as you were when I sent you off to find the girl now asleep in your chamber!"

"Oh, father, but can you not see how I have changed? I'm a woman now."

"You are my little music maker," Kumugwe's voice cracked. "Your beauty has always shone from within. I thought I had lost you!"

Celeste's tears mingling with the salt water surrounding her, though she still couldn't move. Harmony was reunited with her loving father, and it was a beautiful thing to hear. She felt the joy in their hearts.

She forgave the girl who had held her captive.

"And what is this baggage you drag behind you in the tunnels?" the god asked.

"Topsiders from Celeste's village," said Harmony.

Celeste's heart struggled to beat faster. Why couldn't she open her eyes?

"They were so frightened when they saw me that I feared for their safety, so I filled their tunnels with sleep."

"Ah! But let me hug you once more before you make me understand this most unusual homecoming!"

"Hey! Remember me?" Odin's voice sounded more animated than it had been since his imprisonment, and his door rattled unimpressively. "How about releasing me now that your little girl has returned. And why have I not heard from my little buddy in a while? Celeste? Are you still there, Celeste?"

She tried to tell him she was there, that she had been there this whole time, but could not.

"Leave the tunnels with the lions, Harmony, and come with me," Kumugwe spoke quietly. He ignored Odin's plea.

Celeste sensed the two when they entered her room and tried once again to rouse herself.

"It's her!" said Harmony. "It's my runaway playmate!"

Celeste heard Harmony weeping, and even the sound of her lamentation was glorious.

"I didn't know, father. I didn't know I was hurting her. And now horrible people—the very people who threw me to the mercy of your waters—are hurting one of your creatures. Their work threatens the entire planet and even you are not safe. You must come with me, and quickly, and we must find a way to stop them."

"I might help," Odin offered, but his offer went unanswered.

"But what of the girl and those in the tunnels?" he asked, and a flash of fear warmed Celeste's copper blood.

"She was to help me somehow, but look at her. Perhaps if we put them together in one tunnel, they will know what to do for her."

"If their intentions are pure, they will need no tunnel. If not, then their lives mean nothing to me and—save for their eyeballs, which my lions know are my favorite—the topsiders may serve as sustenance for my creatures. It has been too long since I have enjoyed fresh jellied delicacies."

Celeste was horrified by everything she'd just heard and struggled to move, and Odin made a sound of revulsion behind his door.

"Put the topsiders together and I will carry the girl to their tunnel. I will pull them far away from my castle and set them free. The girl will survive, though I do not know the others."

"We must be fast, father. I sensed unrest in the cruel people when I pulled the tunnels away from the poisoned water and Zoya, the creature who has been greatly wronged."

Celeste felt herself lifted and carried through the water and sensed a shift in the atmosphere when she was deposited in a sleepy-air-filled tunnel. Helpless to move, she could only wait until the tunnel filled with sea water, and the topsiders, whoever they were, awoke. She knew they would panic as she had before she learned she could breathe underwater. She hoped they were good people.

She felt the swift pull of the tunnel and then a soft drifting when Kumugwe released it. It wouldn't take long before she'd sense the struggle of the waking villagers.

Cool water filled the undulating tunnel slowly and her body rose until it touched the top of it. And then, violent swirls of water buffeted her. The sleepers, now wide awake, were panicking in an oxygen-depleted trap.

"Chimney! NO!" She heard Nick's voice—it was Nick and Chimney!—as he expelled the last oxygen from his lungs.

"Help!" She heard Chimney's last cry and then waited, tortured by her inability to help two of her best friends.

Another soft wave of water jostled her before a moment of serenity, and then she felt arms around her.

"I'm scared, Nick." Chimney's voice was clear and strong. They had survived the transition from gasping to breathing freely. "What's happened? How'd we get here? Is she dead?"

"No, Chim, she's alive. See? She's breathing too."

She heard Nick's trembling voice, and as he gathered her more closely to him, the blood in her veins began to warm and the back of her head began to tingle.

"Wake her up, Nick, I wanna go home!"

"I'm not sure how to do that, buddy."

"Well, kiss her or something. Isn't that what they do in the stories Maddie used to tell us?"

Celeste's heart skipped a beat and she wondered if the smile on her lips showed. And then she felt Nick's warm lips upon hers, and every inch of her flesh felt like melted butter.

The feeling startled her—had she melted away again?—and in her fear she jolted from his arms, opening her eyes wide and witnessing the astonished expressions on the two boys' faces. She returned to Nick's arms, and the two pulled Chimney into their embrace.

"I wanna go home," Chimney whimpered once the awkward moment had passed. "But they have Blanche. I saw her through a window, and I know she saw me and she was scared like me."

"It's true," said Nick. "And are we really breathing underwater?"

Celeste just smiled. She couldn't take her eyes away from his. She couldn't believe he had risked his life to find her.

He returned her smile, and after another awkward silence, he continued.

"One minute we were with Orville and we were looking for you—this huge dragonfly showed us where to go—and all of a sudden we were in this tunnel and a really white girl was pulling us through the water and we fell asleep. I don't know what happened to Orville."

"Can we get her outta there?" Chimney asked.

Celeste believed she could find her way back to Zoya, but didn't know how she would rescue Blanche from the submarine and its cruel people. And if she found a way, would Chimney's sister survive the journey back to land? She had no reason to believe the girl's intentions had suddenly evolved to a state of what Kumugwe considered to be "pure." She would surely perish underwater.

"We'll try, Chim. I know the way." She grabbed both boys' hands and pulled them out of the tunnel. "Now follow me and swim as I do. Let your arms relax and flap your feet as if you had a big fish tail."

She looked at Nick then and smiled again. When he smiled back, she felt her strength return. And she felt more than just the mark on her head tingle.

~ 50 ~

[Harmony]

"THERE! NOT MUCH FARTHER." Harmony pointed to the edge of where the sick water spread insidiously toward them. She and Kumugwe had covered the great distance between Kumugwe's castle and the suffering octopus faster than Harmony could have imagined. She knew it was possible only because the water god was with her.

"What is this atrocity?" Kumugwe boomed, and then coughed when he inhaled a ribbon of foul water. "Where is the creature?"

"She is deeper still inside this poison, kept alive by the wicked scientists and their mechanical contraptions camouflaged by her body. Do you hear her heart beat, father?"

Kumugwe seemed to listen, and Harmony noted his fury building.

"Stay behind me, daughter." He waved her back with a gentle swish of his hand, moving himself back and away from the pink water as he did so.

"What will you do? They've done unspeakable things, and you see now how they've transformed the water into something even you cannot endure."

"This is true. I cannot endure it for a moment longer."

Harmony watched as Kumugwe filled his lungs with clean water. His massive chest expanded until she thought it might burst, and then she realized what he was about to do.

With a gentle, steady exhalation he blew toward the atrocity until the poisoned water dispersed. Slowly, Zoya's nearest limbs came into view, no longer camouflaged, and Harmony feared for her.

The creature's weak voice called to her. "You are too late. They have gone."

"When? Where? They've escaped, father, and without a thought about me!" As much as she despised the woman who'd given birth to her, the realization that the woman had abandoned her yet again—presumably to die with the topsiders—hurt even more deeply somehow.

"Yes, Harmony, I too can hear my creatures when I am near them." Kumugwe's brow furrowed and he gazed far beyond Zoya.

"You will not see them, Kumugwe," Zoya spoke. "The moment Harmony departed to move the topsiders away from harm, Lilith commanded the others. The man and girls filled my two hollowed arms with things called kiddiwinks from the cavern. There were many sharp, heavy objects too."

Harmony opened her eyes wide in anticipation of her next words, already feeling the horror of what Zoya was about to say.

"With blades of white fire they severed my laden limbs from my body. After that, a powerful blast ejected their metal orb from me and battered my insides. I watched as the orb sent out unnatural arms to hook and pull away my severed limbs."

"But, how are you still—"

"Alive?" Zoya finished Harmony's question. "They left without taking the heart they created to keep me animated and able, though barely, to maintain my concealment. I cannot die while the contraption clinks on. I do not know that I can tolerate the sound of its hideous beat any longer. And yet, I cannot stop it."

"But wait!" Harmony closed her eyes. "Celeste speaks to me. The key! Something about a key. She tells me what I must do to stop your pain." Her eyes flew open and she looked at the orichalcum-embossed spear Kumugwe carried, the one Celeste had returned to the sea. In Kumugwe's great hand, it seemed to have increased in size to match its bearer.

Harmony looked into Zoya's compassionate eyes then and wailed, and through the music of her sorrow, she felt Zoya smile.

"Do it, child," the octopus whispered. "I should have died long, long ago. Even my own children have gone before me."

Feeling the need for her father's permission to perform a hideous task, she turned to Kumugwe and extended her hand toward his spear. He met her gaze and, sensing her intentions, handed her the weapon.

The villagers had called it the Spear of Sorrow, and now Harmony understood why. She marveled at the beauty of its design and knew it had the power to do what its owner wished.

She wished for it to flood Zoya with peaceful memories of a time before her horrors began. She wished for it to kill her without pain.

Harmony closed her eyes again to hear another message from Celeste, who told her to aim the spear near the top of Zoya's bulbous head, away from her eyes. There she would find all three hearts. She shuddered, and saw Zoya close her sad eyes.

Thud-thud-clink, thud-thud-clink, thud-thud-clink . . .

Her aim true, Harmony hurled the spear and watched as it plunged into the soft flesh of the magnificent octopus.

Thud-clink, . . . thud . . . , and then, a whispered "thank you."

Zoya's ravaged body relaxed and flattened into the sediment on the sea floor. She was gone.

Many moments passed in silence before Kumugwe moved to retrieve his spear, and when he turned back to face Harmony, she saw rage in his eyes.

"How could this have happened in my realm?" he bellowed. "Topsiders will pay for what they have done to my waters!"

Harmony gasped when he grabbed her hand, and before she could stop the powerful god, he lifted his spear and his chest high and then slammed the blunt end of the weapon down.

An instantaneous shockwave spread out from where they suddenly stood on nearly dry ground. Harmony watched in awe as the water rose in great waves in a circle around them and rolled away in every direction. The planet beneath them shuddered in response.

"They weakened the planet with their experiments, father!" Harmony shouted to Kumugwe, who looked startled by what had just occurred. "Your brother! Celeste and the boys! Your lions! Hurry!"

Diving into a retreating wave, Harmony swam as fast as she could northward toward the castle. Kumugwe was soon right by her side. She noted apprehension in his face, which did nothing to alleviate her own dread over the repercussions of her father's brash act.

When they reached the castle, all was in ruins and sea lions were swirling away in every direction.

"Odin!" Kumugwe shouted, and from deep within the ruins, Harmony could hear the sky god shout back.

"What have you done, brother? Your walls have fallen in on me!"

"Help us!" Harmony felt her mind fuse with Celeste's again and sensed she was in grave danger—a swirling, tumbling, out-of-control sensation gripped her.

Without a word to Kumugwe, she swam off in pursuit of the girl who was more than just a girl. Odin would remain weak as long as he was trapped underwater, but she knew he wouldn't die. She was not so sure about Celeste, and she was less certain about the girl's friends.

She sensed they were very far away and feared the growing tsunami would pull them along too quickly as it grew, too quickly for her to reach them in time. Ultimately, the wave they were in would crash against the enormous cliff wall to the north, the one from which Harmony had first lured Celeste to her sandcastle. She didn't even want to think about what the wave would do to the south.

She swam faster and tried to make contact with the girl. She sensed nothing but the fast-approaching northern wall, and then, was it them? Three bodies clinging to one another rolled away from her, but she was closing the gap. When she flapped her legs harder—desperate to rescue the hapless topsiders—something felt different, but she had no time to wonder.

"Harmony! Stop!" Kumugwe's voice startled her, but still she pushed forward, oblivious to a new danger ahead.

An enormous boulder crashed through the water in front of her just as she thought she could close the distance between her and the topsiders, and she barely stopped herself from slamming into it. She turned to witness Kumugwe's rapid approach and then a great WHOOMP of rock-fall cut him off from her, leaving a newly formed granite island between them.

Stunned and torn between her rescue mission and her father, she remained in one place as she felt the power of the tsunami subside.

Once again, she was too late.

~ 51 ~

[The Village / Orville]

"WHAT ARE THOSE horrible things?" Orville heard someone cry.

"How could they? How awful!" said another.

"Those poor boys! Why did they spare you, Orville?"

Orville looked back around at the faces in the crowd and shuddered. Everyone around him, including his beautiful Riku, had eyes the color of alabaster.

"I . . . there were only two . . . What has happened here?" He stared into Riku's blank eyes and felt disturbed by his inability to focus.

"Do not look puzzled, beautiful man. We can see you, and one another, and what you have experienced. Do you not feel the power of this new flux?" Riku held him tightly.

He did not.

"But, what does this mean? How will this help us?" Squinting in the bright sunlight, he searched the sky again for Noor. "I could not help two of the most kind-hearted beings in our village."

Before he could concentrate on what he was seeing and hearing, huge gusts of wind forced Orville and those around him to brace. Then, like newly bloomed flowers following the arc of a stray sun, all turned their faces to the north.

"Another wave approaches!" someone shouted.

"We see it, you know," another responded.

"The wall!" Orville remembered. "Bridger's wall will hold! I'm sure of it." But he wasn't, really.

He saw Mason pushing his way toward him through the wind and the crowd in a manner unlike the man, and it frightened him. He moved away from Riku, unsure of the man's intentions.

"Come with me. Get ready." Mason grabbed his arm and moved him away from the crowd.

"Get ready for what, good man, and where are you taking me?" Orville was too startled by the eccentric man's forcefulness to protest right away, but he finally pulled free from Mason's strong grasp.

"She's almost here. Fly me up to her as she passes over. She's expecting us." Mason's speech had changed too. It was abrupt and direct.

Moments later the sky darkened and Noor hovered overhead.

"Now. Fly me up to her. She's too big to land." Mason wrapped his arms tightly around Orville's shoulders and closed his eyes.

"Do as he says," Noor spoke to him, and without taking a moment to consider what he was about to do, Orville extended his damp wings, gave them a forceful shake, and took to the sky.

"Sorry, Layla," he heard Lou far below, "but there ain't no way these feathers'll lift you off the ground."

Orville landed on the flat of Noor's back with Mason still clinging to him, and as soon as both men's feet were planted, Noor flew north. In a flash they were over the wall Bridger had built to stop the last wave and Orville could see that the approaching wall of water, greatly diminished over the distance it had traveled, would be no match for the barrier.

Though he was no longer near the villagers, he could hear them all cheering.

"Close your eyes and see," Noor told him. He wasn't about to question the fire-breathing dragonfly. He closed his eyes and could see as if through the eyes of every joyful villager. The vision made him dizzy and he fell backward onto Mason, who was already seated. The man laughed.

"Mind-blowing, right?" Mason sounded like nearly every other man he'd met. There was no indication at all of a scattered mind.

"Right. Where are we going, Mason?" Orville needed to ask, but his memory, or rather Celeste's memory, gave him the answer. He shook his head in an effort to separate his knowledge of the mountain from Celeste's, but couldn't. They were on a direct path toward Old Man Massive.

"So you know," said Mason, and Orville was aware that his own thoughts were now pooled with everyone else's.

He knew what it had felt like being connected to Celeste without the need to speak, but this new melding of minds and visions was overwhelming. Orville hesitated before answering, unsure of what he knew to be true and how it might be influenced by what he wanted to believe.

"But why are we heading to Old Man Massive? How can the mountain spirit help us?" He remembered Celeste telling him how Old Man Massive had protected and advised her after she'd run away from the children's home, so perhaps his spirit was still communicating with her.

Orville could only hope for that to be true.

Visions of the innocent boys and the horrifying crabs flashed through his mind, and he directed his next question to Noor. "Why, Noor? What good did you expect would come from us finding the water hole below that house?"

"Events unfold as they must," she said.

"And now you sound like Merts." Orville was not amused. "Two young men died needlessly and we are no closer to finding Celeste or Harmony, the crippled child you said she was to help. Was it Celeste you dropped into the water? Tell me, please, and why?"

"Close your eyes again and feel," said Noor.

Orville looked into Mason's alabaster eyes to find some kind of message, but Mason just smiled. Orville obeyed, and waited. What was he supposed to feel other than the wind ruffling his feathers and the sense of expectation and hope in the hearts of all the villagers?

He felt that.

He also picked up vibrations from Old Man Massive, and the closer they got to him, the stronger they felt.

"Can you hear them now?" asked Noor.

Orville squeezed his eyes together tightly and tried to interpret what he felt and heard. Softly at first, and then stronger as they neared the fallen cliffside, he could hear them.

Boom-boom, boom-boom, boom-boom—three distinct hearts beating slowly. It sounded and felt like three hearts beating in the bodies of three people deep in slumber.

Excited by the possibility that one of the hearts could be Celeste's, Orville opened his eyes in time to see an unusual new island south of where Old Man Massive's cliffs once stood.

And even more unusual, beyond that he saw something leaping from the water. It was a young woman with long hair and skin as white as the snow that had just fallen, her powerful tail as white as the rest of her.

When Orville caught the alabaster mermaid's sea-green eyes, he sensed her fear and watched as she disappeared beneath the water near the island. One moment later, Noor circled in a slow wide arc around the crumbled mountain.

Though barely discernable, the face Orville saw in the boulders as he peered over Noor's side to the land below had to be that of Old Man Massive.

"It . . . is done," the deep voice boomed slowly from granite lips. Orville acknowledged the mountain was speaking to Noor. "They . . . are safe within."

As Noor continued her glide around the collapsed mountain, Mason jumped to his feet and leaned precariously over her glistening wings.

"Take us down, Noor," said Mason. But before they landed, he began to shout below.

Orville stared at him in wonder and disbelief.

"Celeste! Can you hear me, Celeste? If you're in there, please answer me!" Mason's voice was powerful.

"Who are you, my good man?" Orville was baffled, but Mason ignored him.

"Answer me, daughter! Your daddy has come to bring you home!"

Somewhere in the deepest recesses of his brain, Orville could feel the villagers holding their collective breath.

And he held his.

~ EPILOGUE ~

CELESTE SAT BOLT UPRIGHT in a dry, dark cave and held her head in her hands. Pain burned between her temples and she saw stars and swirls of color flashing in her brain. It took several moments before she remembered what had just happened.

"Nick? Are you there? Chimney? Where are you? Where are we?"

Hearing nothing but the echo of her own heart, she crawled around on the wobbly rocks blindly searching for her friends.

~ ~ ~ ~ ~

Far, far away from the village, a great wave crashed onto a muddy shoreline, leaving behind a cracked submarine and two enormous, severed octopus limbs from which bizarre objects squiggled out.

~ ~ ~ ~ ~

And in the village, people and creatures regained their normal vision and gazed, expectantly, into the sky.

~ ~ ~ ~ ~

END
Look for the last book in the Waterwight series in 2018!

~ Acknowledgments ~

I could never have written any of my books without the constant encouragement and support of my husband, Mike, who believes in me—and in the power of my storytelling! He gave me a wonderful idea about my character Mason, and I heard Zoya's heartbeat while he pulled me on my paddleboard behind his kayak on Twin Lakes, where an insistent dragonfly also visited me. Mike has provided me with a lifetime of experiences for tickling my muse.

My buddy John Orville Stewart, namesake for one of my most significant characters, continues to inspire ideas during our morning walks. He reminded me about the importance of teamwork, and also suggested an archer character, though he could not have foreseen what I'd do with that suggestion!

Carol Bellhouse, thank you for entertaining me with brilliant bubble bath edits of my manuscript, and Stephanie Spong, thank you for constantly questioning my plot, my thought process, and my deadlines. Both of you, my cherished author friends, have encouraged me to talk through my most outrageous ideas, and have helped me to maintain my focus (most of the time).

Sherry Randall, thank you for suggesting we experience a "float," thus inspiring the idea for how I could use suspended animation!

Erin Sue Grantham, thank you for encouraging me to write fantasy. Waiting for your book!

Cindy Jewkes of *Good Tales Editing*, thank you for proofreading my manuscript given a ridiculous time constraint. You found errors I never would have seen! If there are any proofing errors in this manuscript, they are there only because I continued to edit after you proofread.

Olivia McHargue, thank you for requesting that I include a horse named Layla in Book II. I hope you like this silent mare. Just wait till you see what happens with her in Book III!

Ben Howe, thank you for your painting of Old Man Massive with a doorway! You inspired an idea I modified at the end of this book.

Many thanks to Tom Austin and Jennifer Stewart, who provided valuable feedback before publication, and to Aiyana Feuereisen Kemp and Camila Martinez, who routinely checked in on my writing progress.

Thanks also to Leadville locals who continue to support my writing with their services and promotion: Beth and Kenny Donoher at *Silver City Printing*, Brenda Marine at *B&B Shipping and More*, Elise Sunday at Fire *On The Mountain*, Marcia Martinek at the *Herald Democrat*, and Christine Whittington at *Colorado Mountain College*. Thanks also to Lisa Marvel at *The Book Haven* in Salida for your author events.

And, of course, thank you, kind readers. If you enjoyed Celeste's continuing quest, please consider posting a review!

~ About the Author ~

LAUREL McHARGUE was raised in Braintree, Massachusetts, but somehow found her way to the breathtaking elevation of Leadville, Colorado, where she has taught and currently lives with her husband and Ranger, the German Shepherd.

She established *Leadville Literary League* to promote local literary endeavors and the arts, and she also has been known to act.

Visit Laurel in Leadville and/or check out her blog where she writes about her adventures.

www.leadvillelaurel.com

~ A Personal Note from Laurel ~

I would love to hear from you!
Connect with me here:

Facebook: Leadville Laurel (author page)
Twitter: @LeadvilleLaurel
LinkedIn: Laurel (Bernier) McHargue
Web Page: www.leadvillelaurel.com
Email: laurel@strackpress.com

Check out my other books on my Amazon Author page and
let me know what you think!
The Waterwight Series is not yet over.

Watch for Book III
in 2018

And remember, we struggling authors/musicians/artists/actors
love positive feedback, so if you like what we do, please
consider writing reviews of our work! If you don't like what
we do, well, if you can't say something nice . . .

SYNONYM GLOSSARY

Abate	End, stop, halt
Abhorrent	Hateful, repulsive, disgusting
Abrupt	Sudden, hasty, quick
Abundant	Plentiful, copious, ample
Affront	Insult, injury, disrespect
Agitate	Shake, mix, disturb
Alleviate	Ease, lessen, relieve
Ambient	Surrounding
Amble	Stroll, wander, mosey
Amorphous	Formless, shapeless, vague
Androgynous	Genderless, asexual, neuter
Animate	Live, conscious, sentient
Anomaly	Irregularity, difference, abnormality
Aversion	Dislike, hatred, loathing
Bedraggled	Unkempt, disheveled, untidy
Benevolent	Kind, caring, compassionate
Boisterous	Energetic, noisy, overexcited
Brash	Hasty, foolhardy, impatient
Brazen	Bold, shameless, blatant
Brusquely	Abruptly, harshly, roughly
Buffet	Rock, bang, strike

SYNONYM GLOSSARY

Bulbous	Round, bulging, globular
Buoy	Float, sustain, lift
Camouflage	Disguise, conceal, hide
Carnage	Killing, bloodshed, massacre
Catastrophe	Disaster, upheaval, tragedy
Celestial	Heavenly, cosmic, astronomic
Censure	Criticism, disapproval, scorn
Churn	Mix, shake, toss
Circumnavigate	Orbit, circle, revolve
Cleave to	Stick closely to something
Colossal	Huge, massive, gigantic
Composure	Self-control, poise
Concentric	Sharing the same center
Conglomeration	Hodgepodge, collection, mass
Conjure	Mesmerize, charm, trick
Contempt	Dislike, disrespect, scorn
Contort	Twist, warp, deform
Contrite	Sorry, regretful, apologetic
Crass	Blundering, tactless, insensitive
Curmudgeon	Killjoy, wet blanket
Dank	Clammy, soggy, damp

SYNONYM GLOSSARY

Deluge	Flood, surge, downpour
Demise	Death, end, passing
Despicable	Dreadful, wicked, vile
Detritus	Trash, litter, garbage
Diaphanous	Delicate, transparent, gauzy
Disconcerting	Disturbing, alarming, upsetting
Distraught	Upset, worried, troubled
Eerie	Spooky, creepy, weird
Elude	Avoid, escape, flee
Emaciated	Thin, scrawny, wasted
Empath	Shares feelings of others
Enunciate	Pronounce, speak, vocalize
Eons	Years, eternities, eras
Errant	Wayward, stray
Erratic	Unpredictable, irregular, inconsistent
Ethereal	Fragile, ghostly, unearthly
Exuberance	Excitement, enthusiasm, cheerfulness
Feign	Fake, pretend, sham
Flux	Fluctuation, change, mutability
Forlorn	Lonely, pitiful, abandoned
Formidable	Tough, difficult, intimidating

SYNONYM GLOSSARY

Frantic	Panicky, hysterical, worried
Futile	Useless, pointless, unsuccessful
Gelatinous	Jellylike, gooey, viscous
Gossamer	Delicate, sheer, ethereal
Guileless	Honest, open, straightforward
Hapless	Unlucky, unfortunate, ill-fated
Imminent	Looming, forthcoming, pending
Incantation	Chant, prayer, spell
Incessant	Non-stop, ceaseless, persistent
Kinship	Similarity, connection, understanding
Lure	Bait, trap, entice
Lurk	Loiter, wait, skulk
Malice	Nastiness, cruelty, meanness
Menace	Threat, danger, hazard
Mesmerize	Hypnotize, captivate, charm
Minion	Follower, underling, assistant
Miniscule	Tiny, little, miniature
Nacreous	Iridescent clouds
Nebulous	Unclear, hazy, ill-defined
Nefarious	Wicked, evil, despicable
Nictitating	Third eyelid or membrane

SYNONYM GLOSSARY

Nuptial	Marriage, union
Oblivion	Forgetfulness, extinction, obscurity
Ominous	Threatening, warning, menacing
Oppressive	Repressive, overbearing
Pallid	Pale, ashen, colorless
Palpable	Intense, physical, substantial
Patronizing	Superior, belittling, demeaning
Pearlescent	Having a pearly luster
Perch	Sit, rest, balance
Perplex	Baffle, confuse, mystify
Phosphorescent	Luminous, bright, warm
Plaintive	Mournful, sorrowful, sad
Plummet	Fall, plunge, drop
Precipitously	Hastily, swiftly, rashly
Preen	Groom, clean, smooth
Protuberance	Protrusion, outgrowth
Raucous	Loud, harsh, hoarse
Realm	Kingdom, dominion, territory
Recede	Retreat, withdraw, ebb
Resolute	Firm, unyielding, unwavering
Resound	Echo, resonate, boom

SYNONYM GLOSSARY

Resourcefulness	Inventiveness, creativity, imagination
Reverberate	Echo, resound, vibrate
Revulsion	Disgust, distaste, horror
Ruckus	Disturbance, commotion, uproar
Rudimentary	Basic, elementary, undeveloped
Scrutinize	Study, examine, analyze
Serene	Calm, peaceful, quiet
Sodden	Soaked, wet, drenched
Soufflé	Egg-based baked dish
Subtle	Understated, indirect, elusive
Sumptuous	Superb, extravagant, lavish
Sundry	Various, assorted, different
Surreptitious	Secretive, sneaky, stealthy
Tarnation	Damnation
Throng	Mob, crowd, group
Tranquil	Calm, peaceful, restful
Trepidation	Fear, anxiety, foreboding
Trite	Tired, commonplace, worn
Trudge	Trek, hike, slog
Undulating	Rolling, heaving, rippling
Unencumbered	Unburdened, free, released

SYNONYM GLOSSARY

Unfathomable	Profound, deep, vast
Unison	Agreement, harmony, togetherness
Vapid	Lifeless, weak, watery
Vertigo	Dizziness, faintness, unsteadiness
Vex	Anger, irritate, annoy
Void	Emptiness, vacuum, bareness
Wary	Cautious, mistrustful, suspicious
Wince	Flinch, cringe, grimmace
Wistful	Thoughtful, reflective, longing
Wizened	Wrinkled, shriveled, aged

QUESTIONS FOR DISCUSSION

1. Are the characters' names significant?

2. What does the story tell us about human nature?

3. How does communication work in this story?

4. Who are the gods, and how are they important?

5. What is the significance of the following:
   a. Dreams
   b. Fathers
   c. Fluxes
   d. Camouflage
   e. Different colors
   f. Music
   g. Time
   h. Darkness
   i. The idea of rebirth

6. What happened to the planet? Why?

7. What is the significance of copper-colored skin?

8. How do special powers change in this book?

9. How has Celeste grown in this book?

10. How are Celeste and Harmony similar? Different?

11. What will happen next?

Made in the USA
Columbia, SC
12 April 2019